CW00853815

Robert the Allotment Cat: A Winter's Tail

ISBN: 9798421580591

First Printing 2022

Published by Long Way Round Publishing (UK)

www.LongWayRoundPublishing.co.uk

E-mail: LongWayRoundPublishing@gmail.com

Other Robert books

Robert the Allotment Cat and Friends

Robert the Movie Star

To My Amazing Friends

Jeannie and Paul

who do so much to rescue animals in need

and to

Pip, who loves Animals and Hallowe'en

You All Embrace the Magic

Robert the Allotment Cat: A Winter's Tail

Chapter One

Autumnal Reflections

The sun was shining through the dahlia leaves, the breeze causing bright dapples of light to flit across the deep black of my fur and light brown of the earth in the plot, warming both comfortably. I was contentedly dozing in the early afternoon, my tummy pleasingly full of the breakfast I'd been served in the clubhouse, followed a couple of hours later by a generous helping of my favourite crunchy treats. These had been a present from some human visitors who had come to the Allotments specially to see me. (I often strolled into the clubhouse sometime in the morning for some treats - my "elevenses" as Betty called them).

Today my visitors had been a man and a lady whom I'd met a few times before. The man is what humans call "a nawthor". I have no idea what that is, but apparently it's to do with writing words in humanese and making books out of them. He is bald, but I'm not sure if *all* human nawthors are bald, because some are ladies and I've never seen a bald human lady. Perhaps lady nawthors have to shave their heads? (Humans are strange – it's *so* much easier if you have fur!)

In fact, that very human wrote my story, which became a book. So of course, this set me thinking about everything that had happened since I'd walked into the Allotments as an Outling Cat and then became an Allotment Cat (which is quite convenient for new readers)…

Basically, I'd been an Outling Cat – that is a cat of no fixed abode as opposed to a Home Cat who lives in a house and lets humans share this space and feed him or her – for as long as I can remember. I had a vague long-ago memory of being a tiny kitten, snuggling up to my mother with my litter brothers and sisters but not much after that. If things aren't very good for us cats, we tend to blank those bad memories out, so really my whole recollection was me just living life as an Outling cat, moving from place to place to hunt small animals like mice, voles and birds, stealing food (usually thrown out or left unattended by humans), hooking the occasional goldfish out of a garden pond and, if I was really lucky, gobbling up a Home Cat's food if it was left outdoors for them (which is simply an open invitation in my opinion).

Then there was the constant slog of finding shelter from the weather, especially in winter, hiding in sheds and garages, under bushes, sometimes up trees. Many was the time that I'd be chased off by humans and Home Cats and, of course dogs. In fact, it was because I'd been tricked by a Home Cat into being chased by a dog that I'd found myself by a busy main road. Cars are a constant hazard of course, but I was able to get across the road thanks to following some humans using a pedestrial crossing (I *think* that's what it's called anyway) and then finding my way into the Sunnyside Allotments.

I didn't know what an allotment was then, but I soon learned, thanks to a crow called Henry, that an allotment is an area of land where lots of different humans grow things – fruit, vegetables, flowers. These humans are known as *plot holders*. There were other cats living on the allotments and they soon accepted me as one of them. This was mainly because the human in charge of the allotments – a nice, kind human called Betty – decided that I needed a home and could live on the allotments too. So, we Allotment Cats get regular food, treats, nice comfy beds and veterinary care if we need it. And we're allowed to roam where we like in the allotments, which is great. The humans are happy too because we hunt mice and scare birds away from their precious seeds. Having said that, there's lots of other animals and small beings called *Fae* that live in and around the allotments too, and I became friends with several of them. This was just as well, because when a nasty human called Mr Grasper wanted to throw us all off the allotments and build shops, restaurants and car parks on them as part of a new sports stadium complex, all we animals and Fae united to scare off his hench-humans who tried to destroy the allotments!

Meanwhile, the plot holder humans had set up a campaign to save the allotments and I became the "face of the campaign" on *soshul meejah* with my own pages on *Facey Friends* and *Nitter-Natter.* As a result of this, lots of humans backed the campaign. Unbeknownst to the plot holders, we cats used *Facey Friends* and *Nitter-Natter* to contact cats and other pets around the world, which *really* caught the humans' attention, although the plot owners never twigged that we did it ourselves.

Cutting a long story short, the allotments were saved when I found a box of special papers called *deeds*, which said that the allotments' original owner, a nice human called Mr Goodman, had given the allotments to the plot holders, so that horrible human Grasper didn't own them after all! I became really famous and lots of visitors came to the allotments to meet me (and the other cats too, of course). Betty said she knew a nawthor who could write a book about me and the campaign. Well, naturally the nawthor had to get the full *true* story from me, but seeing as we cats communicate in Kittish, which isn't just sounds like Humanese but smells and taste, what we both had to do was –

'Hullo mate! You look thoughtful.'

I purred happily at this interruption as my big ginger friend Red Fred slipped through the dahlias with surprising grace for such a hefty cat and sat next to me. Fred has a very strong local accent (it's even stronger when you smell it in Kittish), so what he said sounded like: '*'Ullo mayte. Yow look fortfool.*'

'Hi Fred,' I replied. 'I was just thinking about how I came to the allotments and all the adventures we had when that mean Mr Grasper wanted to build on the allotments.'

'Oh yeah,' said Fred, absently, as he started to have a wash (I had to nudge up a bit as when Red Fred spreads out to wash, he takes up a lot of space), 'That was exciting, wasn't it? How many moonths ago did all that happen?' [1]

---

[1] Of course, you humans tell time differently to us cats, don't you? A cat *moonth* is roughly what you'd call a fortnight, give or take a human day or two. It's all to do with sleeping, which we cats can do very, very well and how we divide our days up. So… we can have three cat days of daylight and three cat days of darkness, but to humans that's one day and one night. A moonth is seeing the moon completely changing shape in darkness two or three times and… Look, I didn't say it was simple to understand, did I? To make things easier for you to understand, I'll just describe the passing of time in human terms.

I replied to Fred that it had been about six months since I'd first come to the allotments.

'Time flies, dunnit?' mumbled Fred, stretching one of his hind legs up so that he could give his inner thigh a good lick. 'All quiet now, eh?'

We sat in companionable silence for several minutes, the only sounds being Fred's teeth grinding as they tugged a stubborn grass seed out of his orange fur. I closed my eyes, turning my face towards the sun's rays, enjoying the warmth. Although summer was nearly over and the days (human and feline) had got noticeably shorter and the nights cooler, we were currently enjoying a spell of exceptionally fine, warm weather during the daytime.

It occurred to me that this would be the first autumn and winter I'd had a place to live. No more sneaking into sheds and garages only to be chased away, or wet and shivering under bushes – I could go into the allotment holders' clubhouse pretty much any time I liked, as well as several of their sheds and greenhouses, many of which had cat beds and boxes set aside for us Allotment Cats to use. So I'd be warm, dry *and* well fed for the first time in yonks.[2] And welcome to be there too, of course.

'Lovely day though, innit?' sighed Fred who, having finished his ablutions, lay down and stretched out. His back legs pushed me almost to the edge of the plot. I considered moving and lying down next to Fred to enjoy some more of the sunshine but decided that it might be time to go on patrol and see if anything exciting was happening elsewhere. Besides, I might find another shady spot which let in just enough sunlight to be comfortable.

I bid Fred goodbye, but he was already dozing, his rumbling purr blending with his deep snores, making quite an impressive *purrnorze* sound. I set off along the nearest long rutted footpath between plots up towards the back of the allotments, passing sheds, greenhouses and several other plots on either side of me, most of them still full of so many different kinds of vegetable, or flowers. One or two had been cleared and freshly dug over for planting winter crops. As I approached the line of trees which marked the far boundary of the allotments, I could hear the rumble of the construction and excavation machines from the site of the new sports stadium.

Since the scandal surrounding Mr Grasper's dodgy dealings, a new company had been appointed by Midlandtown Council to finish the job of demolishing the old stadium and building a new one. Unlike the previous company's workers, this lot were a lot nicer and their top human in charge would often come and talk to Betty and the Allotment plot holders committee to let them know what particular work the construction workers would be doing. Betty said he was called the Site Manager, which I suppose meant that he looked at everything. He often used to wear big glasses over his ordinary glasses, so I expect this helped his sight. Mr Site Manager would then listen to any concerns they had and do whatever he could to make sure that any noise and disruption was "kept to a minimum".

---

[2] A Yonk is a Cat Year. (Don't ask)

I think the committee all liked him because they'd always offer him tea and biscuits when he came to meet with them. He liked us cats too – especially me I think, because he'd always stroke me and talk to me. This was only right and proper of course, as I was a nonnyharry trustee *and* committee member. (I always let the humans do the talking at meetings, it was easier to have a doze that way.)

I pushed my way through the thicket of brambles at the end of the plots and found myself on the short area of long grass and wild plants which led to the line of trees and the old, broken wall which divided the stadium site from the allotments. I was surprised to see several of the site workers – all wearing their hard hats and bright orange tabards - on the allotment side. They were knocking down the old wall with big hammers and digging up half-buried bricks with pickaxes and shovels. The bricks were being thrown into a big metal box-like thing called a skip (although I'd never seen it walk, let alone skip).

I edged back into the bramble thicket, concerned that these humans were doing something they shouldn't be doing on our side of the divide – especially by knocking down our wall! Okay, so the wall was pretty broken up to start with, mainly as a result of bad weather over many years, not to mention the trees' roots growing up through the soil under the wall, causing it to fall down in a couple of places, but I was sure the workers shouldn't be knocking it down completely.

'Don't worry – they're workmen and they're supposed to be doing that,' said a quiet little voice next to me. I almost jumped out of my skin, as I'd been so intent on watching the workers, I hadn't seen little Janet creep up alongside me. She often did this. We cats are naturally stealthy, but she was almost *supernaturally* stealthy. Then again, I was certain she could work magic, because she spent so much time with Tiberius, the wise old toad who lived by the pond. He could *certainly* do magic.

'I do wish you wouldn't *do* that!' I grumbled, swiftly licking my bristled-up fur to smooth it down again. We touched noses and sat watching the workmen.

'I can't help it if you're so nervous,' giggled Janet. She was a shy little tortie-tabby cat who mostly lived over the wild side of the allotments, especially by the pond. Since all the excitement and adventures in the past few moonths though, she'd become a lot braver, visiting the clubhouse more frequently and even standing up to Dorothy, the bossy tortoiseshell. Dorothy, of course, thought *she* was the cleverest cat on the allotments and never hesitated to remind us all of this. (She probably was, but it didn't do to tell her this, otherwise her head would never fit through the cat flap in her shed.)

'So what *are* they doing?' I asked.

'They're knocking down the old wall so they can build a new fence between the stadium and the allotments,' said Janet. 'I heard their Site Manager talking to Betty about it the other day. He was showing her where they'd be working. I thought *you'd* know Robert, what with being on the committee and all, because Betty said they'd all agreed to this, especially as the construction people are paying for the new fence.' She paused and looked at me with a smile. 'Perhaps you were just resting your eyes and ears when they mentioned that bit?'

'You really *are* a cheeky Kitbit sometimes, aren't you?' I retorted, but in a friendly voice.

'So you say,' said Janet cheekily, '*But you still can't catch me*!' With that she bounded out of the thicket, veered left and ran at top speed, weaving and jinking between the astonished workers' legs. I followed at a swift lick but didn't make it far because I skidded on some scuffed up slippery grass and slid right into the legs of one very burly workman. He loomed over me and his big, broad, bearded face broke into a wide smile.

'Hey lads! It's Robert, the famous allotment cat!' he said with delight. He bent down, pulled off a glove and extended a big, meaty hand to me. His whole hand could have completely covered my head, but he stroked me with surprising gentleness. 'You're a 'andsome lad aren't yer, Robert me old lad?' he boomed. He looked and sounded exactly like I thought Red Fred would look if he was a human.

Several of the other workmen crowded round and began to stroke me and talk to me in those funny cooing voices that some humans use for babies and animals. I stood up and purred, butting my head against the friendly hands. I even said a few words, saying How Nice it was to be Recognised and What a Wonderful Job they Were All Doing. As always though, I expect all they heard was *'Meow! Meow! Prrrt!'*

I decided to stay a little while and bask in their adulation, especially when one nice young man went over to a nearby pile of the workmen's belongings and produced a ham sandwich from a lunch box. He opened the sandwich and gave me several pieces of thick, tasty ham to eat (I think he ate the bread, but I wasn't interested in that bit of the sandwich). Another workman, not to be outdone, brought over a chicken leg from his lunchbox and broke off a large hunk of chicken for me to gobble down. What lovely, friendly humans and what a difference from most of those I'd come across when I was an Outling Cat.

The big workman sat on a pile of bricks and took off his hard hat. He looked very hot – I noticed that he wasn't wearing a shirt under his tabard. He had a close-shaved head (it's odd how humans shave their fur off). I didn't think he was a nawthor though. However, he made up for the lack of hair on his head with his beard and a lot of chest hair. The big man mopped the sweat from his head with a big spotted handkerchief.

'My granddaughter's read your book, Robert,' he said, tickling me under the chin with a thick, sausage-like finger, making my brain rattle in my skull. 'Wait 'til I tell her I met you!'

'Wanna piccy wiv 'im, Dave?' asked another workman, producing a mobile phone. Dave agreed readily. I was used to having my photograph taken, especially with mobiles, so I sat next to Dave, looking suitably regal, while the other workman clicked away with his camera phone. Then I let him pick me up for a couple more photos. Again, big though he was, Dave – Big Dave as the other workmen called him – was incredibly gentle.

Finally, Big Dave put me back down and straightened up. 'Gotta get back to work, Robert,' he rumbled. 'We 'ave to 'ave this bit o' wall down by close of play t'day. You best get off after that little girlfriend o' yourn, eh?' He winked at me conspiratorially. I'd completely forgotten all about chasing Janet, being distracted as I was by Big Dave and his mates, plus the ham and chicken snack. I winked back at him, then trotted off, tail held high, in the direction Janet had taken. I was sure she'd understand why I hadn't followed her.

After all, one must put on a performance for one's public…

Chapter Two

Dog Days

'Oh, *there* you are at last,' said Janet, looking up from where she was lying by the side of the pond. I noticed how the slight breeze was causing the ripples on the pond's surface to catch the sunlight and twinkle like a patchwork of watery stars. I also couldn't help but notice how the sunlight enhanced the orangey-gold tortie-tabby patches in Janet's fur Not for the first time, I found myself thinking how very pretty Janet was - not just for her fur but also her delicate features and bright yellow eyes.

'Sorry… I got a bit held up,' I said, feeling somewhat guilty at not having chased Janet. I also didn't want to have upset her.

'Oh, that's okay,' she smirked, 'I saw you getting *held up* by the workmen. Nice ham and chicken, was it?'

Before I could think of a suitable reply, I noticed that Tiberius the toad was sitting next to her, in the entrance to his half-buried flowerpot. Like Janet he was basking in the mid-afternoon sun, eyes closed, his warty skin inflating and deflating slowly as he breathed in and out. 'Hello young Robert,' he croaked, slowly opening his eyes and turning his head slightly in my direction. He blinked sleepily, his bronze eyes seeming to drop down into his head before popping up again.

I bowed my head respectfully to Tiberius, in deference to his position as the Allotments' oldest – and wisest – animal inhabitant. '*Salvete nobilis bufo*,' I said, using the Latin phrase Janet had painstakingly taught me previously.[3]

'*Salvete nobilis feline, cultis hortis amici,*' he responded. I was sure I detected a hint of a smile in his voice, but with a mouth as wide as Tiberius's, together with his naturally solemn demeanour, it was hard to tell.

'You're looking well, Tiberius,' I said. 'I thought you'd be hypernating by now.'

'You mean *hibernating,*' corrected Tiberius. 'Yes, I was all set to do so, then we had this spell of warm weather, so I decided to stay awake a little longer. We toads have a saying: "*While there's still crawlers and fliers, keep your eyes open and your tongue ready.*"' As if to emphasise his point, his long, sticky tongue shot out of his mouth, snaring a passing fly. Quick as a flash, his tongue was withdrawn into his mouth, taking the fly with it. Tiberius' eyes popped down again to help him swallow his latest snack. They popped up again as soon as he'd finished swallowing. '*That* hit the spot,' he said, in a satisfied way, then belched loudly.

---

[3] Believe me, speaking Kittish-Latin *(Klattin)* is hard to smell. I'm sure Tiberius makes up half of those Latin phases. If I didn't know better, I'd say he looks them up on *Moggle Translate*™ - except I've never seen him use a computer, let alone go online…

Not for the first time I wished I could catch mice as quickly as Tiberius could catch flies, but then I decided that I wouldn't want a tongue as long as that in my mouth. It would probably get in the way when I wanted a drink, although it might be useful for washing myself, and saving me having to bend into all sorts of odd positions. Then again, a toad's tongue was sticky, so I'd probably get lots of fur stuck on it and then I'd be throwing up furballs all the time instead of just now and then.

'Penny for your thoughts?' said Janet.

'Who's Penny?' I asked. 'Has another cat come to live on the allotments?'

'It's a human saying,' explained Janet with a sigh. 'It means I was wondering what you were thinking about.'

I still didn't see where this Penny person (or cat?) fitted into all of this, but I let it go for now. 'Oh, I was just thinking about - er – how useful it must be… um… to have a long tongue like Tiberius,' I said, hoping I wouldn't offend the amiable amphibian.

'We are each and every one of us adapted to our place on the planet,' said Tiberius sagely. 'Even *humans*, although that may seem hard to believe at times.'

'It must be nice to able to sleep all through the cold weather though,' I said, thinking about some of the miserable winters I'd spent out in the world before I came to the Allotments. 'I mean, I was thinking earlier on how good it is that I'm living here where at least I can go into a shed or the clubhouse if it's cold or wet, but even so, at least being asleep you can avoid all that.'

'Hedgehogs hibernate too,' remarked Janet. 'And bats.'

'As do our relatives frogs and newts,' added Tiberius. 'But believe me my young friends, it's not always *safe* when one hibernates. It's a much deeper sleep than *you* could ever undertake. Our bodies' functions slow down to the minimum and we are unaware. We can't just wake up – the weather needs to warm us sufficiently to enable us to do so, and even then it can be dangerous. I've seen too many friends perish when they've awoken to a very warm spell only for the cold to return quickly and catch them unawares. Then there's the dangers of *where* we sleep, usually thanks to the activities of humans. They might dig out the mud where we toads and frogs slumber or set fire to piles of fallen leaves where the hedgehogs hibernate. True, Mother Nature can be cruel at times, but humans can be far crueller. They can't seem to just let things *be.*'

He looked away at that point, gazing across the pond, probably even far beyond it, not just in distance but in time. Then his eyes closed, and he began to breath slowly. I guessed he'd fallen asleep again.

Thankfully, Janet decided to lighten the mood somewhat by changing the subject. 'So, what have you been up to today Robert?' she asked. 'Apart from making friends with the workmen and sharing their lunch, that is.'

I told her about my visitors earlier that day, the Nawthor and his wife.

'Is he going to write another book about you Robert?' she asked.

I considered this for a moment. 'I suppose it depends if I have any more adventures,' I said at length. 'It's all been very quiet round here lately.'

'Even the quiet times can lead to adventure,' said Tiberius, suddenly alert again. I doubted that he'd been asleep at all.

'Do you know something then, Tiberius?' asked Janet mischievously. 'You always seem to know what's about to happen before it does.'

Tiberius looked up at the sky and his nostrils opened wider as he began to smell the air. 'I know that this fine weather will last two more human days,' he said. He turned his jewelled-eyed gaze to us both again. 'Autumn is a time of change and with change you'll often find adventure. Or adventure will find you. Now, if you'll excuse me, I've warmed up enough, so now I need a bit of shade.' With that he turned and shuffled off into the cool darkness of his flowerpot.

I knew better than to question Tiberius further – he'd never give me a straight answer anyway.

Janet gave me a knowing look. She spent even more time with the wise old toad than I did – she was his sort of apprentice after all – but even *she* didn't get straight answers from him.

'Never mind Robert,' she said. 'Let's go for a walk and enjoy some of this nice weather while it lasts.'

We took a leisurely cat-amble up and over the slope – stopping to sniff at interesting smells here and there, marking our own scent to leave a pawshake message. We found ourselves heading towards the overgrown area where the ruins of Mr Goodman's old cottage stood. The cottage had stood empty for some time after old Mr Goodman had died. One night there had been a terrible storm and a huge old oak tree had blown down onto the cottage, crushing most of it into rubble.

'Watch your step Janet,' I said, cautiously testing the stability of the ground. I'd fallen through rotten floorboards into the cellar of the old cottage some moonths before and hurt my leg. Luckily, I'd been rescued eventually. It was just as well I'd fallen down there because I discovered a box containing those important papers called *deeds*. Everyone said how cleaver I'd been to find the box of deeds which had saved the Allotments. I had no wish to fall into the cellar again, so I proceeded carefully. As well as using my paws, I probed carefully with my whiskers to detect those subtle changes in the air above ground where there might be holes.

We needn't have worried after all, because the overgrown area wasn't nearly as overgrown now – several of the plot holders had been busy clearing away much of the rubble of the old cottage, as well as the brambles, nettles and ivy that had grown over and around it. They planned to use some of the old bricks to build a memorial to Mr Goodman. Another odd thing that humans do, but I suppose it helps them to remember things. Or, in this case, remember a person.

'It's a bit different now, isn't it?' remarked Janet, looking up at the few solid parts remaining of the cottage walls, although their uneven, rather jagged shape made me imagine they were giant stone teeth poking up from the ground. It also reminded me rather of the old wall that Big Dave and his fellow workers were knocking down. Most of the plaster covering the cottage's bricks had crumbled away over the years thanks to the weather and ivy growing over the walls, but a few patches of it remained here and there. It was mostly dirty grey or green with moss, but it had once been white when the cottage was still standing, many years ago. I knew this because I'd seen it when I was unconscious in the cellar. I still wasn't sure if it was a dream or not, but it *seemed* real enough.

'I see they've removed some of the tree too. I watched them use a big electric saw to do it.' said Janet, sniffing around the cottage wall. There was a long hollow in the ground where the tree trunk had lain. All across the earth was a carpet of sawdust, flecked with pieces of bark where most of the tree trunk had been sawn up. She nodded towards a large pile of logs placed nearby. 'I hear they're going to make these into nature homes for insects and lizards and the like,' she added

'The roots are still there,' I observed, looking back along the dip towards the remaining part of the tree trunk, the massive tangle of roots sticking out of the ground where the tree had toppled over all those years ago, tearing up the soil as it went. There was a big hollow in the ground under the tangle of roots. There would have been a huge hole thanks to the roots being ripped from the earth, but gradually it had filled up with leaf litter and soil until it was no longer a hole but just a hollow. I guessed that there was still a large part of the root system underneath the ground, but those roots that had been exposed to the air had been largely covered with lichen and moss over the years, so that they now looked like a

'Don't mention it,' I spluttered, attempting to smooth my damp fur. Dog's tongues are very wet, whereas cat's tongues are very dry and rough, ideal for washing one's fur. Rosie further surprised me by telling me that she lived with a couple of Home Cats anyway, which was why she found it so strange that other cats ran away from her.

'I expect they're used to your doggy ways,' I said tactfully. 'But watch your step with the other Allotment cats – they're not all as tolerant as me. You'll need to take things gently with them when you meet them.'

'Oh, I will! I will! I promise!' panted Rosie happily. She jumped up, her tail wagging madly as her human family and Betty came back into the clubhouse.

'It looks like Rosie and Robert are friends, Mum!' said Tom delightedly, hurrying over to stroke me and hug Rosie.

A few minutes later, after plot rental forms had been signed, the first three months' rental paid (I still don't understand what use money is!), it was time for Rosie and her family to leave. Betty and I accompanied them to their car. As the humans were all saying goodbye, Tom unclipped Rosie's lead to let her jump up onto the back seat of the car. At this precise moment, her eyes lit up when she saw the plump Tortoiseshell form of Dorothy walking sedately towards the clubhouse.

'Oooh! Who's that?' she exclaimed. 'That's one of the cats I first tried to say hello to!'

'That's Dorothy,' I said. 'She's probably not scared now she's seen that I get on okay with you, but Rosie, she's not...'

Before I could finish my sentence, by which I would explain that Dorothy didn't like to be grabbed, touched or basically even spoken to unless she was in the mood, Rosie had charged away before a protesting Tom could grab her.

'Oh no, not again!' cried Bex. '*Rosie!* Come back here!'

But of course, Rosie was too excited to hear and bounded up to Dorothy who didn't run away this time but slowly, almost majestically, began to arch her back and fluff out her tail, her ears flattening against her head. '*Oooh! Hello Dorothy! I'm Rosie*!' barked Rosie excitedly. Dorothy's eyes narrowed as Rosie drew near and I could almost hear her claws springing out of her toes.

I looked at Betty who put a hand over her eyes in resignation. I closed my eyes likewise.

Rosie was about to learn a valuable - and potentially painful - lesson…

Chapter Three

Skullduggery Unpleasant

'Well, serves the stupid dog right for running up to me like that,' said Dorothy dismissively, as she licked her paw and then brushed the fur on her head.

'She was only trying to be friendly, Dorothy!' I protested. 'You didn't have to scratch her nose.'

'It was only a light dab,' retorted Dorothy. 'The way that silly mutt howled you'd think I'd scratched its nose off!'

I decided it wasn't worth arguing. Dorothy can be very single minded and besides, I can't claim that I've never scratched a dog's nose before. Hopefully, Rosie would learn from this experience and steer clear of Dorothy in future. I found myself quite liking Rosie.

'I'm with Dorothy on this one,' added Barbara. 'Mind you, it *was* quite funny to see her run back to her humans like that and jump in the car to get away from Dorothy.'

'DDD,' sniggered Dorothy. 'Don't Diss Dorothy!'

I turned to my black and white friend Barbara, who was also washing himself,[4] having acquired a few green smears on his white bib from his mad dash through the asparagus when he fled from Rosie.

'I suppose it wasn't a *bad* scratch,' I conceded. 'And Rosie didn't *really* mean any harm. Next time you see her, give her a chance. She's just a bit… excitable, that's all.'

'Oh well… I'll try,' said Barbara, who is generally a very affable cat and good company.

'Hmpf!' muttered Dorothy, darkly.

'So… what are those humans doing to the old wall, Robert?' asked Barbara.

I explained about the humans' plans to put up a new fence in place of the old wall.

'Humans are always trying to change things,' grumbled Dorothy.

---

[4] Apparently, Barbara is a female name in Humanese. It doesn't bother Barbara though – it's not his real cat name and besides, *he* knows who he is and he's comfortable in his own skin.

'I suppose it will make a better barrier between us and that new stadium,' I said. 'Anyway,' I added, 'The workmen are doing a good job of knocking the old wall down and they seem very nice too.'

'Oh yes?' smiled Barbara. 'Shared their food with you did they, eh Robert?'

'They *might* have done,' I said, airily, inspecting a very interesting beetle that was scuttling along the path where we were sitting. 'I can't help it if humans want to give me treats and things. Besides, we all get to share the nice things they give us, like those comfy new cat beds.'

'That's true,' agreed Barbara. 'I liked those blankets that the kind human lady knitted for us too.'

'Yes, it's good to have nice things,' conceded Dorothy. 'But after all, it's only right. Us cats *are* very special, after all.'

Speaking as a cat, I couldn't argue with that.

The next day was also warm and sunny. I'd been patrolling the allotments during the night, enjoying the different scents, sounds and feelings of the dark. I had watched the dawn break, the sky changing from black to purple to blue, the sun finally breaking through and illuminating the foliage, turning the silvery leaves to green, the flowers slowly opening as the sun warmed their petals. After greeting Betty and having breakfast at the clubhouse, I spent the morning pleasantly enough ambling from plot to plot greeting any plot holders who were tending to crops and graciously accepting any little treats they cared to offer me. I also chatted to my friend Henry the crow, who had his beady eyes on Colin's plot, as Colin was sowing some winter seeds. Colin, in turn, had his beady eyes on Henry. I rounded off the morning by finding a nice shady spot under some bay leaves to curl up for a well-deserved nap.

I was awoken sometime later by someone prodding me.

I opened my eyes blearily to see Red Fred, who was doing the prodding with one of his big paws. With him were Barbara, GG, Janet and ET.

'C'mon mate, wakey-wakey!' rumbled Red Fred.

'Whassup?' I mumbled muzzily, feeling quite grumpy at being disturbed. 'I was out patrolling most of last night. I'm tired. What's so urgent?'

'Th-th-there's p-p-problems *attheclubhouse*!' wibbled ET, wobbling from side to side in agitation. 'D-D-Dorothy is *v-v-veryupset!'*[5]

[5] ET , who is mainly white with tortie patches and a magnificent fluffy tortie-ginger tail, suffers from a condition known as *Wobbly Cat Syndrome*. She can still get around like other cats and do cat things; it just takes her a little longer. Her voice wobbles too when she speaks (this is called *wibbling*), then all her words come out in a rush at the end of a sentence. It's easy enough to understand her with a little patience and practice.

'Oh no! Is Rosie here again?' I said, sitting bolt upright, now fully awake.

'No, it's not Rosie,' said Barbara. 'Not sure what it is but… well… it must be horrible!'

'You'd best see for yourself, Robert,' added GG.

I noticed that Janet was her usual quiet self, but she looked as worried as the others. I didn't like to see Janet upset in any way, so I put on a brave face for her sake. 'Come on, everyone,' I said, sounding bolder than I actually felt as we hurried towards the clubhouse. From the position of the sun and the taste of the air, it was now mid-afternoon.

As we trotted (and in ET's case, wobbled) down the main path near the clubhouse, I saw several cars, which I knew belonged to some of the allotment committee members, including Betty's. Standing slightly to one side of them was the solid, square shape of the Land Rover belonging to Mr Building Site Manager. As usually, it was spattered with mud, some of it fresh, most of it dried on.

'I'll come in with you mate,' said Fred. 'Safety in numbers, eh?'

Safety? What could Dorothy be up to? I thought with alarm.

The other cats waited on the path as Fred and I slipped in through the open doorway into the clubhouse. I must confess that my heart was beating faster than usual, and I felt quite apprehensive.

The first thing I saw was Betty, half a dozen committee members and the Site Manager crowded round the big table where meetings usually took place. The Site Manager was wearing his bright orange jacket and hard hat as usual. He was talking to the committee members whilst pointing at something on the table which I couldn't see due to the humans crowding round it. The second thing I saw was Dorothy, hiding under one of the smaller tables, her ears flat against her head, her eyes wide and staring, her tail bristling like a bottle brush, and she was growling in a low, menacing way. I realised I had never seen Dorothy like this before. She wasn't angry… she was *scared!*

We cautiously padded over to her. I inched forward, not wanting to be on the receiving end of a dab from Dorothy's claws. When a cat is that upset, we tend to lash out instinctively. I should know, I'd had enough scrapes and close calls when I was an Outling Cat.

'Dorothy,' I said quietly. 'Dorothy, it's me, Robert. What's the matter?'

She turned her head slowly towards me and gradually stopped growling, her eyes becoming more focussed.

'On… the…table,' she mumbled. 'Go see…Not nice… Horrible!'

Dorothy didn't reply, but simply swished her fluffed up tail with agitation.

'Go on mate, I'm here if you need me,' said Fred encouragingly. I knew that Fred was a very brave cat usually, but even he seemed put out by Dorothy's reaction and the tip of his tail was twitching madly.

With my legs feeling as wobbly as ET's, I approached the gaggle of humans. They were all talking at once and so nobody noticed me as I silently jumped up onto one of the empty chairs around the table. I took a deep breath and then took a small hop up onto the table…

… To be confronted by a skull! Or to be more accurate, a *cat's* skull.

Everyone around the table jumped and gave an exclamation of surprise – I think I must've given them a bit of fright, suddenly appearing like that when they were contemplating the cat's skull.

Kate recovered first and immediately wrapped her arms around me to lift me off the table. 'Oh no Robert!' she exclaimed. 'You don't want to see that!'

I wriggled free of Kate's grasp. The skull was disconcerting, but it didn't frighten me. Sadly, in my time as an Outling Cat, I had seen cat skulls on more than one occasion, where some unfortunate Outling had perished and its body had lain forgotten and unclaimed, slowly decomposing and returning to nature. The skull was always the last part remaining.

I crouched down on the table and regarded the skull. It was greyish white, almost yellow in places, completely devoid of skin or fur. It was missing its lower jaw, but the teeth in the top jaw all looked intact, the large incisors looking usefully sharp, but even so, it was hard to tell how old it had been when it died. I tentatively reached out with my nose to touch the skull where its nose would have been in life, but now there was just a heart-shaped hole. The bone was surprisingly warm to the touch, but then it was indoors and it had been handled by the humans. I inhaled deeply. There was no smell of cat, nothing to indicate a living, breathing animal, no subtle signals which only us cats can detect from each other to say who/what/where, no pawshake of any kind. Instead, I could smell earth and dust and, warm though the skull was, I felt a cold emptiness… almost a *loneliness*, as though the skull was trying to tell me that it had been buried, alone and forgotten for a very, very long time. I sat back, looking into the cavernous, now sightless eye sockets, wondering who this cat had been and where had he or she lived?

I sat back, my tail twitching with curiosity.

'He doesn't seem too bothered by it,' said Betty. 'Unlike poor Dorothy!'

'She shot under one of the tables,' said Kate. 'Hopefully, she'll come out soon.'

I noticed that two of the humans were Donna and Anji. They were plot holders now, having joined up when the allotments were under threat a few months before. They were what Betty called historians, which is something to do with stuff that happened a long time ago. They had been very helpful though, providing information about the land the allotments were on and who owned it and when. They often changed their hair colour too, which is a very human thing to do. Donna now had bright pink hair, while Anji's hair was now almost white, contrasting very nicely with her light brown skin. Like Donna, she had lots of tattoos on her arms and was wearing various silver and gold bracelets and had a stud through her nose. I think humans call this *joolry*, which I suppose they wear because they haven't got fur with patterns on it like us cats, so they have to make up for it in other ways They probably change their hair colour for the same reason.

It was Anji who turned to Mr Site Manager, obviously carrying on their conversation which I had interrupted, and said: 'And where did you say your workmen found this?'

Mr Site Manager adjusted his smaller glasses and replied; 'About halfway along the old wall, probably buried about two feet down. The lads had cleared the last of the bricks away and were digging out a new foundation trench for the concrete that the new fence's posts are going to be fixed into.'

'And this was all they found?' asked Donna.

'Well actually no,' said Mr Site Manager. 'There were a couple of bits of rotten wood in the earth, so it might have been in a box, but I expect if a whole cat had been buried in a box, the other bones must've rotted away with the box a long time ago.

'Yes, skulls do tend to last a bit longer,' mused Anji, stroking her chin thoughtfully. 'I'm just wondering when it might've been buried and by whom.'

'Was it a rodent scare perhaps?' asked Kate.

'No, they're usually in walls and they're mummified,' replied Donna. (I had no idea why a mummy cat would be in a wall, but there you go). She turned to Mr Site Manager. 'You said it wasn't the only thing you found?'

'That's right. We found this under the skull,' replied Mr Site Manager. He placed a dirty metal band of metal on the table next to the skull. It looked like the sort of thing that I'd seen Donna wear on her wrist; it was quite large, although not very thick, with a gap in it, the two ends a little way apart. Anji picked it up carefully and gently brushed the crusted earth away. The metal looked a sort of browny orange, with green streaks on it.

'Hmm… a cuff bracelet. Is it gold?' asked Donna, peering closely at the bracelet.

'No, it's just basic copper,' replied Anji. 'See where's it's oxidised in the soil and discoloured?' She pointed to the green colouration. 'I don't think it's valuable anyway. Maybe it was a collar for the cat?'

'Looks a bit too big for that,' said Kate. 'Surely it's a bracelet.' The other humans nodded in agreement.

'So someone buried a bracelet with a cat? How odd,' said Betty curiously.

Donna said: 'That's an old wall of course but it's not *that* old – it was put up probably fifty, sixty years ago to separate the allotment land from the stadium when that was built. But the foundations of the wall might be a lot older. There may have been another wall there at some point. The thing is, that part of the land, the border if you like, is a bit of a mystery, historically speaking.'

'I don't think there was a wall or any other building there before,' said Mr Site Manager. 'The lads have been digging down a couple of feet and all they've really found is the usual stones, tree roots and the like. No other bones or boxes or anything like that.'

'Could the cat have died naturally?' pondered Kate. 'You know, and the skull just sunk into the ground over the years?'

'Probably not to that depth,' replied Donna. 'No, I think this cat was buried, with that bracelet, possibly in a box, obviously by someone who cared about it. It was probably someone's pet.'

'Definitely a mystery,' said Betty. 'I wonder why it was buried there, under the wall? Although of course the wall was most likely built after the cat was buried.'

'The old wall's foundations only go down less than a foot,' said Mr Site Manager. 'Which explains why it was so easily undermined by tree roots and subsidence. I think the wall must've been built in a hurry and quite cheaply.'

'Yeah, that figures,' muttered Colin. 'Blooming cowboy builders threw that old stadium up and it falls down a few years later, which is why the Council's having to build a new one now. And it all comes out of ratepayer's money!' Colin was always rather grumpy about things, which probably explained why he was the only human who really got on with Dorothy. (I wondered briefly who these rat payer people were and why rats would need money from humans in the first place, but as I've said before, I'll never understand anything about money).

'Ahem… yes well…' said Mr Site Manager, coughing nervously. 'I can't really comment on how skilful the original builders of the stadium were or how much it's costing the council. I – ah – just thought you'd want to see the skull and bracelet. I can show you ladies exactly where we found them if you like. We haven't finished the foundation trench yet.'

'Oh yes, that'd be very useful, thanks,' said Anji.

'Yes, thanks. We can take some photos and measurements, plot it out on old maps of the land from the history society,' added Donna. 'Let's get on with it though, because we'll need to pick the kids up from school in an hour.'

'I'll take the bracelet to our friend Maeve who works at the archaeology department at Midlandtown University,' said Anji. 'She can maybe clean it up and put some kind of a date to it. That is, if you don't mind, Betty?'

'No, go ahead, please,' said Betty, as Anji carefully wrapped the bracelet in a handkerchief.

After a few quick goodbyes, Mr Site Manager, Donna and Anji left the clubhouse. Colin, Kate and Betty sat down and looked thoughtfully at the skull.

‘Probably it was just someone’s pet or just a feral ca that lived on the Allotments,’ said Colin. He looked across at me and stroked me affectionately. ‘No offence Robert old chap. Here…’ He rummaged in his coat pocket and dropped a few cat treats on the table. I purred happily and began to gobble them up. Colin always had a few goodies in his pockets. I hoped Dorothy wasn’t watching, because they were probably her cat treats.

‘Hmmm,’ said Betty thoughtfully. ‘Buried in an odd place though and quite deep. It might be older than we think. And there’s that bracelet too, of course.’

‘Well, I don’t know about you guys, but I could murder a cuppa,’ said Kate cheerfully. ‘All this talk of skulls and suchlike has made me thirsty. In fact… my throat’s *bone dry*.’ She giggled. Colin and Betty groaned in that way humans do when something is funny but doesn’t really deserve a laugh. ‘I’ll make us all a cuppa,’ added Kate getting up and heading to the kitchen.

‘Do you need any help, Kate?’ asked Colin, making no move to actually get up from his chair.

‘No, no... it’s alright, you sit and rest your *weary bones*, Colin,’ called Kate from the kitchen and laughed.

Betty chuckled at Colin’s pained expression. ‘Well, I think this skull should be put somewhere safe until we decide what to do with it,’ she said, carefully picking up the cat’s skull. She bustled over to her odds ‘n’ ends table, which was covered with leaflets, envelopes, rolls of sticky tape and a variety of cardboard boxes of different sizes. She selected a small box and popped the skull inside, then put the box on a shelf above the table.

‘It’s a mystery, isn’t it, Robert?’ said Colin conversationally.

I miaowed in agreement.

‘So… you’ve never seen a cat skull before, Dorothy?’ I asked. We were having a Cat-Meet, sitting on the main pathway between the plots, discussing the strange events of earlier that day.

‘Of course not! Why should I have?’ snapped Dorothy crossly. ‘*You* might have seen skulls all over the streets when you were a *stray*, but *I* lived in a bookshop before I moved to the allotments!’

Stray. Ouch! Not a nice word in Kittish.

‘You sure, Princess?’ drawled Red Fred, winking at me. ‘I mean… all them books… surely you’d have seen a *picture* of a skull in a book?’

Dorothy favoured Fred with a Withering Look but declined to answer. When I’d jumped down from the table after Betty had put the skull away in the box, I’d seen Dorothy slink out of the clubhouse, with Fred following. She’d been very upset by the sight of the cat skull and I’d felt really sorry for her. In fact, I think we all did. But now, outside in the sunshine, an hour later, she had recovered most of her bravado and sarcasm.

‘R-R-Robert w-w-was *beingnicetoyou*!’ wibbled ET indignantly. ‘Y-y-you sh-sh-should b-be *gratefultohim!*’

‘Oh, don’t worry about it, ET,’ I said airily. ‘Dorothy couldn’t help being frightened.’

'I wasn't *frightened* as such,' retorted Dorothy in a couldn't-care-less kind of way. 'It just gave me a bit of surprise, that's all. I mean… I jumped up on the table and well… there it was. I don't know why Betty and the others were so interested in it. It probably wasn't a cat they knew anyway.'

'Makes you wonder though, doesn't it?' said Barbara. 'I mean, why was it buried there and with that bracelet thingy too? From what you told us Mr Site Manager said, Robert, it must've been a long time ago.'

'Perhaps I should try and Moggle it on Betty's laptop,' said GG brightly. 'What is it humans say online? *Moggle is your friend*!'

'Wh-what's *M-M-Moggle*?' asked ET.

'It's a search engine.' replied GG. 'It tells you things.'

'Isn't that one of those big, clanky, steamy things we've seen pictures on the laptop?' asked Barbara. 'You know, like those old films where that human in the top hat and cape twirls his moustache and ties that woman to the metal rails and there's a steam engine thingy coming? Then this other bloke has to rescue her before it runs over her, but it takes ages for it to get any closer which is really strange!'

'Oh yeah!' exclaimed Red Fred. 'I like the one where the steam engine thingy has to push that magic car along the rails until it gets to the right speed so's it can travel in time and the rails run out, 'cos the bridge hasn't been built yet and…'

'We are not discussing *movies*!' snapped Dorothy crossly. 'Why would I be talking about movies? Anyway, it's not *that* sort of engine, is it GG?'

GG said she was right, but before she could explain any further Dorothy butted in and said in a very smug way: 'Anyway, that Moggle is an *electric* engine!'

'What were we talking about?' sighed Fred, flopping down in resignation. 'I've lost the plot and there's plenty of plots to choose from.' He looked around him and winked at me again.

'Maybe Tiberius knows,' said a quiet little voice. It was, of course, Janet, who had been sitting quietly at the edge of our group, unnoticed by most of the other cats.

'What? Oh, it's *you*, Thingy,' snorted Dorothy dismissively. 'Every time we need to know something you say: "Let's ask Tiberius". "Where are the cat treats? *Let's ask Tiberius*!". "Is it going to rain today? *Let's ask Tiberius*!" "Why is Thingy so annoying? *Let's ask Tiberius*!"'

Janet looked down at her feet.

'Don't be *mean*, Dorothy!' I said crossly. 'Janet's right. Tiberius knows most things. He remembers a lot of things that have happened, even if he wasn't there… er… Isn't that right Janet?'

Janet brightened up a bit. ‘That’s right Robert,’ she said. ‘It’s the *Avorum Memoria Bufones’*.

We all looked at her blankly.

‘Er… that means *The Ancestral Memory of Toadkind*, I think…’ stammered Janet, a little embarrassed.

‘*More* made up words! Well, *I* don’t think that warty water dweller knows everything!’ retorted Dorothy. ‘*You* go and ask him if you like. *I’m* not bothered! What does it matter who buried some dead Home Cat or stray or whatever hundreds of yonks ago with a cheap old human bracelet? It’s not like we *knew* him.’ With that she turned around and stalked off, tail in the air. ‘Or her!’ she added as she disappeared into a forest of Dahlias in the nearest plot, petals dropping to the ground in her wake.

We were all silent for a moment.

‘I think she might have a point, mate,’ said Fred at length. ‘I mean, bit of a mystery an’ all, but it’s not like the poor fella’s still around is it? Or his human, come to that.’

‘I suppose you’re right,’ I sighed. I looked at Janet and noticed again how the colours in her fur seemed to subtly shift and change in the sunlight and how delicately her whiskers twitched as she blinked. ‘But hey – come on Janet. Let’s go and ask Tiberius anyway, eh?’

‘Good idea!’ agreed GG. ‘And I’ll sneak onto Betty’s laptop and try and Moggle it, see what I can find out.’

‘I’ll stay here and make sure no-one steals the Dahlias,’ chuckled Fred, stretching out on the warm earth. ET wobbled over to him and plonked herself down beside him. GG scampered off in the direction of the clubhouse, while Janet and I set off to the pond.

As we headed away, I heard ET ask Fred in a confused kind of way: ‘S-so-so F-F-Fred. Wh-where d-d-does th-this M-M-Moggle *thinglivethen*?’

Chapter Four

Tracking Tiberius

As things turned out, asking Tiberius for his insight into the mystery of the skull wasn't at all easy. When Janet and I arrived at the pond, as the sun was sinking lower in the sky and the shadows were lengthening, Tiberius was noticeable only by his absence.

'He's not at home,' said Janet, looking up from the flowerpot, which, as ever, rested on its side, partly buried in the soft earth close to the edge of the pond.

We looked out across the pond, just as a cool breeze caused the water to ripple, causing the last part of the pond not in shade to twinkle and flicker with golden light. This reminded me of the fairy folk, the Fae, who lived "on the other side of a shadow" as they referred to it. Occasionally they came to our side, flitting between their world and this, which – in ways I couldn't quite grasp – was the same place but a step sideways.

'Perhaps we can ask Oakroot the gnome instead,' I suggested. 'He's been around a long time; he might have seen something.'

'We could if we could find him,' replied Janet. 'But I expect he's on the Fae side right now. Maybe Tiberius is there too? He often likes to talk to Oakroot.'

Suddenly, I saw a blur of movement out of the corner of my eye, and good cat that I am, I instinctively pounced. I looked down and found that I had trapped a big greeny-brown frog under my paws. The frog squirmed and wriggled, then suddenly froze, with its front legs stretched over its head, its eyes retracted into its head and its back legs tucked up to its side. I was wise to this trick, having encountered frogs when I was an Outling Cat. They freeze like this to pretend they're dead in the hope that predators will leave them alone. Sometimes it works, but frogs don't taste that nice anyway. At least, not raw.

I leaned down to say: 'Listen froggy, I know you're alive. I want to talk to you.'

The frog suddenly started wriggling again. 'Mercy Mr Moggy! Mercy!' croaked the frog in agitation. 'I ain't done nuffin'! I don't taste nice! I ain't an edible frog – they all live down in Kent! 'Ave a heart – I got a wife and two hundred tadpoles to support!'

'It isn't the time of year for tadpoles.' I said evenly.

The frog blinked, then carried on babbling: 'No, o' course it ain't. I meant *froglets*, I got four hundred froglets to support!'

'That doesn't even add up!' sighed Janet, crouching down to face the frog. 'How can two hundred tadpoles become four hundred froglets?'

'Didn't say they was all from *this* year's clump of spawn, did I?' wailed the frog. 'Please don't eat me! Finbarr – that's me, that is - ain't done you no harm!'

'We're not going to eat you. At least we won't if you answer a few questions and stop wriggling and whining!' I snapped. Frogs weren't anywhere near as clever at toads. Maybe toads have got bigger brains because they are so warty and taste really nasty, so with less predators they've been around longer than frogs and have had time to grow their brains.

'We need to find Tiberius,' said Janet patiently. 'You know? Tiberius the wise old toad?'

'Oh yes, oh yes!' said Finbarr, nodding enthusiastically.

'Well?' said Janet, her patience by now beginning to wear as thin as mine.

'Well what?' replied the frog, looking confused.

'Well… where have you seen him?'

'I ain't seen 'im!'

'*You said you had seen him*!' I almost exploded, pushing my paw down on Finbarr, causing him to protest loudly. I relented and raised my paw slightly to let him speak.

'No, your mate here asked me if I *knew* him,' said the frog, re-inflating himself indignantly, glaring at Janet. 'She said: *"You know? Tiberius the wise old toad?"* And I do! I know him! Everyone in th' pond knows him! And everybody beyond th' pond too.'

Janet bent down lower until her pink nose was touching Finbarr's slimy snout and she spoke very slowly and deliberately: 'What I *meant,* my frustrating froggy friend Finbarr, was; have you seen him around *today?*' Although naturally shy and quiet, Janet could be quite direct when the need arose. I think she felt more confident around me. I felt quite happy about that, for both of us.

I lifted my paw to allow Finbarr to sit up. He blinked and ran one of his front paws over his snout, deep in thought. Then his eyes lit up and his mouth opened in a wide grin and he nodded his head delightedly, obviously remembering. Janet and I leaned forward expectantly.

'No,' he replied flatly. 'Not seen him today. Can I go now? Gotta get ready for hibernation you know. Was thinking of sleeping in the mud at the bottom of the pond. Nice an' warm there. You should try it. Oh, 'course you can't. You live on th' land, don't you?'

'Oh, just hoppit!' I snapped, in exasperation. Finbarr didn't need telling twice. He splayed his large, webbed feet out onto the ground, his powerful back legs contracted then expanded, allowing him to leap with, I conceded grudgingly, quite graceful legerity a long way out across the pond, landing in the water with a neat splash. A second or two later, his head popped up out of the water. 'Well, a "*Thank You*" would be nice!' he shouted. I growled and took a step towards the pond and the frog's head disappeared with a loud plop! I was glad he'd swum away. I didn't want to get my paws wet.

'*That* was a waste of time,' sighed Janet.

'You're telling me!' I grumbled. 'No wonder so many animals want to eat frogs. It's pointless *talking* to them!'

We wandered up the slope and away from the pond, alert for any sign of Tiberius or indeed anyone else who might know where he was. Our tracking brought us to where the old wall stood or, more accurately, *had* stood. Now all the bricks had gone, apart from a handful of broken ones and flakes of mortar. The wall had been replaced by a long trench which ran all the way to the far wall of the allotments, which bordered a grass verge alongside the busy main road. The workmen had long since gone home for the evening, the stadium building site beyond silent and still in the fading light.

'That must be where they dug the skull up from,' I said.

We trotted over and cautiously peered into the trench. I don't know why we were being so cautious – perhaps we were half expecting to see a whole pile of cat skulls. But there was nothing remarkable to see. Just a reasonably deep trench with quite smoothly dug sides. Here and there the odd tree root poked through, or an odd stone or piece of old brick lay.

Janet sniffed carefully. 'Just smells of earth and sweaty humans,' she muttered.

I nodded in agreement, although I was sure I could detect a hint of ham sandwiches, although that might just have been fanciful thinking on my part.

By now dusk was falling and we hurried on, ready to cut through the bramble bushes and back onto the allotments. Suddenly we heard a *twit-twhoo-hoo* noise. We both froze and looked around us, beginning to arch our backs slightly. We looked around us quickly, our eyes alighting on a russet-brown shape sitting on the low hanging branch from one of the tall trees which stood in front of the newly dug trench. It was an owl – a Tawny owl to be precise. The owl regarded us with its wide yellow eyes, no doubt sizing us up as potential prey. But seeing as we were a lot bigger and more capable of defending ourselves than a mouse or a vole, the owl lost interest in us and twisted its head away in that disconcerting way owls can, to look behind where it was perched.

'I'm probably going to regret this,' I said to Janet, 'But I suppose we could ask the owl.'[6]

'Hellooo!' I called, trying to mimic the owl's way of talking. 'We're looooking for a tooooad. Have you seeeeen one?'

The owl spun its head back round towards us. 'Whoooo?' it said.

'Tibeeeeriuuuuus the toooooaaaad,' replied Janet, following my lead.

---

[6] Just to explain at this point: you humans have got it totally wrong when you talk about "the wise old owl". They're not wise at all. In fact, they're incredibly dim. Most of the little brain space they have in their skulls means they are mainly focussed on hunting, eating and flying. If you want a wise animal, try a toad. But I don't expect they look as cute to humans as owls.

'*Whooooo*!' responded the owl.

'Tiberius! The smartest animal on the allotments!' I snapped, adding under my breath: '*Unlike you.*'

'Twhoooo!' said the owl again.

'That's right, a toad,' added Janet eagerly.

'Whoooo?'

'Ah forget it, this is pointless!' I muttered. 'Come on Janet, let's go and find someone with a working brain.'

As we walked away, I heard the owl say with a hint of smugness: *'Twit!'*

The next creature we encountered also gave us a bit of a start. We were walking down one of the pathways when a long snout topped by pointy ears suddenly poked out from behind a compost heap. We needn't have worried too much. It was Ruby, the fox vixen who had been so helpful in defending the allotments a few moonths before. I'd had my share of run-ins with urban foxes as an Outling cat, but Ruby was less urban and much more rural in her nature. This was probably because she didn't need to compete with the

Allotment Cats for food scraps, although I'm sure she did occasionally gobble up any cat food we left unattended in our sheds if the mood took her.

'I say, hello Robert old chap!' said Ruby in her clipped, slightly throaty way. 'And little Janet too. How are you both?'

We exchanged greetings with Ruby and asked her whether she'd seen Tiberius.

''Fraid not, old chums,' replied Ruby. 'Haven't seen the warty one for a few days as it happens, but then again, I've not been over by the pond. You could try asking old Brock the badger – he was rooting around in the next row of plots over. He said he was soon orf to some ceremony or other. Tiberius will probably be in charge of that. You know how our old amphibious oracle likes a good ceremony.'

Janet looked thoughtful. 'Hmmm... a *ceremony*... I think Tiberius said something about that a few days ago.'

Talk of a ceremony put me in mind of the Gathering that Tiberius had organised back in the summer, calling together all the inhabitants of the allotments and several from the world of the Fae by some powerful magic. However, it didn't feel like that now, either in the air or by the smells and sounds around us.

'Well, let's go and ask Mr Brock,' I said. 'Thanks for your help, Ruby.'

'Anytime old bean,' said Ruby affably as we set off past the compost heap and across the next path to the adjoining section of plots.

By now it was almost fully dark, but our keen night vision, acute hearing and sense of smell allowed us to find our way easily enough. Besides, we needn't have worried. We spotted the white stripes of Mr Brock's face very clearly, as he used his powerful front claws to dig a hole in the soil of an as-yet-to-be rented plot which was rather overgrown with weeds and tall grass. He dipped his long snout into the hole and then jerked his head up, his jaws chomping on something squishy.

He looked over to us. 'Nice couple o' grubs under this grass!' he rumbled. 'Beetle larvae. I like a nice crunchy beetle but a good, fat beetle grub makes a change.'

I nodded politely. We cats will eat insects now and again – Crane Flies being a favourite – but that's more for the hunting practice than anything else.[7] Besides, insects' long, bristly legs tend to get stuck between your teeth.

Janet asked Mr Brock whether he'd seen Tiberius.

'Just off t' see him now as a matter of fact,' replied Mr Brock, licking the grub juice off his snout. 'I'm attending the Equinox Ceremony. Thought you'd know about that, young Janet, you being his famulus and all.'

---

[7] I know for a fact that Home Cats catch and eat Crane Flies just to freak their humans out. Besides, they're easier to catch than buzzing flies.

'Oh fiddlesticks!' exclaimed Janet. 'Is that today? I'd completely forgotten!'

My head was spinning by now. 'What's an equeebox and what's a familynus?' I asked plaintively.

'*Equinox* and *famulus*,' corrected Janet. 'The equinox, well, it's sort of how the planet year divides up, sort of into quarters, each quarter covering a season. This'd be the Autumnal equinox, isn't that right, Mr Brock?'

'Yup,' replied Mr Brock. 'Very important one this one. Day 'n' night aligned, light 'n' dark equal lengths.'

I nodded. 'I see,' I lied, unconvincingly. 'And what's that other thing?'

'I'm a *famulus*,' said Janet proudly.

'I thought you were a feline?'

'I am, but a famulus is a – well – a sort of assistant to a wise being who practices magic.'

'Like an apprentice,' added Mr Brock helpfully. 'A pupil, one who learns a craft.'

'It sounds quite important,' I said, impressed. 'I always thought you knew more about things than you let on.'

'Maybe,' sighed Janet. 'But I can't be much good if I forgot that it was the Equinox!'

Poor Janet sounded terribly upset. I put a paw out to pat her back in sympathy. Her fur felt very soft and warm beneath my paw pads.

'Don't worry youngster!' said Mr Brock cheerfully. 'I won't tell Tiberius you forgot, and you won't either, will you Robert?'

'Of course not!' I exclaimed, eager to cheer Janet up. I was pleased she see that she brightened up at this.

'Come on then, you two,' said Mr Brock briskly. 'Orf we go!' He barrelled through the cabbages on the nearest plot.

'Where are we going anyway?' I asked, as we hurried in his wake. I couldn't help but feel the plot holder who rented this plot was going to be pleased with the pathway of crushed cabbages. Janet and I were able to slip and skip between the plants gracefully.

'The pond!' called Mr Brock.

'We've just come from there!' I muttered.

As it turned out, Mr Brock took a circuitous route which led us to the far end of the pond, furthest from the allotments rather than the one closest to the allotments, where

Tiberius tended to stay by his flowerpot. The far end was bordered by a thick growth of trees at the top of the slope, beyond which, I guessed, lay the outside world.

We skirted around the edge of the overgrown area where the ruined cottage lay, avoiding the worst of the undergrowth, then cut across towards the treeline on the slope. We emerged from the treeline to see a strange collection of allotment inhabitants forming a circle. There were half a dozen toads, four crows, three hares and two hedgehogs. They were forming a circle at the centre of which sat Tiberius on top of a large stone. Several heads turned towards us as we approached. It put me in mind of a smaller version of the Gathering in the summer, except then it seemed that every animal in the allotments had been present.

By now the moon had risen, full and shining brightly, illuminating the circle of animals and turning their fur and feathers silver. Faint ripples on the pond below the slope reflected the moonlight back to us.

'Ah, Robert! Janet! And Mr Brock!' said Tiberius brightly. 'Just in time! Please join the circle. I am about to begin the ceremony.'

'Wotcher Robert!' said one of the crows. I realised that it was Henry.

'Hello Henry. I didn't think birds liked being out and about at night,' I said, as we took our places (Mr Brock took up quite a lot of space and everybody had to shuffle round and squeeze up a bit). 'Apart from owls, that is.' I added, thinking about the unhelpful owl we had spoken to earlier.

'*Owls!* They wouldn't know the equinox from a nole in th' ground,' sneered Henry. 'Anyways, us crows is intelligent, we is. Even humans says so, all h'official and scientific like. An' we don't mind stayin' up late when it's for summat important, like this.'

Tiberius croaked loudly, which I assume was the amphibious equivalent of clearing his throat, indicating that he wanted to get on with the ceremony.

'Oops, this is my bit this year,' said Henry. He hurriedly turned to the assembled gathering. He spread his wings, looking sharply around the circle, his bright black eyes glinting in the moonlight..

'All are gathered here,' he cawed. 'Fur, feather and 'Phibian, united to celebrate the *Equinoxal Equilibrium.*' I noticed that suddenly he sounded quite well spoken, unlike his usual matey patter. This was probably the voice he used on special occasions. He dipped his beak respectfully to Tiberius. '*Loquere major nobilis bufo.*'

Tiberius nodded in acknowledgement. '*Benedicat te amicum Corvus*,' he responded. Then he sat back on his haunches and raised his head to the sky, spreading his front legs wide. His bronze eyes glittered in the moonlight.

'As we celebrate the Autumnal equinox, we acknowledge the turn of the year's wheel,' he intoned. 'Day and night are of equal length, light and dark are in equilibrium. From here the dark will reign until the light returns at the Solstice. Let us not fear but let us celebrate the cycle of the seasons.'

'*We shall not fear!*' responded the other animals.

'Nor will I,' I added quickly.

A hare looked at me with irritation. If I could blush with embarrassment, I would have. I had to fight the urge to wash, which is the cat equivalent of blushing.

'Don't worry, just try to keep up,' whispered Janet. 'Everyone has to start somewhere.'

'Et rota volvitur!' said Tiberius, his voice rising. *'Transit annus!'*

'*We shall not fear*!' responded everyone. I managed to respond in time with the others. I stole a quick glance at the hare, who nodded towards me approvingly. Somehow this made me feel quite proud.

'We welcome the Autumn; we fear not the dark!' cried Tiberius. *'Autumnus grata!'*

'Autumnus grata!' we responded.

As the last sound of our chant died away, a cool breeze sprang up, rustling the leaves and branches of the trees and wafting the grass, gently caressing our fur, or feathers, or skin, then rippling across the water of the pond, breaking the moon's reflection into a thousand miniature silver stars.

'The breath of Autumn," whispered Janet.
And with that breath of Autumn, we all seemed to hold *our* breath for several seconds until the breeze died away. Then, as one, we all relaxed.

Tiberius dropped forward onto all fours again and looked around the circle. 'I thank you all for your attendance,' he croaked. 'Go in peace and safety.' He hopped down from the stone. There was a general croaking, snuffling, cawing and snouting in response. Janet nudged me and we both said *'Miaow!'*

The hares bid the group goodbye and lolloped off, while the hedgehogs simply crashed off into the undergrowth in a search for slugs. Mr Brock snuffled over to the toads and began a conversation with them. Three of the crows cawed loudly and launched themselves rather gracelessly into the air. Henry was just about to take off when I called out to him.

'Y'all right Robert mate?' he said, lowering his wings. 'Did yer enjoy th' ceremonials then?'

'Er – yes, very interesting,' I said. 'But Henry… you sounded so… different.'

'*Posh* in fact,' put in Janet with a smile.

Henry chuckled in his throaty corvid way. ''Ah, we crows, we's good mimics, ain't we?' he said with a wink. 'That was me tephylone voice that was.'

'You mean *telephone* voice?' I said.

'That's wot I said,' replied Henry a bit huffily. '*Tephylone.*'

I decided not to push the point. 'Betty sounds a bit different when she talks on her mobile, so do some of the other humans. I've noticed that,' I said. 'Do they have to?'

'Ah, not s'much on mobiles,' said Henry thoughtfully. 'But they does on their proper tephylones. I lissens to 'em when I sits on the tephylone wires. Ol' 'Enery picks up a lot 'e does. So I uses me tephylone voice for speshul events like this.'

'How do you hear what humans are saying just by sitting on the telephone wires?' asked Janet. 'Surely you need an actual tephylone – I mean – telephone?'

'Ah, that's a crow secret, that is,' said Henry, with another wink, running his long wings feathers down his beak in a conspiratorially way. 'Anyway, it's past ol' 'Enery's roostin' time, so I'd best be orf. Wanna get a decent branch. See yers!' With that he flapped his big wings, causing quite a breeze of his own and flew off into the night sky, the *whup-whup-whup* sounds of his wing strokes getting fainter, the further away and higher he went.

'Crows, eh?' said Janet with a sigh. I nodded in agreement. Crows might be cleverer than owls, but it was murder to get an answer to their secrets. Rather like Tiberius in fact.

'Toodle-oo both!' said Mr Brock brightly as he rumbled past us, having finished his conversation with the toads. 'The night is young, but I still need to find some grub. Or grubs.'

We trotted over to where Tiberius and his toad followers were beginning to amble down the slope towards the pond.

'Ah, my young friends,' said Tiberius. 'You may not have met my fellow toads. May I introduce Benedict, Ophelia, Constanza, Malachi, Cumberbatch and Osric.' The toads nodded gravely as we greeted them.

'We must hasten now, as the weather is changing and we must seek our hibernation quarters,' said one of the female toads. I noticed she and the other female toad were somewhat bigger than the male toads.

'You're quite correct Ophelia,' said Tiberius. 'But I think Robert here needs to ask us something.'

Ophelia squinted at me, narrowing her bronze eyes, which is quite a difficult feat for a toad to achieve. 'Oh, it's *you*!' she said, as though recognizing me from somewhere. 'You look different without the long ears and big back legs.'

''Don't be so daft!' snapped a wizened little toad who, if anything, seemed older than Tiberius. 'That was *hundreds* of years ago!' He turned to look at me. 'Took you long enough to find your way back here then?'

'Malachi, *please* don't confuse Robert so,' said Tiberius heartily. 'He has much to learn in *this* life, let alone past lives.'

Before I could ask about these "past lives", recalling my strange dream when I was in the cottage cellar, Janet quickly interjected and started telling Tiberius about the cat skull and where it was found. I added what I knew and asked Tiberius if he or the other toads knew anything about how it had come to be buried under the old wall and with a bracelet.

The toads all looked at each other quizzically. One by one they shook their heads.

'As you know, we toads share long memories,' said Tiberius. 'We also tap into the memory of the water, which circulates around the world and connects to itself through space and time. But I'm afraid the burial of the cat is something we didn't observe. However…' He paused, deep in thought.

'Yes?' I prompted, by now rather tired of all the mystery and mysticism that night.

Tiberius looked at me thoughtfully and then said: 'Remember, young Robert, all life is linked. You may just as well look to a tree for the answer. For as a tree's roots are connected to the fungi trails in the soil, so they in turn are linked to other trees and plants and carry memory, so that tree may be where your answer lies.'

'Any particular tree, Tiberius?' asked Janet.

'Ah, my little famulus, you can help Robert find that answer,' beamed Tiberius. 'And now we must go and seek our rest.'

He and the other toads began to hurry down the slope with a surprising turn of speed. They pushed into the thicket of reeds at the water's edge and then slipped into the water itself. Suddenly, we were alone, beneath the night sky, the twinkling stars and the moon and their reflections on the dark water of the pond.

'Well, *that* was helpful,' I grumbled sarcastically. 'I suppose he thinks we need to go and ask all the trees by the old wall what they saw!'

'Maybe,' said Janet with an air of mystery. 'You just need to know how to talk to trees properly… and when.'

'Oh, don't *you* start with all that!' I muttered crossly. 'You're as bad as Tiberius with all the mystery stuff sometimes. I've never heard a tree talk in my life!'

'I'm not saying I have all the answers,' said Janet impatiently. 'But I'm sure *you'll* work it out on your own Robert, as you know *so* much!'

Before I could say anything else, Janet turned away and ran up the slope and disappeared into the treeline. I was about to follow her to apologise for being so grouchy but thought maybe it was best to let her cool down. After all, if Dorothy had spoken to Janet like that, I'd have leapt to Janet's defence. All I'd done was upset her just as badly as Dorothy could. The fact that I was Janet's friend made it worse somehow.

I sat by the pond, feeling ashamed by my outburst. I also felt something else, a kind of hollow feeling, deep in my chest. It took me a few minutes to realise what it was. For all that I had spent most my life as an Outling Cat, fending for myself, needing no friends or human help, I was an Allotment Cat now.

For the first time in many moonths I felt *alone*.

Chapter Five

The White Cat

I wandered disconsolately around the edges of the Allotments. My emotions were completely mixed up; I felt lonely, sad and angry all at once. I would have given anything to find Janet, touch noses with her and apologize for being so short-tempered. But no matter where I looked, she was nowhere to be found.

Most of my anger was directed at myself for allowing myself to be so short-tempered, but the truth was, part of that anger also came from the fact that I never seemed to get a straight answer from anyone – Tiberius, Janet, Mr Brock, the other Toads; they all knew - or seemed to know - more than me. Even more annoyingly, they seemed to know more about *me* than I did myself!

In short, I felt thoroughly miserable.

I explored the overgrown area and cottage ruins thoroughly – being careful to avoid the hole to the cottage cellar – but there was no sign of Janet. I caught her smell of course, but it was one of many, laid down as part of a mishmash of all the animals and humans that had been here recently. I decided to head towards the divide between the Allotments and the stadium building site, as she often walked that way to get to the pond.

As I approached the divide, I was aware of the trench dug where the wall had been, a long, dark expanse, with the silhouettes of the nearby trees standing like tall, black sentinels. Trench and trees were thrown in stark relief by the far-off security lights at the main stadium construction sight. My heart sank; there was neither sight nor sound nor smell of Janet.

By now, my feeling of being alone was overpowering any feelings of anger and I desperately wanted some company to cheer myself up. Whether it was one of the other Allotment Cats, Ruby or Mr Brock, I didn't mind. Even Finbarr or the owl would have relieved that awful feeling of loneliness. Perhaps I was feeling it so strongly because it was such an alien emotion to me. I'd spent so much of my life alone but since coming to the Allotments I had discovered not just a sense of belonging but also friendship. To have upset one of my friends had plunged me deep into despair.

'Come on Robert, pull yourself together,' I muttered to myself. 'Let's get onto the Allotments and find Fred. He'll cheer you up!' Truth be told, even Dorothy at her snarky best would have been a welcome face right then.

I trotted along the line of the trench, planning to pass the bramble bushes which marked the boundary of the overgrown area and then cut down one of the paths into the allotment plots. Just then, the moon came out from behind a cloud, its silvery light creating even sharper dark shadows. Suddenly, I felt a chill in the air. It wasn't a breeze but felt more like the times I'd stood by the clubhouse fridge when someone had opened the door to fetch a bottle of milk. But it was as though I'd stepped from a mild Autumn night into a freezing Winter night. I stood still, wondering what had happened, my tail twitching madly in agitation. Then, slowly and surely, I felt my tail fur begin to bristle, my whiskers tingling. I sensed that someone or *something* unknown was in the vicinity. I turned in a full circle, looking all around me and then my eyes fell upon the source of my agitation.

It was a cat.

A white cat.

In fact, it was the *whitest* cat I'd ever seen. I had the impression that it was glowing but decided that this was just the effect of the moonlight on its fur.

The cat was sitting quite still a few yards from the trench, staring ahead in the direction of the stadium, further back where I had just walked from. Then it stood up and began to slowly walk towards the trench and the waste ground leading to the stadium. There was something about the way it walked which bothered me, because somehow it didn't look quite *right*.

I instinctively lowered myself to the ground, my back legs poised to spring, bottom rising, tail madly thrashing. It's not that I wanted to get into a fight at all, but this cat was obviously not an Allotment Cat. Maybe it was a Home Cat who'd taken a wrong turning somewhere, which did occasionally happen, although any such interlopers were soon chased out of the Allotments by us residents. Or possibly it was an Outling Cat looking for somewhere to live, in which case he or she might be welcome, but it was my residential duty to challenge any strange cats and ask their business.

Besides, the cat only looked about as big as me from this distance and therefore wouldn't be *too* much of a physical threat. (You have to consider these things before you run up to a stranger shouting the odds).

I inched forward, then scooted along faster, still keeping low to the ground. Having black fur would give me the element of surprise in the dark, but I had already planned to break cover a little way from the white cat, just to prevent it from lashing out at me in surprise. Hopefully it would also take that opportunity to run away.

Just at that precise moment, the cat's head spun round and he – I felt from its build that it was a male – stared in my direction. Realising that he'd seen me, I sat up to show myself, smoothing my fur down. I began to slowly walk towards the cat, noting that he wasn't displaying any sign of aggression. Nor fear, come to that. In fact, this strange cat didn't seem to notice me at all.

'Hello there!' I called amiably. 'Are you lost?'

The white cat didn't reply.

I drew closer and then sat down quickly. I was now perhaps two shed lengths from the cat and I realised that I couldn't actually *see* his fur. It was as though he had no fur and his whole body was white. I tried to make out what colour his eyes were. Like his body, they just seemed to be white, but were also white with dark pupils, eyes that seemed to look right through me. In fact, I realised with a sudden jolt that *I could see through him*! It was like the times I'd looked through the windows of the clubhouse or one of the greenhouses on a misty day when everything outside seemed blurred and indistinct. I could just make out tufts of grass, a nearby bush, as though looking through a white mist – except that this white mist was cat-shaped and I was looking *through its body*!

My fur bristled again and I arched my back, a long, low growl rumbling up from my throat to end in a protracted hiss. Looking back, I know that what I felt then wasn't just everyday fear of the unknown but total, deep-rooted, ancestral, bladder-loosening fear for my life! I felt rooted to the spot, willing my legs to propel me away from this strange apparition, but unable to move. I don't mind admitting that my bladder failed me at that point, as my back paws suddenly felt damp.

However, the white cat-thing (I decided it wasn't male or female at this point), made no move to attack, but simply turned its head back towards the stadium. Suddenly, it darted towards the trench, making no sound, not even a swish of air as it moved. I couldn't even say that its feet touched the ground as it moved. It wasn't so much running as simply *gliding* towards the trench.

Then suddenly, it was gone!

I finally got my legs to work and I leaped backwards – which is an exceptionally good manoeuvre if you can do it – flipped around in the air, landed on all fours and ran in the opposite direction. I screeched to a halt by the cover of a big tree, then turned to look back to where the white cat-thing had been. It wasn't there. Swallowing hard and willing myself to be brave, I cautiously walked back along the trench line. My heart was pounding madly, but although I was still afraid, I *had* to see where the cat-thing had gone. Had it jumped into the trench, or leaped over the trench to run across the waste ground towards the stadium?

I sniffed the ground as I passed the spot where I had stood and drew near to where the white cat-thing had been. I could smell myself quite clearly and there was a faint smell of Janet from earlier that day, but there was absolutely no smell of another cat! I reached the spot where the mysterious creature had been and tiptoed to the edge of the trench. I cautiously peered in but saw nothing but darkness. If the white cat-thing had been there, I'd have surely seen it. I looked in both directions but couldn't see nor smell a cat. The only smell I could detect was earth and human sweat from the workmen, mingled with the dusty smell from the building site and a hint of chicken and ham.

I sat up and scanned the waste ground beyond. I didn't feel like jumping over the trench to investigate so far away from the Allotments. But by the moonlight and the distant security lights I had a good view of the area. The ground was much less bumpy and full of holes than it had been when Grasper's workmen had dug it all up with their noisy machines some moonths before. The new workmen had pretty much flattened it down, so there was nowhere for a cat to hide unless it reached the stadium building itself. Again, I saw no sign of the white cat… or whatever it was.

I backed away from the trench, my fur still bristling, and another growl forming in my throat. I can't claim to be the world's bravest animal, but I'm no scaredy-cat either. However, on this occasion, I turned tail and fled towards the Allotments, crashing through the plots in a blind panic.

I realised then that what I had seen was something I'd heard about but had never been totally convinced really existed.

I had seen a ghost!

I charged pell-mell through the plots until I collided with the solid ginger mass of Red Fred who was patrolling at his usual measured, leonine pace. It was like hitting a furry marmalade-coloured wall. Fred hardly moved but I rebounded and ended up on my back looking up into the night sky. I swear I saw more stars than there should have been at that point.

'You alright mate?' rumbled Fred, looking down at me with concern. With his heavy accent it sounded more like *'Yow owroight mayte?'*, but it was this sense of normality and familiarity which allowed me to breathe more easily and calm down somewhat.

I sat up and babbled out my story about the ghost-cat-thing. Fred listened patiently, then asked me to repeat it more slowly. I took a deep breath and did so. Fred's brow furrowed in concentration. I saw his cheeks twitch slightly, causing his whiskers to vibrate.

'You're trying not to laugh, aren't you?' I muttered crossly.

'Oh, I'm sorry mate,' chuckled Fred. 'But you've got to admit, it *does* sound a bit far-fetched. I mean, I know odd things go on in the Allotments, but a ghost cat? I think it might've been a trick of the light. It was probably just some white-furred Outling or Home Cat who'd got lost and the moonlight an' shadows made it look sort of ghostly.''

'Was the *Gathering* "a trick of the light" too?' I snapped. 'The strange mist that carried us there, the standing stones, all the animals gathered in perfect peace?' I was trying not to be angry at my friend's disbelief, but truth be told, I was starting to doubt myself.

'That's diff'rent mate,' said Fred, reasonably. 'That was *magic*, that was.'

I sighed. I had no wish to argue with Fred. 'Perhaps you're right,' I said. 'What with that cat's skull being dug up near there and all that mystic stuff with the Equinox ceremony and all… maybe I was just feeling a bit on edge.'

Just at that moment, GG slipped through a row of bean canes, followed by Barbara. 'Hello you two,' said GG. 'What's wrong, Robert? Barbara and I saw you running like a pack of dogs were after you.'

'You didn't see *us* though,' added Barbara, 'You were going too fast.'

'Robert thinks he's seen a ghost,' said Fred, but without any hint of mockery in his voice.

'Really?' exclaimed GG. 'Do tell us, Robert!'

I sighed and repeated my story. Telling it for a third time made me realise how ridiculous it must sound. Barbara sniggered, but not unkindly. However, GG wasn't laughing. She looked thoughtful.

'That cat skull…' she mused. 'It was dug up by the workmen from under the wall's foundations, wasn't it?'

I nodded.

'Well, what if the skull belonged to the cat whose ghost you saw? That is, if you did see a ghost, of course,' said GG.

'What would a ghost want with a cat's skull then?' asked Barbara in a confused voice.

'No, I meant the cat whose skull it was,' explained GG. 'When it was alive. The skull inside its fur.'

'Ah, I see…' said Barbara slowly. He then spoiled it rather by adding, 'I think.'

GG patiently explained that whoever the unfortunate cat was, it had died and been buried. Some years later the wall was built on top of where it was buried. Then when the workmen knocked down the wall, they dug up what was left of the cat, namely its skull.

'So that ghost-cat-thing I saw,' I said. 'That's the ghost of the cat whose skull they found?'

'Exactly!' said GG, with some relief. Barbara nodded vigorously to show that he understood too.

'So, if it *was* a ghost that I saw, why hasn't anyone seen it before now?' I asked.

'I don't know,' said GG. 'Maybe digging up the skull disturbed it, woke it up?'

'And it saw Robert and decided to haunt him, I suppose?' said a sharp, sarcastic voice which made us all jump. Dorothy stalked out of the darkness, rather like a tortoiseshell apparition herself, her face a wearing a look of disdain. She had obviously been listening to our conversation. 'What utter rot!' she added. 'Fancy being frightened of a white stray.'

'Huh! Not like you were terrified of the skull earlier today, was it, Princess?' retorted Fred.

'That was *different*!' snapped Dorothy, defensively. 'It took me by surprise, that's all.'

'You have to admit Dorothy, it does sound strange,' said GG. 'I wonder if Janet might have an idea about it?'

'I was looking for Janet,' I said miserably. 'We – er – well, we had… words and she ran off.'

'Oh, who *cares?*' snorted Dorothy. 'So Thingy got upset. Maybe she's decided to go off and hibernate like that awful amphibian she adores so much. At least we won't have to listen to all that mystic mog mumbo-jumbo anymore.'

I narrowed my eyes at Dorothy, trying to give her a dose of her own medicine with a stern Look, but it was dark and she wasn't facing me anyway. But I gave the back of her head a good hard Look anyway.

'Tell you what, why don't we *all* go up to that trench at the boundary now and maybe see who or what it was?' said GG brightly. She turned to me and added, kindly: 'I'm not saying you didn't see *something* Robert, but whether it was a ghost or not, we don't know. So, let's find out. Whatever it is, it may still be around.'

Barbara and Red Fred agreed. I nodded reluctantly because I had no real desire to go near that spot again. However, I reasoned there was safety in numbers, so I felt a bit bolder about doing so. Besides, I was rather hoping that we *would* all see the strange ghost-cat-thing again. Even if it *was* just an ordinary white cat – which would put my mind at rest – it would prove that I *had* seen something.

'Yow comin' Princess?' said Fred as we turned to leave. Dorothy was still washing, making no move to join us.

'It's a ridiculous waste of time,' she sniffed.

'Oh well, please yowself, Princess,' said Fred in an off-paw sort of way. 'I thought you wouldn't want to miss a chance to be proved right, that's all. Oh well…' With that he slipped me a sly wink and set off, slipping between two sheds, tail held high, with me trying to walk bravely alongside him, Barbara and GG trotting along just behind us. A few seconds later we heard pawsteps behind us. We turned to see Dorothy hurrying to catch us up.

Before we could say anything, she said crossly: 'This is just to prove there's no such thing as ghosts, okay?'

'Okay Princess,' chuckled Fred smugly, setting off again. 'If yow say so.'

From just behind us we heard the cross retort: '*And don't call me Princess!*'

'Well, *this* is exciting!' Dorothy was being sarcastic, but she had a point. For the past few hours, we had all been sitting perfectly still, our front paws tucked neatly under our chests, just a few yards from the trench, watching and waiting for a sign of the white-cat-ghost-thing. But, apart from a mouse who probably turned white with shock when he broke cover and saw five cats staring intently at him, we'd seen nothing, white or otherwise. (The mouse fled to safety, although we were tempted to give chase!). By now the eastern sky above the stadium building site was growing lighter, and the rumble from traffic on the busy main road which ran past the stadium site and the Allotments was increasing. The human world was waking up.

'It'll soon be light,' observed GG. 'Should we call it a night? Or a day even?'

'Let's give it just a few more minutes,' said Barbara. 'I'm sure Robert saw something and whatever it was may come back before dawn.'

I smiled to myself, appreciating Barbara's support, even if he didn't think I'd seen a ghost.

We sat quietly for more minutes. We heard the tweeting of birds, the dawn chorus starting up as the sky grew lighter still.

'I saw a really weird thing the other day,' said Fred conversationally, more to break the silence than anything, I guessed.

'What was it?' I asked, hoping that it might add some weight to my ghost-cat-thing sighting.

'It was one of the plot holders, that bloke Sandy,' said Fred. 'He was looking at birds in a tree.'

'Nothing unusual about that, Fred,' I said. 'I look at birds in the trees all the time.'

'I know, but I mean he was looking really *hard* at 'em,' said Fred. 'He had these sort of long glasses things which he held up to his eyes.'

'Hmm, that *does* sound odd,' I agreed.

'He was using Binockilers,' piped up GG. 'They're like spectacles which humans use to see things that are a long way off. They haven't got such good eyesight as us, after all.'

'Oh right,' said Fred. 'But I couldn't work out why Sandy was so interested in *those* birds. There's birds around the allotments all the time.'

'Maybe he was playing that game that they play on their phones,' said GG. 'You know, *Irritated Birdies*.'

'He wasn't using his phone though,' replied Fred. 'And the birds didn't seem annoyed to me.'

Dorothy sighed impatiently. 'Oh, for goodness sake! He was *birdwatching*!' she snapped.

'I know he was...' began Fred but Dorothy cut him short.

'I mean, it's a thing they do. When I lived in the bookshop there were lots of books on Birdwatching in the Hobbies section. Birdwatching must be his hobby.'

'Hobbies?' said GG. 'Aren't they those small people that live in round houses in the side of hills and go on quests and things and...'

'No! *Hobbies!*' exclaimed Dorothy impatiently. 'It's things that humans do to stop themselves getting bored. Like some of the plot holders do allotmenting as a hobby and show their vegetables and flowers to other humans to win prizes. Or… or collect stamps and things.'

'Oh yeah,' I said. 'I've seen something like that. Some humans take their really *posh* Home Cats out for the day to show them off against other really posh Home Cats. Funny old business that. I wouldn't want to sit in a cage all day and have strange humans poking at me.'

'Well, you're quite happy when strange humans come to the allotments and poke at you and give you treats,' muttered Dorothy. She could do sarcasm very cuttingly. I pretended to ignore her.

'Oh well,' said Fred, standing up and stretching, arching his back and standing high on his toes. He yawned extravagantly. 'It's nearly dawn and we haven't seen whatever it was you saw, mate, so I reckon it's time to head back to me shed for a couple of hours' shuteye until Betty rocks up with our breakfast.'

The others began to slowly unfurl themselves and stretch, yawning. I reluctantly followed suit a few seconds later, just as they began to make their way around the bramble bushes and back to the allotments. The sky was still dark behind the bushes, the growing light not yet reaching the undergrowth.

Suddenly there was a wailing sound which sounded like '*W-w-w-w-woooo*!' Everybody froze in their tracks, ears twitching madly. Before anyone could speak there was a rustling from the brambles and suddenly a white cat shape burst through and rolled across the grass towards them!

Well! What happened next was a real cat-atsrophe, I can tell you! Fred, Barbara, Dorothy and GG fluffed up, their fur bristling and they all yowled and hissed. Dorothy swore and spat as she scrambled up the trunk of one of the tall trees. GG and Barbara pelted off in opposite directions. Before I could react, Fred barged into me as he ran past, sending me flying backwards into the trench.

Luckily, I landed on all fours, although this turn of events had completely confused me. I had no wish to be in the trench where the cat skull had lain and where, possibly, the ghost-cat-thing had disappeared into. I also suspected that the white cat shape that had scared everyone silly *wasn't* the ghostly apparition though. Hoping I was right, I leapt up the side of the trench, hooked my front claws on the lip and pulled myself up….

…. To come face to face with ET who had wobbled over to the trench. ET is, of course, mainly white, which explained everyone's surprise when she had crashed out of the darkened bushes. The perfect ghost cat lookalike to tired feline minds, in fact.

'Oh h-h-hello R-R-Robert,' she wibbled. 'I s-s-saw you all over h-h-here and tried to *getthroughthe* br-brambles, b-but I got stuck! I st-st-struggled and th-then *fellthrough* b-b-but everyone *ranaway*. I m-m-must have *surprisedthem*.'

'Very possibly,' I said, with a smirk.

She looked at me in confusion. 'Wh-what are you d-doing *downthattrench*?'

'Oh, just inspecting the workmanship,' I said airily as I pulled myself out onto the grass. 'Nice and straight, good smooth sides. Those workmen have done a good job.'

ET nodded, or maybe just wobbled her head. It was hard to tell sometimes.

'Anyway ET,' I said brightly, attempting to restore my dignity. 'I'm just heading back to my shed for a snooze.'

'Oh, g-g-*goodidea*!' enthused ET. 'I've b-b-been *outallnight* h-h-hunting m-mice. I'm qu-qu-quite *tirednow*.

As we strolled and wobbled towards the allotments ET stopped and flopped around to look up into the branches of a tall tree nearby. A few yellowing leaves fluttered down with a rustle as Dorothy climbed higher in the branches to safety, not having seen that the scary white apparition had, in fact, been ET.

'Wh-why i-i-is D-D-Dorothy *upthattree*?' ET asked me, puzzled.

'Er… she's birdwatching,' I said, as we turned away. 'It's her hobby, you know.'

Chapter Six

Catnip Capers

Over the next couple of (human) weeks, the weather turned much cooler and more unsettled, with frequent rain. The nights were definitely colder and I found myself spending more time snuggled up in my cat bed in Betty's shed during the night. And on particularly cold days I'd spend time curled up in any of the cat beds in the clubhouse in between my regular patrols and feeding times.

The allotments were changing too. Many of the vegetables on the plots had been picked, their stalks now withered. The plot holders were then digging the plants up and throwing them on compost heaps, then digging the soil over to plant what they called "winter crops", such as broad beans, onions and garlic. Meanwhile, the leaves on the trees were rapidly changing colour from their usual green to yellow, brown and red before they began to fall from the trees and carpet the ground.

I noticed several plot holders raking up the leaves on and around their plots and adding these to their compost heaps or putting them in special bags or bins to make a type of compost called "leaf mould", which apparently would help vegetables and flowers grow better. I wouldn't know about that, but I've always found leaf mould quite soft and comfortable to poo in.

In fact, I overheard a long conversation between Colin, Kate and Donna on the rival merits of leaf mould made from different kinds of leaves. Well, I say *conversation*, it was more Colin expounding on leaf mould while Kate and Donna nodded politely and said 'Uh-huh' at certain intervals and fidgeted quite a lot. Eventually Kate whipped her mobile phone out of her pocket and said 'Oh, excuse me, I've got to take this,' and wandered off with her phone to her ear. It was odd though, because I hadn't heard it ring and she didn't seem to be talking to anyone. Shortly after, Donna hurried off with apologies to Colin saying she needed to catch Betty before she left for the day to ask her something extremely important, although I knew that Betty had *already* left for the day and was sure I'd seen Donna talking to her just *before* she left.

As I've said before: Humans can behave very oddly at times.

On those nights when it wasn't raining or too cold, I'd venture cautiously over to the boundary area to stand watch, to see if that strange white ghost-cat-thing came back. Once or twice I even found Red Fred or Barbara there. When I asked them what they were doing they said they'd simply been "just passing", but I knew they were looking for it too. However, none of us saw anything out of the ordinary, apart from the new tall metal fence that the workmen had put up.

In fact, it had been quite interesting to watch the workmen put the fence up each day. To begin with, a very large truck had been driven over the waste ground to the boundary trench. Then Big Dave had pulled a long, thick hose from the back of it and held it above the trench. Then a gloopy greyish liquid had poured out of the hose, almost filling the trench. I heard one of the workmen call this stuff "concrete". As Dave walked along the trench pouring the concrete into it, the other workmen placed tall metal poles along the trench at regular intervals and held them there. After a few minutes they let go of the poles which stood up by themselves. I was so curious by this point that I ignored the rumbling noise from the truck and walked over to take a look. The concrete in the trench had become hard, a bit like water does when it freezes, but this was much, much thicker, making it look and feel like stone, which held the metal poles in place. I realised then using concrete was how humans built a lot of their houses and other buildings.

After Big Dave had filled the trench and all the poles were firmly set into the concrete, the workmen had a break, so there were ham sandwiches and pieces of chicken again. Of course, they invited me to share in their meal and yes, a fuss was made of me and more photographs were taken.

The day after the poles had been set in concrete, the workmen started attaching big metal panels to them to create a new fence. I thought this was a bit of a shame because the workmen would then be on the other side of the very tall new fence and there would be no chance for them to share their meals with me. The fence had lots of little round holes in the metal, so I could look through to the stadium site and waste ground if I wanted to, but unfortunately the holes weren't big enough for any of the workmen to pass any bits of ham or chicken through to me. Still, before they put the final panel up, they did have a lunch break, and Big Dave had brought a plastic tub of chicken and ham pieces especially for me.

'I'll miss seein' yer, Robert,' he rumbled, with genuine sadness in his voice. 'Might see if I can get meself a plot in your allotments sometime, then I can see yer when I'm growin' fresh veg for me missus.'

I told Dave that this was a very good idea by rubbing myself around his legs.

It occurred to me that now, what with the trench having been filled with solid concrete, not to mention a heavy metal fence sat on top, that any ghost cat would find it very difficult to escape from the trench. Then again, I remembered, solid objects didn't seem to be something that had bothered whatever-it-was that I saw that night, so if it wanted to get out, it could easily do so. The thought of that made me shiver.

Thankfully, the other cats seemed to have recovered from their shock when ET had burst out of the brambles. In fact, once they realised that it had been ET and not a ghost-cat, everybody thought it was amusing. All except Dorothy that is, who snootily claimed that she wasn't startled or scared, she'd simply seen a particularly plump bird up the tree and had decided to try to catch it. When ET innocently asked if she'd been bird watching, we all fell about laughing, which led to Dorothy flouncing off in a moody sulk which lasted a full two days.

There was one thing bothering me more than anything about the ghost-cat-thing or even if Big Dave would ever be able to share his lunch with me again; I hadn't seen Janet since that fateful evening of the Equinox when I'd upset her. I'd asked the other cats (except Dorothy) if they'd seen her around, but nobody had. However, as Red Fred wisely pointed out, Janet was very adept at moving around the allotments and not being observed, being very shy by nature. This made me think that Janet didn't *want* to be seen, particularly by me. This was a very sad thought indeed. All I wanted to do was to say sorry to her for being so unkind.

As for the whole mystery of the cat skull and the copper bracelet, nothing further had been discovered by the humans. I'd listened in on a conversation between Betty, Kate, Donna and Anji. It seemed that Anji's friend Maeve from the University had been away "on a dig" for the past few weeks (which I assume meant she had been busy on an allotment plot of her own somewhere). But she had promised to analyse the bracelet upon her return. As for GG looking up some information about the bracelet online, she hadn't been able to sneak a peek at Betty's laptop. Betty was either using it or remembering to take it home with her when she left each day. Perhaps she had her suspicions that another plot holder was posting messages from me on *Nitter-Natter* and *FaceyFriends*, so wanted to post my messages herself. It was a bit annoying, because GG hadn't been able to post any *real* messages from me either! It might keep my human fans happy, but my animal fans would be able to tell the difference.

So, all in all, I was really fed up! (And not "fed up" in a good way).

One morning, I was sitting outside the greenhouse which I'd decided was one of my hangout homes, still feeling miserable, despite this day being sunny, dry and reasonably warm for a change. Leaves were fluttering gently from the trees to create a brightly coloured blanket on the empty plot next to the greenhouse. I was idly watching two squirrels leaping between two oak trees arguing over a particular acorn, which one of them had in its mouth. It didn't seem to occur to the dozy bushy-tailed tree rats that there were hundreds of acorns both in the trees and lying on the ground around them. But even watching them squabbling was failing to cheer me up.

'Oh, there you are mate! Been looking for you everywhere.' I looked up as Red Fred peered round the corner of the greenhouse.

'Oh, hi Fred,' I said, glumly.

'Bit down in the dumps, are you?' said Fred. 'I'll tell you what'll cheer you up – Betty's making nipknots in the clubhouse. The catnip harvest is in!'

My ears pricked up at this and my attention was fully engaged. I'd seen the plot where the catnip grew and it smelled lovely, always worth a sniff whenever I passed by. Fred had told me soon after I arrived in the allotments that the catnip harvest was an eagerly anticipated event by the Allotment Cats. Usually, there would be at least two harvests of the delightfully delicious plant, but due to the uncertainly about the allotments' fate earlier this year, the first harvest hadn't taken place.

I'd been told that Betty would dry the leaves out, grind them up and sew them into little kitty toys which she called nipknots, made out of spare bits of fabric. People would then buy these toys for their own cats and Betty would put the money into the Allotment Cats' Vet Fund. As I've said, I don't really understand money, but apparently this was all for our benefit in case we got ill and needed the vet. All I knew was, the nipknot toys were great fun, as Betty had given me one soon after I'd stopped being wary of her and ventured into the clubhouse. It smelled delicious and made me drool and was great fun to kick around, leap on, chew and play with.

'Well come on mate – they cut the 'nip down a few days back and they've got the dried-out leaves in the clubhouse,' said Fred excitedly. It was unusual to see Red Fred quite so animated – he was usually a very laid-back sort of fellow.

'Let's go!' I said with genuine enthusiasm, as I stood and stretched. If catnip wouldn't lift me out of the doldrums, nothing would!

'Hang on a mo,'chuckled Fred crouching down and lifting his bottom into the air, his tail wiggling with anticipation. I followed his gaze over to the grass by the trees where the two squirrels had come down from the trees and were now engaged in an energetic tug-of-war for the prized acorn, each with it jaws clamped round the acorn. They were making muffled, angry chittering sounds. It looked for all the world like they were kissing.

Suddenly Red Fred sprang forward, propelled by his powerful back legs (I thought briefly how Finbarr the frog would have approved of a leap like that). He landed directly in front of the squirrels with a shout of '*Boo!*' causing them to leap into the air in fright, their bushy tails bristling out even more than usual. The precious acorn dropped to the ground as they streaked up the nearest tree, scattering fallen leaves in their wake, all rivalry forgotten.

I had to chuckle as I saw Fred flop down onto his side laughing, blending very nicely with the orange leaves. The squirrels glowered at him from the tree, swearing and waving their tails. One of them even shook a fist at Fred angrily.

'I'll bop you on the snotbox, you big stripey so-and-so!' it chittered.[8] Fred just rolled onto his back and laughed some more, before flipping over and standing up.

'Yeah, yeah, yeah, you and whose army?' said Fred dismissively, padding towards me nonchalantly. He winked at me. 'I always enjoy stirring up squirrels.'

Just as Fred reached where I was standing, I saw a smaller squirrel bound across the grass, snatch up the fallen acorn and skitter up another tree. The two bigger squirrels were horrified at the loss of their coveted acorn and chittered at each other madly.

'If *you* hadn't dropped it…!'

'Well, *you* were frightened of that moggy, so *you* dropped it!'

'Oh yeah? Like *you* were gonna tangle with the moggy?'

---

[8] The squirrel actually swore a lot whilst saying this, but this is a family book, so I've edited the bad words out. And I thought us cats could swear when we wanted to!

'I *could've* done! I only ran after you to protect you 'cos you was so frit!'

'Frit? *Frit*? You callin' me a coward are ya? Are ya?'

'Come on then!'

We left them to their sweary argument and headed off to the clubhouse. All that fuss over one acorn. I mean, what's the attraction with acorns? I suppose it's a squirrel thing.

A minute or so later, we entered the clubhouse. I could smell the heady aroma of the catnip before I saw it – and what a sight it was! The long committee table was covered with bundles of dried catnip plants and a heap of brightly coloured pieces of fabric, along with a selection of cotton reels. Betty was sitting at one side of the table industriously stuffing powdered, crushed catnip into individual sausage-shaped pieces of fabric, then sewing the side and ends of each one up, before snipping the loose fabric at the ends with scissors to make tassels.

She was being assisted by a younger lady who'd recently joined the allotments team. She was named Phillipa, but everyone called her Pip. Right now, Pip was pulling the dry leaves off the catnip plant stalks, putting them in a bowl and grinding them up with some sort of tool thingy. Betty would then take a handful of the crushed catnip from the bowl to stuff into the fabric she was sewing. The completed nipknots were being dropped into a cardboard box on the floor next to the table.

Betty and Pip were chatting amiably whilst working and hadn't seen Fred and me as we trotted over to a stack of empty cardboard boxes which were awaiting shredding for compost.

I wasn't entirely surprised to find Dorothy, Barbara, and GG lurking behind the boxes. They were sniffing the air, taking in the heady scent of the catnip. We all greeted each other and settled down to watch Betty and Pip at work.

'Reckon we'll be given some new nipknots when they've finished?' said Barbara. 'Mine's almost completely lost its scent now.'

'I reckon so,' said Fred. 'Mine's gone all manky after I've kicked it around. Pity the catnip smell doesn't last long.'

'Well, the good news is they always grow plenty of catnip on the plot,' added GG.

'Anyway, they surely can't be selling *all* the nipknots they're making,' observed Dorothy. 'After all, surely we Allotment Cats come first for the catnip?'

'Yes, but they sell the nipknots to raise money for our vet care,' GG pointed out.

'Yes, well… I still like a nipknot of my own though,' replied Dorothy.

I sniffed the air again, drawing in the delightful catnip aroma. The fact is, green, growing catnip smells very attractive to us cats, it even makes us feel a little dizzy and playful. But when it's dried and put inside toys, well… it *really* makes us feel very strange and very, *very* happy and playful. Right now, the aroma of the dried catnip was causing me to feel rather light-headed and wanting to purr with pleasure.

Just then, Betty's mobile phone started to ring. She picked it up off the table and spoke into it. 'Hello? Yes, yes, this is Mrs DeGatto… uh-huh… At the gate?... You unloaded it *there*? Why didn't you call me?... Yes, I *know* you've called me *now*! But… oh never mind! We'll have to manage!'

Betty plonked her phone down onto the table. She looked very flustered.

'What's up, Betty?' asked Pip, looking concerned.

'Oh, it's the delivery men with those fertilizer sacks,' said Betty crossly. 'They were due to deliver them here – we got them in bulk to sell to the plot holders, remember?' Pip nodded. 'Well, because the gate to the Allotments is locked – like it always is – they've only gone and unloaded all the sacks at the gate! I mean, why didn't they call me when they arrived? I'd have gone up and unlocked the gate so they could drive their van up to the clubhouse!'

'Can't they do that now?' asked Pip.

'Oh no, they've "got another delivery",' said Betty, making those odd quotation mark signs that humans do with their fingers. 'So they've just driven off and left the sacks there. Now I'm going to have to drive up to the gate and load them into my car!'

'Oh, how stupid of them!' agreed Pip. 'Never mind Betty, I'll bring my car up as well and help you. I reckon we can load them into the car boots okay, maybe onto the back seats as well. We'll sort it.'

With that, Betty and Pip stopped their nipknot work, got up and hurried out of the clubhouse. In their haste, they didn't notice us behind the cardboard boxes. A few seconds later we heard two car engines start up, then the cars move off down the road towards the allotment gates.

'Well, that sounded odd,' I said.

'That's tradesmen for you!' said Dorothy disapprovingly.

'Definitely,' agreed Red Fred. 'But look – they've left the catnip on the table… and the nipknots are in that box. Shall we go an' have a sniff?'

'I'm sure they wouldn't mind if we just had a *sniff*,' agreed Barbara.

'Just a sniff after all,' I added.

'Well, come on then,' said Dorothy, already heading towards the table. 'They'll be back soon and they won't want us messing with the catnip, so we'd better hurry up!'

Within a very few seconds, we'd all jumped up onto the table and were sniffing the dried catnip plants. The smell was overpowering! My eyes went out of focus and my body suddenly felt very light, almost as if I could float up to the ceiling. I realised that I was beginning to drool. The catnip seemed to have had the same effect on the others and they were beginning to weave unsteadily across the table.

'Oh, thash sho gooooood,' muttered Dorothy indistinctly. 'Letsh… letsh have a shniff… of the sthtuff… inna bowl…' She poked her head into the bowl and put both her front paws onto it.

Of course, the bowl tipped over, spilling the finely ground catnip across the table. As one, we all dived on it, poking our noses into it, inhaling the amazing heady scent. I felt lots of tiny bits of catnip leaf tingling inside my nose. I sneezed, blowing a cloud of catnip into Barbara's face. He in turn sneezed, blowing more catnip onto Dorothy. Within seconds we were all sniffing and sneezing, laughing delightedly. I didn't think that I'd felt that giddy since I was a kitten. In fact, my brain seemed to be telling me I *was* a kitten! Of *course* I was a kitten… it felt so *right*!

I flopped down happily and then, through bleary eyes saw a familiar face looming over me. It was Janet!

'Hello Robert,' she purred. 'You look like you're having fun.'

I grinned up at her stupidly and tried to focus my thoughts. 'Ja… Janet. I'm… sho…sho shorry I upshet you…' I mumbled muzzily. 'I mish… mished you.'

'I f-f-*foundher*!' wibbled ET, her face also filling my vision. 'Sh-she-she *wasoustide* the clubhouse. W-w-we c-c-*couldsmellthecatnip* from outside!'

'It's alright Robert, I forgive you,' said Janet, delicately touching noses with me. I sneezed loudly, causing Janet to back into ET, who fell into the pile of catnip plants. She rolled around for a few seconds to regain her balance, in the process crushing several of the dried leaves.

'L-l-look, ET's making…h-h-her own catnip powder!' laughed Barbara.

'Shorry I schneezed on you, J-J-Janet,' I slurred. 'Ish – ish the catnip – ish making me all li-li-light headed.'

'Don't worry Robert,' said Janet primly. 'I'll have a little sniff myself.' She bent her head to the table and began to sniff the powdered catnip. She sat down promptly and sneezed. 'Oh, that's rather good,' she purred.

'Oh look, ish… ish… Fingy!' said Dorothy, almost delightedly. She tried to stand up, but couldn't manage to, so she crawled across the table to Janet. 'I-I- know your namesh really Janet, Fingy,' she said, 'But I-I only call you Fingy cos… cos… you're sho nice an' an – I'm sho nashty. No-nobody lovesh me!'

Janet regarded Dorothy evenly and said nothing.

Dorothy started to sniff uncontrollably. We cats can't cry like humans but we can wail and that's exactly what Dorothy started to do… very loudly.

'Shush! Shush Princhesh!' giggled Fred. 'They'll hear you up at th-the gate!'

'But everybody *hatesh* me!' wailed Dorothy. '*Awwwwwoooolll*!'

'W-w-we don't hate you, Do-Do-Doroffy!' I babbled, trying to quieten her down. 'You're n-n-nicesh really. An-and p-p-pretty.' I flopped down next to her. Janet meanwhile was busily investigating a relatively undisturbed patch of catnip which hadn't been inhaled or sneezed all over the table. I muzzily hoped she hadn't heard me telling Dorothy she was pretty.

Dorothy started to knead my tummy with her paw. 'Oh Wobert! Dear, dear Wobert,' purred Dorothy. 'You're sh-sho kind.' She waved her head around blearily taking in the other cats and waved a paw in my general direction. 'Ishn't he kind everyone?' she added. The others all slurrily agreed.

'*Awww* look!' cooed Dorothy, peering at me. 'You've g-o-gone aaaalll slit-eyed and dribbly! Thish catnipsh the biz, ishn't it? You *handshome* beast you, Wobert!'

'*Handshome*, me?' I stammered. 'Yesh, yesh, I shuppose I am. Hey everyone, I'm handshome! Doroffy shez sho!'

'I'm g-ggoing to play with the nipknots!' shouted Barbara and with a cry of 'Wheee!' leapt from the table straight into the cardboard box of nipknots, which upended, spilling Barbara and nipknots all over the floor. "Come b-b-back nipknotsh!' wailed Barbara. 'Come back, for flipsh's sake.' He began to pounce at them, but instead of trying to grab them one by one, he tried to grab them all at the same time in every direction. It was quite exciting to behold.

'Hey, look at me!' exclaimed ET. 'I've gone all wobbly and I sound funny!' I was amazed to see ET walking up and down in perfectly straight lines but without the hint of a wobble that I could see. Her eyes were as glazed as everyone else's, but the catnip seemed to be affecting her in quite a different way. No wobble to her walk and no wibble to her voice either.

'I think… I think… I know what's going on,' said GG very slowly and deliberately. 'The catnip is usually in those -nuh-nuh-nipknots we play with and the fabric controls the o-o-odour. But this is *raw* catnip and it's… it's… *lovelyyyyy…*' She collapsed onto her side and started to snore loudly.

Somewhere, seemingly from far off, I heard the sound of two cars drawing up outside. Then I heard footsteps coming into the clubhouse.

'Oops! I forgot to close the door,' came Pip's voice.

'Don't worry,' said Betty. 'We were around and… *oh I say*!'

I focussed my bleary eyes on Betty and Pip – or several blurry Bettys and Pips standing in the doorway looking aghast at what they could see. And I expect what *they* could see was catnip plants strewn across the table and on the floor, powdered catnip all over the table, floating in the air and in the fur of several Allotment Cats. These same Allotment Cats who were lying on the table in various odd poses, except for ET who was walking from one end of the table to other and back again in perfectly straight lines. Red Fred was snoring loudly under the pieces of fabric which fallen on top of him. I caught sight of Barbara skittering across the floor, batting three nipknots ahead of him and growling at them to stay still.

'I - er - think we shouldn't have left the catnip out, Betty,' said Pip quietly.

'You don't say,' sighed Betty, wearily.

Chapter Seven

Pumpkin Pandemonium

'Can't see the attraction myself,' said Red Fred as we regarded the ever-growing display of pumpkins on a row of trestle tables outside the clubhouse. 'Apart from the colour of course. Orange is a good colour.'

'There are a couple of green ones too. Oh - and two or three white ones,' observed Barbara.

'Yeah well… but they're *mostly* orange,' said Fred. 'I reckon pumpkins are s'posed to be orange, except when they're not. And anyway, like I was sayin', it's not as though you can *eat* 'em.'

'Well… I think *humans* can eat them,' I said. 'I saw some of the plot holders preparing pumpkin pie in the clubhouse kitchen.'

'Yeah, and pumpkin soup!' added Barbara.

'But *cats* don't eat pumpkins, do we?' said Fred. 'And besides, even if we did, we wouldn't be lining 'em up so's we can brag about whose pumpkin is the biggest, or heaviest or roundest.'

'It's a competition,' I said. 'You can win a prize for the best pumpkin.'

'Oh yeah, they do this every autumn,' added Barbara. 'All part of the Fayre.'

The Fayre, of course was the Sunnyside Allotments Autumn Fayre. I'd been told by the other cats that these Fayres were held every so often when the Allotments were opened to the public, usually at the weekend. Today was a Sunday and the weather was fine. A good number of visitors were expected.

The wide grassed area near the clubhouse had been carefully covered with wooden decking, upon which several stalls and tables had been set up. Although most of these were selling fruit, vegetables and flowers grown on the allotments, along with lots of freshly potted plant cuttings and seeds, there were quite a few selling different kinds of food. In fact, there were so many delicious smells filling the air; bacon, pork, chicken, fish, as well as exotic spicy aromas. My nose was twitching pleasantly and my mouth was beginning to water at the thought that there may be a few titbits on offer for me. Many of the food stalls had brightly coloured flags proclaiming the stall holders' nationalities. Of course, most of the vegetables and spices in the food had been grown right here, on the Allotments.

The Pumpkin competition was all part of the various festivities planned for later that day and several long tables had been set up on the paved area outside the clubhouse, where plot holders and several people we hadn't seen before were arranging pumpkins. In fact, this year, Sunnyside Allotments were playing host to an extra-special Pumpkin competition, as proclaimed by a large banner hung across the wall of the clubhouse. GG had read it to us earlier. It said:

Grand Pumpkin Competition!
Organised by The Pumpkin and Gourd Growers Association - PAGGA
(Midlandshire Branch)

Barbara added: 'Of course, people don't just eat them or judge them against each other. They carve them too. They make horrible faces on them and then stick candles inside to light them up.'

'That'd be for Hallo Evie then,' I said brightly. 'I used to see humans do this when I was an Outling Cat. There'd be pumpkins outside their houses, sometimes inside their houses too, they put them in the windows. All with faces carved on them and lit up. Then there'd be lots of human children all dressed up in strange clothes and masks going door to door to get sweets off people. Come to think of it, some of the big humans dressed up in odd clothes too.'

'Well, I think there's a competition for that too,' said GG, nodding towards a separate table on the decked area, festooned with pumpkins and various carving tools. 'But I don't think any of these pumpkins in the competition are going to be carved.'

'It's actually called *Halloween*' said a quiet little voice next to me. 'And the carved pumpkins are called Jack o'lanterns.' We all jumped and looked round as Janet suddenly appeared. She had a very disconcerting way of *not being* there one moment and then suddenly *being* there the next.

We all greeted Janet with nose touches. Was it my imagination or did Janet take just a little longer touching noses with me?

'So, what is it then, this Halloween?' I asked.

'Well, it's an ancient celebration,' said Janet. 'Tiberius has mentioned it once or twice although he's always hibernating when it's on. I think Oakroot could tell you more, because his people, the Fae have quite a bit to do with it. It all has to do with spirits and ghosts and things like that. Anyway, it's not actually Halloween for a few days yet.'

'Maybe he could tell you about your ghost cat, mate,' said Fred, giving me a sly wink. 'You never know, it might've been out early for Hallo Ever.'

I winced inwardly. Fred was a good friend but after several weeks of no ghost cat sightings, I could tell he didn't believe that I'd seen a ghost cat. At best, he – and everybody else – thought I'd been mistaken and had just seen an ordinary white cat. All, that is, except Janet, who had listened patiently to my story and had expressed her belief in what I'd seen. In fact, she'd not been at all surprised that a ghost cat might exist, especially as it had appeared at the spot where the cat's skull had been dug up.

Thankfully, the subject was forgotten as our attention was diverted by the arrival of two men, not plot holders that we recognised, puffing and panting as they pushed what looked like an extra wide wheelbarrow up to a table. The wheelbarrow contained what seemed to be a huge round ball covered in blankets. The men carefully removed the blankets to reveal an enormous pumpkin, quite the biggest I'd ever seen. Carefully, almost reverently, they hefted the massive vegetable out of the trolley and wrestled it onto a square of green cloth on one of the long wooden tables. It was so big and heavy that the table began to sag alarmingly in the middle. I saw Betty hurry over with another trestle to put under the middle of the table to strengthen it. The men grunted their thanks, and then started to carefully polish the pumpkin with what were surely special cloths, making its orange skin shine.

I noticed a small knot of Sunnyside plot holders including Donna standing together watching the two men and muttering to each other.

'Bloomin' disgrace, I calls it,' growled Digby, one the oldest plot holders, tugging his flat cap down on his head aggressively. 'Every year, wherever the PAGGA competition is, those two shows up with their bloomin' mutant pumpkins. And they wins! T'aint right it isn't!'

'Yerrrs,' grumbled Old Ted, another elderly plot holder.

Donna had her arms folded defiantly watching the two men who were smirking across at the little group, making a big show of polishing their pumpkin.

'Who are they anyway?' Donna asked Digby.

'It's them two rag an' bone men from over Skank End way, innit?' muttered Digby darkly. 'Floggitt and Leggett. Floggitt's the one with the white hair and silly eyebrows and Leggitt's the greasy one.'

'*Antique traders* and house clearances, actually,' chuckled Leggitt, who had obviously been listening. He had oily black hair, long sideburns and a pencil moustache, and was wearing a dark trilby hat which seemed too small and was tipped back on his head.

'And I think you'll find this is an *open* show,' added his companion, Floggitt, who possessed fuzzy white hair which stuck out at odd angles, and huge bushy white eyebrows. 'That means *open to everyone*, whether they are plot holders on these Allotments or indeed, any other.'

'No need to be so smug,' said Donna. 'Tell me, how did you get that pumpkin to grow so large? Steroids, was it?'

'Ah-ah-ah, now, now, dear, you don't expect us to reveal our horticultural secrets, do you?' said Leggitt, grinning widely showing a gold tooth glinting amongst his other rather yellow teeth. He gave Donna a sly wink.

Donna bristled visibly and I felt sure I saw her spiky hair stand up straighter, rather like a cat's would. It was quite impressive to see. 'I'm not your *"dear"* and I doubt you use natural compost and plant food either!' she snapped.

'I heard they've got a secret allotment somewhere and that they uses industrial fertilizer what's banned because it's toxic to insects!' added Digby.

'Nothing says we have to use your pinky-green, politically correct, tree-hugging, "environmentally friendly" ethically sourced manure donated by disadvantaged ex-dray horses,' sneered Floggitt, making quotation marks with his fingers when he said the words "environmentally friendly".

'Besides,' leered Leggitt, 'You're all just jealous 'cos we've grown the biggest pumpkin here!'

'Size isn't everything!' retorted Donna, turning her back on them and walking over to another table which contained a selection of odd-shaped gourds and turnips. I had to admit, some of the vegetables looked quite amusing.

Digby and Old Ted also turned their backs on the grinning Floggitt and Leggett and shuffled off with as much dignity as they could muster.

Not for the first time in my life, I found myself baffled by human behaviour. From the look on the other cats' faces I could see they were also in a state of extreme bafflement.

'Shall we go for a wander round the Fayre?' suggested Barbara. 'I see they've started letting those public humans in through the main gate, so it's going to be busy soon. We can check out where the food stalls are. I'm sure there'll be a few snacks on offer.'

We all agreed that this was a good idea and set off for a leisurely stroll around the various stalls and tables that had been set up on the decked area. I noticed strings of coloured lights, as yet unlit, strung between the trees.

I came across Pip, who was in charge of some sort of game where people were invited to throw balls which had been painted to look like human eyes into the open mouth of a large wooden jack o' lantern. It seemed to be an extremely popular game, especially for children who were eager to win a prize. (The prizes seemed to be a selection of fluffy toys, including a few unrealistic black cats which were supposed to be me, I expect).

Several people were, as mentioned, busily preparing pumpkin pie and pumpkin soup in the clubhouse kitchen, as well as making hot drinks for the visitors. There were tables and chairs set up both inside and outside the clubhouse for people to sit down to eat and drink. Betty had her own table just inside the clubhouse entrance with lots of information leaflets about the Allotments and forms for people to apply for plots although there were only about four spare plots left now, I'd overheard.

On another table next to Betty's were a pile of my books and a cardboard sign which said:

Read the Adventures of Robert The Allotment Cat and Friends!
Buy a Signed Copy
And
Meet Robert in Person!

Well, I guessed that because there was a sign by the books, it made sense that they were signed copies, but I didn't know who or what this "Person" was. I realised that the Nawthor himself was sitting behind the table. I hadn't recognised him at first because he was wearing a hat. I expect that, being bald, all Nawthors must wear hats to keep their heads warm. I thought it would be a good idea to wander around near the book table in a little while, so people could buy copies and make a fuss of me. There would be photographs taken no doubt and, of course, cat treats and toys would most likely be forthcoming from my Adoring Public. While I was doing that, the Nawthor could do whatever it was Nawthors had to do when they weren't writing.

There was a sense of excitement in the air (along with the delicious aromas) as the visitors began to arrive and wander around the stalls. It was a bright, sunny day, not too cold, just "brisk" as Betty called it, so a good number of Public were expected. Of course, the Public would do that thing where they handed over money for whatever they bought to take away or to eat and drink.

The Plot Holders' Committee had been discussing the money thing from the Autumn Fayre a couple of days beforehand. Before I fell asleep, I heard them say that this money would be used to keep the Allotments in good repair, boost our Veterinary Fund and hopefully donate to a local charity which looked after poorly Outling Cats.

Personally, I'd never considered myself to be a *poorly* Outling Cat before I came to the allotments, although I'd seen plenty of sickly, poorly Outling Cats, quite a few of whom had been Home Cats but had been abandoned by their humans. Hearing their stories was one of the many reasons why I'd never trusted humans until I came to the Sunnyside Allotments. It was then that I realised that *some* humans could be genuinely nice. I sometimes wondered if I'd once been a Home Cat who was pushed out of a human home to become an Outling, although most of my early life was a blank, because we cats simply forget any bad times and live for the moment. As far as I knew, I'd always been an Outling Cat until I became an Allotment Cat… And being an Allotment Cat was a much better thing to be.

I saw a group of children, accompanied by Kate, walking down the driveway. I recognised them as being members of Kate's class from the school where she was a teacher. They often visited the Allotments where they had their own plot which they tended with great enthusiasm. As soon as the children saw Fred, Barbara and me they squealed with delight and hurried over and were soon stroking and patting us and talking excitedly.

'Miss! Miss! Can we give Robert and his friends the cat treats now? Can we? Please Miss!' piped up one girl.

'Oh yeah! Can we? Please Miss!' chorused several other children.

Kate sighed, smiled and rummaged in her shoulder bag and pulled out a big bag of cat treats, which she opened and put a small handful of cat treats into each child's outstretched hand. 'One at a time now!' said Kate in her special teacher's voice. 'Save some for the other cats too!'

'Good luck with that!' mumbled Red Fred, his mouth full of treats. 'We're here, they're not!'

This was true; Dorothy didn't like a lot of fuss from non-plot holders. Come to think about it, she didn't even like a lot of fuss from plot holders either. She'd no doubt be skulking around somewhere. Janet was shy anyway and had made herself scarce as soon as the children had run over to us. As for ET, I felt sure she'd turn up in her own time, as she was quite nervous of big crowds. Hopefully, there might even be some cat treats left for them when they eventually showed up.

After we'd eaten our cat treats and been thoroughly fussed over, Kate managed to shepherd the children away to have a look at some of the other attractions. We wandered around the stalls, rubbing ourselves against people's legs and purring, which elicited a lot of delighted comments and several more cat treats.

My nose twitched at the familiar smell of catnip and looked up into a stall selling all sorts of "cat accessories" – food bowls, blankets, cat carriers, toys and, of course, Betty's homemade nipknots. Much as I'd have liked to jump up to sniff the nipknots, I thought the better of it. Betty hadn't exactly been cross with us after the nipknot incident (Betty never *really* got cross with us, no matter what mischief we got up to), but she *had* been somewhat flustered upon finding us lying amongst the mess we'd made of her catnip harvest.

My memory was very hazy, so I assume she and Pip had carefully picked us all up and put us in our cat beds, because that's where I woke up a little while later. Thankfully, the effect of catnip wears off very quickly, but it often leaves us cats feeling a bit confused and embarrassed, wondering what all the fuss was about and trying not think if we *really* acted like hyperactive kittens. Most of my friends trotted off - and in ET's case wobbled off - into the allotments to have a good, distracting wash as soon as their heads began to clear.

Certainly, Dorothy had beaten a hasty retreat as soon as she'd focussed her eyes on me from the cat bed next to mine. Her body language made it clear that whatever it was she'd said to me, it had been the catnip talking. In a way, I was glad of this, especially as Janet had forgiven me for being so snotty towards her. The last thing I wanted was to upset her again! Thankfully, she didn't seem to have noticed what Dorothy had said about me being handsome (even if it was true).

As for the nipknots, Betty and Pip must have carried on making them somewhere away from the allotments, because they didn't leave any more unattended catnip in the clubhouse. Much as I liked catnip, I had to agree that this was maybe just as well.

As is often the way with cats, we all wandered off in different directions around the Fayre after a while. I found myself next to another outdoor table where Colin was selling sacks of Sunnyside Allotment-grown compost. And who should be there but Rosie and her family! Rosie was actually quite subdued and not just because she was on her lead. She was lying on the ground with her head resting on her outstretched front paws looking quite bored. Her adult humans, Bex and Jason, were standing there listening to Colin expounding the virtues of his oak and maple leaf mould compost. Their eyes looked somewhat glazed and unfocussed, although they both jumped when Colin dipped his hand into a bowl of compost displayed on the table, grabbed a handful of it and waved it under their noses.

'Just smell that! That's nature at its best, that is!' he exclaimed.

'Ooh – er – it's… very…nice,' mumbled Bex, her nose wrinkling.

'It smells like cat poo!' said Jason, backing away a few steps.

'Well, it all makes for good manure,' said Colin without missing a beat. 'Perfectly natural, eco-friendly product that is. Great for your garden.'

At this point Rosie saw me and jumped up, her tail wagging madly. She bounced towards me, almost jerking Bex off her feet.

'Hello Robert! Great to see! How are you? Are you enjoying the Fayre? I was until we stopped at this stall, been here ages!' She remembered to breathe at this point and, panting madly, plonked her bottom down suddenly. Her nose wrinkled and she looked around. 'Can you smell cat poo? No offence.'

'Oh… umm… Hey! Where's Tom and Amelia?' I said, quickly changing the subject.

'Oh, they wandered off *ages* ago!' panted Rosie. 'Two minutes of this guff about leaf mould and they'd had enough. I mean, I *like* leaf mould and I *love* leaves especially at this time of year when your humans have raked all the fallen leaves up in the garden and then you can go and leap in them and scatter them everywhere! But I mean, there's only so much you can say about leaf mould isn't there?' She took another deep breath, her long pink tongue lolling in and out of her mouth.

'Colin seems to manage to say quite a lot about it,' I observed.

Bex took advantage of the distraction caused by Rosie jerking her lead and started to stroke me and tickle me under the chin, saying "Oh, Robert, you look so handsome today!"

Jason meanwhile had managed to extricate himself from Colin's leaf mould lecture thanks to another hapless human wandering up to the stall and being immediately latched onto by Colin. Jason joined Bex in stroking me, whilst Rosie wagged her tail excitedly and tried to lick me, although I managed to discreetly keep my distance. Talking to a friendly dog is one thing, being slobbered on by one is quite another.

'Well, we'd better find the kids, hadn't we?' said Jason, nervously eyeing Colin who was failing to convince his latest victim of the benefits of leaf mould and might suddenly turn his attention to Bex and Jason again. They said goodbye to me, as did Rosie in her snuffly, excitable way and set off quickly to look for Tom and Amelia.

I watched Colin's exchange with the harassed-looking little man who had made the mistake of stopping at his stall. He was wearing a raincoat and a beret and had one of those fussy little square moustaches sitting just under his nose and looking quite lost. I noticed that he was wearing bicycle clips around his ankles. There was no sign of a bicycle though.

'B-b-but I live in a flat,' protested the man. 'I've only got a couple of window boxes. I don't need a lot of leaf mould compost.'

'Have you got a balcony?' asked Colin. 'You could put a couple of nice big planters on there, leaf mould'd be good in them.'

'I-I keep my bicycle on the balcony,' stuttered the man. He pointed to his bicycle clips as if to convince Colin of this fact.

'Can't you put it in the hall?' said Colin. 'Then you'd have room on your balcony for some plant pots. Look here – smell it – it's good stuff that!'

'*Ewww*! It smells of cat poo!' gasped the little man. 'I'm allergic to cats! Er… and… and I'm allergic to their poo too! I really must be going.' He made a rather theatrical display of sneezing to emphasize this point, then pointed at me in a way that suggested I was his salvation. '*Aaachoo!* And there's a cat over there! And I've started sneezing! *Aaachoo!* Oh, dear me! I must run!' With that he hurried off.

Colin looked crestfallen. 'Smells of cat poo indeed!' he muttered to himself. 'It's good natural leaf mould, that!' He sniffed the bowl of compost to reassure himself. His nose wrinkled and he took a step backwards in surprise. He looked around in agitation, then focussed his gaze on me, his eyes narrowing somewhat.

I decided it was time to wander over to the clubhouse and see how my book sales were going. I just hoped they were selling better than Colin's leaf mould compost…

I spent a very pleasant hour alongside the Nawthor in the clubhouse. I sat on his table most of the time, posing for photographs with the Nawthor and with people who came to buy the book. He was signing each book with his name and using a rubber stamp which made an ink pawprint to sign for me. Several people had brought me treats. The Nawthor carefully rationed the treats to me and put the various packets and boxes in a bag slung across the back of his chair.

'We can save those for later. After all Robert, we don't want you getting too fat, do we?' he said, tickling me under the chin. 'Not like me, eh?'

'You said it, Guv,' I replied (which of course just came out as *Miaow*).

'I was wondering,' said a man who was buying a book for his children. 'Or rather the children were wondering…'

'Yes?' smiled the Nawthor, knowingly.

‘Well… how did Robert tell you his story? He can’t speak and, well, ha-ha – you – er – surely don’t speak Cattish, do you?’

‘It’s *Kittish* actually,’ said the Nawthor. ‘Actually, it’s funny you should ask that. What happens is…’

‘*Ladies and Gentlemen*! *Boys and Girls!* It’s time for the Grand Pumpkin Competition prize giving!’ bellowed a man’s voice from outside the clubhouse.

I hopped down from the table and hurried outside, curious to see what was happening with the pumpkin competition which had been causing so much bad feeling with the plot holders. I’d been idly watching the judging on and off from the clubhouse for the past hour. This seemed to consist of two rather self-important people – a man dressed in a tweed suit with an unlit pipe in his mouth, together with a lady dressed in a tweed twin set and hair that looked like a blue helmet – wandering up and down the tables, touching and peering closely at the pumpkins, and, in the case of the large ones, wrapping a tape measure around them. The man and woman would then jot down notes onto clipboards they were carrying. I assumed that this was how posh cats were also judged at posh cat shows, although personally I’d be a bit put out if someone tried to measure my tummy with a tape measure. I know Dorothy certainly would.

Just as I wandered outside, I saw another couple of ladies walking up and down putting little coloured cards next to some of the pumpkins, followed by coloured flower-like things made of silk.

‘What are they doing?’ I asked GG who was sitting outside the clubhouse watching these strange proceedings with detached interest.

‘Oh, they’re putting out prize cards and rosettes,’ replied GG. ‘They show which pumpkins have won an award.’

‘And what are they doing now?’ I asked, as the two judges started wrapping two tape measures round the massive pumpkin owned by Floggitt and Leggett, who were standing nearby, but further apart from the other exhibitors, looking very smug.

‘Oh, they’re measuring the pumpkins,’ said GG. ‘Obviously that one is so big they need two tape measures to go round it. They did that earlier on. It looks like they’re confirming their measurements. I expect that one is in line for Best Pumpkin in Show.’

I marvelled at GG’s extensive knowledge of such things.

‘And they just get those pies cards and rozzits for winning?’ I asked.

‘Oh no, if they’ve won special places like Best in Show, they get a trophy,’ said GG. She nodded to a small table in front of the pumpkin show tables on which lots of ornate silverware was laid out. ‘Those are trophies.’

Most of the trophies looked like cups on a tall stem fixed to a base. The cups had a handle on both sides. I guessed that if humans had to drink tea or coffee out of such big cups, they’d probably need to hold both handles. A couple of other trophies looked like little plot holders digging with a spade and a particularly big trophy was shaped like a pumpkin. I guessed this was for Best in Show.

By now a fairly large crowd had gathered on the paved area to watch the judging, including Donna, Anji and their kids Veema and Arnie, Digby, Old Ted, Betty and a few other plot holders I recognized. The judges were standing by the tables beaming and looking even more self-important. Another rather less self-important man was calling out the names of the winning pumpkin exhibitors. The winners would then walk up to the judges who would hand them a trophy and shake hands. They would then all pose for a photographer to take photographs. I recognised the photographer as being from the local newspaper. He was often here, taking pictures of various happenings at the Allotments, such as the plots maintained by Kate's class, or, of course, me.

We watched proceedings for a couple more minutes until I yawned, realising I was quite bored of this. 'I'm just going for a wander,' I said to GG. She mumbled a reply as she had just started to have an extensive wash.

I padded under the judging table and trotted along to the nearest plot and slipped through its rickety fence into the next plot, which was planted out with cabbages. I looked up as I walked, noticing that the sky was darkening somewhat, shading to a darker blue, whilst the sun sank lower, changing from yellow to red, colouring the thin band of clouds on the horizon into a fluffy red ribbon. It was now late afternoon and would soon be twilight. At that precise moment, the strings of coloured lights strung around the stalls and paved area were switched on, to cries of "*Ooh!*" and "*Aah!*" from the people still milling around.

I could still hear the awards officer calling out the prizes for the pumpkin show. It still didn't sound overly exciting. I guess you needed to *really* like pumpkins.

I was still looking back at the activity by the clubhouse, intending to cut through a row of late runner beans into the next plot. My progress was abruptly halted when I bumped into a solid object which had been obscured by the bean plants, causing me to sit back on my haunches in surprise.

'Can't you watch where you're going?' came a familiar grumbling voice. A couple of seconds later Dorothy poked her head through the rows of beans, scowling. 'It's bad enough with all these people making a racket and wandering all over the place without you blundering around!' she added.

'Oh, sorry Dorothy, I wasn't looking where I was going,' I said, in what I hoped was a placatory tone. I didn't think she was going to remark how handsome I was today, and I certainly didn't want to get a clout round the ear from her.

Dorothy attempted to ease herself through the beans with something of a struggle, trying to maintain her feline dignity, even when her rear end got stuck and she had to strain to pull her bottom through. The plot holders had given her the nickname of Dorothy Dumpling which was quite appropriate but not something I'd mention to her personally. At least, not unless it was from a safe distance.

'Aren't they all going home soon?' grumbled Dorothy, looking towards the crowds around the clubhouse and milling around the stalls.

'I think they will be soon,' I said, diplomatically. 'It's getting late and…'

I broke off as we heard a rustling and crunching noise from the beans, which had started to quiver. Neither of us were surprised when ET crashed through the plants and staggered to a wobbly halt in front of us.

'Oh h-h-hello R-R-*RobertandDorothy*,' she wibbled. 'A-a-all those p-p-*peoplearound* t-t-today! Th-th-they m-m-make *megoallwobbly!'*

Dorothy began to say that she agreed but broke off when she saw ET's head weaving from side to side even more than usual. 'Looking for someone?' she asked impatiently.

'Y-y-yes,' wibbled ET. 'I-I-I've b-b-been f-f-following *astrangecat*. H-h-he s-s-seems to h-h-*havedisappeared*.'

I felt a shiver run along my spine and my tail began to bristle in and swish in agitation. I noticed that my whiskers were tingling too. 'Strange cat?' I asked. 'What did it look like?' Was it my imagination or was a strange chill creeping over the plot where we were standing? This had nothing to do with sun beginning to set and the air getting naturally chillier.

'I s-s-saw it, it w-w-*waswhite*,' wibbled ET. 'I-I-I think i-i-t's a b-b-*boycat*. H-h-he c-c-can *moveveryfas*t. A-a-*andqueietly*!'

'That sounds like the ghost-cat-thing I saw that night!' I exclaimed.

'Oh, what rubbish!' snorted Dorothy. 'There's no such thing as… as…' Her eyes grew wide and round, her ears flattening against her head as she slowly rose on her toes, her fur bristling from her head to the tip of her tail. She was staring past me.

'It's behind me, isn't it?' I gulped, beginning to rise on my toes too. Dorothy nodded, mutely.

I slowly turned round to see the ghostly white cat wafting through the beans without disturbing so much as a leaf. As before, it was brilliantly white, as though it was lit from inside, and it moved with an unnatural silence. I could just about make out a hint of fur on its body although it was hard to tell, as I could also see the bean plants vaguely through its body.

'Oh th-th-that's h-h-him,' said ET delightedly then frowned. 'D-d-did y-y-you say g-g-*ghostcatthing,* R-R-Robert?'

I noticed that the ghost-cat-thing was looking directly at me, its white eyes locking onto mine. I could see the merest hint of a pupil in each of its eyes, but otherwise they were blank. I felt as though it was looking deep into my mind, searching my very soul. The ghost-cat-thing opened its mouth, but no sound came out. Instead, the temperature around us dropped even further and to my alarm I could see little fronds of frost forming on the bean plant leaves and on the beans themselves.

'*RUN!*' I hissed and pelted through the plots towards the clubhouse. ET must have wobbled off in the other direction, but I was aware of Dorothy streaking along beside me, hissing madly. Out of the corner of my eye I saw the ghost-cat-thing keeping pace with us, but its feet weren't touching the ground. In fact, they seemed to be barely moving. The apparition was almost flying forwards, simply wafting through any plant or compost heap or scarecrow in its path as though they weren't there!

As we burst out of the last plot I veered towards the clubhouse, with Dorothy just behind me. The ghost-cat-thing began to turn in our direction closing the gap between it and us. I reached the pumpkin competition tables and hurtled underneath the nearest one, dodging around two trestles, hoping to distract the ghost-cat-thing. I exited onto the paved area and almost collided with Rosie, who was sitting quietly (for a change) watching the pumpkin awards being given out with her human family. Young Tom was holding her lead, looking quite bored.

'Oh, hallo Robert!' barked Rosie jumping up, her tail wagging excitedly.

Of course, I didn't stop, my legs seemed to have taken on a life of their own and I streaked past her and back under the judging tables. I felt, rather than saw, that the ghost-cat-thing was right behind me and I was dimly aware of Dorothy thundering along in the same direction a few feet away.

Looking back, I can't say with absolute certainty that I saw everything that happened next, but I'm fairly sure that I heard Rosie shout something like: 'Hey you! Stop chasing my friends!' with which she yanked her lead from young Tom's grasp and chased after the ghost-cat-thing. I ducked under the trestle at one end of the table in an attempt to distract my ghostly pursuer and Rosie attempted to do the same, but instead she crashed into the trestle knocking it down and causing the end of the table to sag. By now I was at the middle trestle and ducked round it. No doubt the ghost-cat-thing simply went *through* the trestle, whilst Rosie probably tried to run round it. However, her lead, which was flying loosely behind her wrapped itself round the central trestle and jerked it away after her as she ran out from under the table. The heavy trestle clattered along the ground and brought Rosie to a sudden halt as it pulled sharply on her collar.

By now I was dodging around people's feet heading for the open clubhouse door and looked back. Several pumpkins and gourds were rolling off one of the tables having been dislodged by our passing. I could see the lady judge holding her hands to her cheeks, her mouth wide open, while the male judge was holding the large silver pumpkin trophy in air to protect it from the carnage erupting around him. As though time itself had slowed down I saw the long table on which Floggitt and Leggett's massive pumpkin rested toppling slowly forwards, having lost its end and middle trestles. The giant pumpkin was sliding from the table towards the paved area, Floggitt and Leggett leaping forwards to save it. Of course, they didn't reach it in time and the massive vegetable hit the paving stones with a wet *crunch!* It exploded outwards in a shower of orange skin, pulpy white pith and hundreds of bullet-like seeds which sprayed across the paving stones. Then time seemed to roll forwards at its normal speed. The scene was one of people shouting and jumping out of the way as pieces of pumpkin flew through the air towards them.

I screeched to a halt. I caught a glimpse of Dorothy – or rather a tortoiseshell blur – heading behind the clubhouse. Rosie was sitting up panting and looking around in confusion, her lead still wrapped round the heavy trestle. What I *couldn't* see though was the ghost-cat-thing. It was as though it had never been there.

The newspaper photographer was snapping away with his camera at the scene of mayhem, focussing on Floggitt and Leggett who were on their knees weeping at the remains of their prize pumpkin.

Leggitt scrambled to his feet pushing the photographer aside, his face bright red. He started towards Rosie, his fist shaking. 'That ruddy mutt's cost us the competition!' he roared. 'Wait 'til I get my hands on it!'

At this point Tom and Amelia ran up and threw their arms around Rosie to protect her.

'Don't you *dare* touch our dog!' shouted Amelia bravely.

Leggitt snarled a curse in reply but then took a couple of hasty steps backwards as Jason pounded up. Leggitt obviously didn't want to argue with a grown man, coward that he was. He trod on a piece of pumpkin and skidded backwards, vainly trying to keep his balance. He fell bottom-first onto the largest piece of pumpkin that was left intact and which was being cradled protectively by Floggitt, still on his knees. Needless to say, the large piece of pumpkin burst apart, showering pith and skin into Floggitt's face.

Floggitt leapt up, spitting pumpkin seeds out of his mouth and furiously wiping pumpkin pith from his face. Unfortunately, he hadn't noticed two large pieces of pumpkin rind which had landed on his eyebrows, making him look more surprised than angry, whilst a large chunk of pumpkin was sitting in the middle of his fuzzy hair like a badly fitted hat. By now people in the crowd were laughing uncontrollably at the spectacle they'd just witnessed. Donna, Digby and Old Tom were literally holding themselves up with hysterical laughter, whilst Anji was doing her best to tell their children that it wasn't funny, before she too collapsed with laughter.

Floggitt and Leggett were now remonstrating with the judges and the awards officer.

'You were going to award us Best in Show for our pumpkin!' shouted Floggitt. 'You were just about to announce it when those blasted animals destroyed it!'

'Well, um, maybe, *possibly*,' stammered the male judge, nervously, 'But we hadn't actually *announced* it…' He was holding the silver pumpkin trophy away from the two angry men in case they should make a grab for it.

'And the rules state that the pumpkin must be intact and whole!' added the awards officer.

'Yes, when it's being *judged*!' shouted Leggett hotly. 'You'd judged it, hadn't you?'

'The show wasn't *concluded!*' retorted the lady judge. 'And as your pumpkin met with its unfortunate – um – accident, it cannot be eligible to be placed.'

'But you'd already awarded it Biggest Pumpkin in Show!' wailed Floggitt.

'Well, that's some consolation, surely?' said the male judge, attempting a smile.

'That's no *consolation* at all! We don't want *consolation* prizes!' bellowed Leggitt.

By now, other exhibitors, including Donna, Digby and Old Tom had gathered round and were joining in the argument, telling Floggitt and Leggett to Go Away in various colourful terms. The photographer was still snapping photographs gleefully – this was going to be a much better story than he'd anticipated.

'Show some dignity in defeat man!' Digby shouted at Floggitt. 'You lost! Accept the result!'

'Yeah, show some dignity – or as much as you can with an orange face!' sniggered Donna, to Floggitt's clear annoyance.

'You certainly know how to liven things up around the Allotments, Robert,' said Barbara as he sat down next to me to watch the excitement. 'I was in the clubhouse cadging treats and heard all the excitement so came for a look.'

'Did you see it Barbara?' I asked. 'The white cat? The ghost-cat-thing? *Please* tell me you saw it!'

'Oh yes, I did, said Barbara. 'It's scary alright. Made me bristle when I saw it. But after the table collapsed, it just, well, *disappeared!*'

'I *knew* it!' I said, more to myself than to Barbara. 'I *knew* it was a ghost cat!'

‘Well, that was exciting,’ came a familiar human voice. I looked up to see the Nawthor together with Mrs Nawthor, Betty and Pip. All three were standing there, arms folded, watching the argument. By this point Floggitt and Leggett, still angrily protesting, were being escorted away by a couple of show officials. ‘Is it *always* this exciting at the Sunnyside Allotments Betty?’ he added with a chuckle.

‘Not *all* the time,’ said Betty evenly. ‘I wonder what made Robert and Dorothy so frightened?’ She reached down and rubbed my head. ‘You’re okay now aren’t you, Robert?’ she smiled at me. I purred in acknowledgement.

‘Well,’ said Pip, ‘It looked like they were running from something. I saw it, it was white. It *might’ve* been a cat. But there aren’t any white cats on the Allotments, are there?’

‘Or maybe a stoat in its winter coat?’ added Betty, straightening up. ‘You know, like an ermine? I couldn’t be sure, it moved so fast.’

‘I saw *something* too,’ agreed the Nawthor. ‘But it was there one minute and gone the next!’

They stopped talking to cheer and clap along with the crowd who were delighted to see Digby being awarded Best Pumpkin in Show and proudly receiving the silver pumpkin trophy.

I turned to Barbara. ‘Did you hear that?’ I said with astonishment. *‘The humans could see it too!’*

Chapter Eight

Phantom Photo

'They say there's no such thing as bad publicity, Betty,' said Pip.

'Except for Floggitt and Leggett that is,' added Donna with a chuckle. The other members of the Plot Holders Committee laughed in agreement as they rustled through their copies of the *Midlandtown Clarion* newspaper. They were seated, as ever, around the long committee table in the clubhouse, cups of tea and coffee gently steaming on the table in front of them. I was occupying my usual position in the middle of the table, with my paws tucked under me, my eyes half-closed, letting the buzz of conversation drift lazily past my ears. It was late afternoon of the day after the Autumn Fayre and outside the clubhouse, the sky was just beginning to darken as the sun set.

'Hmmm, maybe,' conceded Betty absently, as she peered at her laptop. 'I wouldn't want people thinking this sort of thing happens all the time at Sunnyside Allotments. We do actually *do* normal things, like simply grow vegetables. Ah, here's the *Clarion's* online version. Oh dear, there's even more photos of the giant pumpkin disaster.'

Several of the plot holders got up and crowded round behind Betty's chair to look at the online photospread from the Autumn Fayre. These photos drew even more laughter from the committee.

'I just hope we won't be held legally liable,' added Betty with a hint of nervousness in her voice. '*Could* we be held legally responsible, Mr Waite?'

All eyes turned towards Jonathan Waite, the Sunnyside Allotment's lawyer from the legal firm of Knockard and Waite. Mr Waite had been involved in sorting out the legalities surrounding the ownership of the Allotments following the events earlier in the year. He was a neat little man who wore what I'd heard described as an old-fashioned winged collar (although I'd yet to see it fly. If it did, I'd try to catch it for him). Mr Waite was currently studying a copy of the *Clarion* which was spread out on the table in front of him. I was lying on the table opposite him. When Mr Waite cleared his throat, my ears pricked up and I opened my eyes fully. He didn't usually say a lot, being content to let the rest of the committee do all the talking and occasionally making a decision. If he was going to speak, it would definitely be worth listening to.

'Well, I don't think so, Mrs DeGatto,' he said, looking across at Betty over his half-moon glasses. 'The Allotments do have valid third-party insurance and besides, the – um – *incident* with the large pumpkin technically occurred under the auspices of the PAGGA show, not the Autumn Fayre as such.'

I wondered what these Orspeeseez were and where they'd been hiding during the show. Mr Waite continued: 'Besides, I believe all entrants to the pumpkin competition sign a disclaimer to the effect that any damage or accident befalling their own pumpkins, along with any violation or act of aggression towards their pumpkins, from other exhibitors will not be deemed to be the responsibility of PAGGA or of the venue at which the show is staged.' He paused, then added: 'I must say, I had no idea that vegetable shows could generate such high passions.'

'Yeah, well, if you think pumpkin growers can be highly strung, you should see what the carrot growers get up to,' muttered Colin, darkly. 'Now *there's* a bunch you don't want to get on the wrong side of!'

'I never knew a bunch of carrots could be so dangerous!' said Pip, mischeviously, prompting a great deal of laughter from the other committee members. Even Mr Waite smiled.

Colin didn't laugh but frowned instead. 'Just be warned,' he muttered, folding his arms. 'Root vegetables are a serious business.'

'Well, they do say "money is the *root* of all evil",' put in Pip, generating more laughter.

'I would say therefore,' said Mr Waite raising his voice slightly over the laughter, 'That the two gentlemen to whom the large pumpkin belonged, Messrs…' he peered at the newspaper to check the names, although I was sure he knew perfectly well what they were, '… Floggitt and Leggett… would have no legal claim for damages against Sunnyside Allotments.'

'Thank goodness for that,' said Betty, snapping the lid of her laptop shut. 'We still don't know what it was that chased Robert and Dorothy but whatever it was, it caused us a lot of bother. That said, the Autumn Fayre was a great success. Now, if we could move onto other business…'

Thoughts of the ghost cat (I was sure now that it *was* a cat, not a thing *looking* like a cat) made me shiver, but I needed to investigate the matter further. I stood up, stretched, then shuffled forward to look at Mr Waite's newspaper with the slightly-bored-but-showing-polite-interest expression we cats have perfected over centuries of association with humans.[9] The report about the Autumn Fayre had resulted in a double page spread of photographs, showing the various stalls, some of the jack o' lantern pumpkins carved with gruesome faces by the children, Pip's Throw-an-Eyeball game, plus various shots of visitors and plot holders. There was, of course, a photograph of me looking very majestic. However, one whole page was taken up with photographs of the giant pumpkin and a quite astonishing sequence of it falling to the ground and bursting apart.

I peered closely at each photograph. I could see Rosie in some of them, as she ran out from under the table dragging the trestle behind her with her lead wrapped round it, then her sitting looking surprised as she was abruptly halted by the weight of the trestle. Behind her the table had tipped and the pumpkin was falling, Floggitt and Leggett, arms outstretched vainly trying to catch it. I could see myself and Dorothy in one photo, both running towards the edge of the photograph and looking blurry as we ran. There was a spectacular photograph of the pumpkin exploding and showering skin, pith and seeds through the air, with onlookers jumping back, surprise on their faces.

---

[9] We practice this expression from kittenhood. Often in front of a mirror.

What I *couldn't* see however, was the ghost cat. It simply wasn't in any of the photographs.

The following day, we Allotment Cats assembled in the clubhouse. It was mid-afternoon and, apart from us, the clubhouse was deserted. Betty had gone home for her lunch a little while ago and Pip had gone shopping for more Halloween decorations. She'd been very busy that morning decorating the clubhouse for Halloween, hanging orange and black paper garlands along the walls and ceiling, and placing various strange little model figures on the tables. To me, they looked just like ordinary humans wearing odd clothes, but GG had told me that they were witches, vampires and zombies. There were also a couple of impossibly large spiders, as well as lots of fake spiders' webs and strands of cobwebs.

'Pip obviously likes Halloween,' said Barbara, sniffing at one of the little figures. This, according to GG, was a zombie. I must admit, studying the figure more closely, it did look like this particular human was rather poorly and quite shocking to look at. He was very thin – you could see his ribs. He also had bits of flesh hanging off or missing altogether and was wearing raggedy clothes. His arms were outstretched, fingers looking like claws, and his eyes wide and staring.

'Poor fella looks like he should be in hospital,' observed Barbara. He looked up at the paper streamers and cobwebs. 'And humans do this for *fun*?'

'Halloween is seen as a bit of fun nowadays,' said Janet quietly. 'But it was quite a big festival in olden days for humans. It was all to do with the spirits of the dead walking the Earth.'

'What about ghost cats?' I asked. 'I don't see any figures of those.'

'Well – um – witches were supposed to have black cats as companions, I think,' said Janet.

'You'd be alright then mate,' chuckled Red Fred, nudging me playfully. 'Didn't I hear Pip saying earlier on that you'd be the ideal cat for Halloween?'

'Yes, I heard her say that,' I replied, nudging him back, equally playfully. 'She also said you were the right shape and colour to be a pumpkin, Fred.'

This brought a snigger from Barbara and Janet.

As ever, Red Fred took all this good naturedly and chuckled. 'Humans can be really weird,' he said. 'I mean, look at all those fake cobwebs Pip's put all over the place. I've seen the plot holders spend ages dusting real cobwebs out of their sheds and yet they're decorating the clubhouse with 'em.'

'Never mind all that now, let's look at what GG's found on the laptop!' This was Dorothy, who was sitting on the long committee table next to GG, who, having opened Betty's laptop, using her long claws, was now tapping away at the keys with great determination.

For once, Betty had left her laptop behind when she'd gone for lunch. I'd been sitting on my favourite couch in the clubhouse at the time next to Barbara, whilst ET was snoozing on one of the cat beds. We'd been waiting for just such an opportunity so I quickly jumped up onto the table and made a point of laying on the laptop whilst she was putting her coat on. When she'd turned round and saw me, she'd smiled at me and said she wouldn't disturb me, just keep an eye on the laptop for her. Pip had still been in the clubhouse decorating it but had left soon afterwards to get some more decorations. She had locked the clubhouse door behind her (being mindful of the catnip incident no doubt), but hadn't realised that the rear kitchen window was slightly open, so it was a simple matter for us cats to nip in and out. Barbara had quickly rounded up the other cats now that we had a golden opportunity to use the laptop and soon all seven of us were in the clubhouse. Whilst GG was busily opening the laptop and "booting it up" as she said (although no actual kicking was involved), with Dorothy supervising proceedings, the rest of us had been examining the Halloween decorations. It's hard to stay focussed on one thing when you're a cat and there are lots of other interesting things to sniff and poke at.

We all jumped up on the table, except for ET, who was keeping watch out of the glass pane in the clubhouse door and crowded round the laptop. GG had found the *Midlandtown Clarion's* webpage and had opened the online version of that day's paper. There was the report from the Autumn Fayre with even more photographs from the Fayre and, naturally, of the giant pumpkin incident. GG told us that the big, bold headline over the pumpkin photos said: *Pumpkin Pulped*!

I'd told the others that I hadn't seen the ghost cat in the newspaper photographs, much to the annoyance of Dorothy, who now fervently believed in the ghost cat, having been chased by it. ET had also confirmed the ghost cat's existence, as had Barbara. I was sure now that Fred and GG believed us - after all, who would dare argue with Dorothy? - whilst Janet had never doubted me to begin with when I'd first told her about my encounter with the ghost cat.

We all studied the photographs carefully. 'Some of these are a bit out of focus,' I said. 'The ones in the newspaper were sharper.'

'This often happens,' explained GG, peering intently at each photograph. 'They always use the best ones for the actual newspaper itself and put more of the not-so-good ones up on their website to fill the space.'

'Hang on,' said Janet, pointing her paw at a photograph near the bottom of the screen. 'What's that?'

We all peered closely at the photo, which resulted in a lot of jostling. Perhaps not surprisingly, Dorothy batted us away with her paws and peered at the photograph. 'There it is!' she cried. 'The ghost cat!'

'Er… is it okay if we have a look?' I asked cautiously. Dorothy graciously stepped aside so we could look. Sure enough, the photograph showed a blurry white shape, almost like a wisp of smoke or mist wafting around – or possibly through – the upturned table. Was that a glimpse of a tail I saw?

'You sure it's not just a smudge on the photo?' said Fred, wrinkling his nose at the screen. 'Sometimes happens, dunnit?'

'It's possible,' said GG. 'Like I said, they probably didn't use this photograph in the printed newspaper because of this mark. I think it's called a lens flare and…'

'No!' said Dorothy defiantly. 'That thing chased me – well, us – and that's what it was like when it moved, sort of blurry and misty.'

'It certainly looks like that's where I saw it,' agreed Barbara. 'I saw you both and Rosie run out from under the table, then that ghostly cat appeared just as the table fell over and then, well… it was gone.'

'I-I-I s-s-*sawittoo*,' wibbled ET from across by the door. 'B-b-but I r-r-ran th-th-*throughtheplots*.'

'So why did it chase *us*?' demanded Dorothy. 'It would have been easier to chase ET!'

'Th-th-*thanks*!' muttered ET sarcastically.

'You know,' said Janet slowly, 'I don't think it was chasing *you* Dorothy. I think it wanted Robert.'

'Why would it want *him*?' snorted Dorothy sourly.

'Why would it want *you*, Princess?' pointed out Red Fred pointedly. Dorothy shot him a Look, but Fred continued unabashed: 'The way I see it is, Robert saw it in the first place, right? So maybe it recognises Robert?'

Dorothy opened her mouth as if to say something then shut it abruptly. We were all silent for a few seconds as we considered this point.

I broke the silence. 'But why did it *chase* me?'

'I don't think it was *chasing* you,' said Janet. 'You and Dorothy were both scared – yes you were, Dorothy – you ran off, so it ran after you. Then of course Rosie ran at it and there was all the business with the pumpkin, lots of humans shouting and suchlike, so maybe it was scared off by that? Perhaps… perhaps it wants to *tell* you something, Robert?'

We looked at each other as we considered this. Once again, I broke the silence first: 'Well, it could've just asked!'

'P-p-perhaps i-i-it c-c-*can'ttalk*,' wibbled ET. 'A-a-at l-l-least n-n-*notsoyou* c-c-*canhearit*.'

'Good point, ET!' exclaimed Janet. 'After all, if it's a ghost, well… oh, it's a pity Tiberius is hibernating because he might know how …'

'Here we go!' snorted Dorothy crossly and flopped down at the other end of the table. 'Typical Thingy! "*Let's ask the toad*!". Never mind that I got chased all over the allotments then had bits of pumpkin pulp showered on me, on no!'

'Now, now Princess,' admonished Fred. 'Janet's right. I mean, we don't know how to talk to ghosts do we?'

Janet looked around at the Halloween decorations. 'You know,' she said quietly. 'It's Halloween in a couple of days' time. If ghosts are meant to come out on Halloween night… well… maybe *that's* the time to talk to a ghost cat!'

Chapter Nine

Pip 'n' Tip

Halloween started just like any other day. It certainly didn't *feel* like it was going to be a special day. It was quite cloudy, although the clouds were moving fairly quickly in the keen breeze, exposing patches of light blue sky and letting the sun peek through occasionally. However, it did little to warm the rather chilly air. I was patrolling around the allotments on the lookout for anything strange or out of place, but it all looked like a perfectly normal autumn day.

I pounced on some dry, fallen leaves which blew past on the wind. (Some feline instincts are hard to ignore. After all, if it moves, it might be edible). I watched as the breeze plucked more leaves from the trees and sent them careening into the air, their different shapes and colours combining in a frantic arial ballet. They reminded me of the humans I'd seen in television clips on Betty's laptop from the programme *Starchly Go Dancing* (or something like that), whirling around in their colourful costumes in time to music.

It made me think that humans might be strange in many ways, but fair play to them, they'd perfected this dancing thing. It was usually quite glamorous and reminded me of birds doing their strange courtship rituals. I'd watched plenty of male birds "courting", which basically meant preening and flitting about in front of the dowdier females, trying to catch their eye and show how handsome they were. Humans probably used to do the same sort of thing before they hit upon the idea of dancing. Although nowadays most of them probably saved themselves the bother of learning dance steps by just posting photographs on *FaceyFriends*. That said, us male cats – well, us *handsome* male cats that is – just swagger around with our tails held high looking macho, which works on the females just as well. I hadn't swaggered in front of Janet though – well, not much anyway – she was very shy, so I hoped she'd appreciate my natural charm. I wouldn't dare swagger in front of Dorothy, especially after what she said to me during the catnip incident. She'd either bop me round the head or, more worryingly, actually *like* my swagger, which would make things *very* complicated indeed.

'Penny for 'em Robert?' croaked a familiar voice.

I looked around and then up. There was Henry the crow sitting on a fence post, his keen little black eyes following every movement of the leaves.

'Oh, erm… I was just thinking about… umm… how you birds attract mates,' I stammered. 'You know, courtship sort of stuff.'

'Oh yerrs,' said Henry, hopping down from the post. 'Not the right time o' year for that though, Robert. Spring's the time. More food around for the little chickies to eat, right?' He looked thoughtful. 'O' course, us crows keeps the same mates. Me 'n' me missus Cora, we bin together for ages. Mind you, we only keeps the same mates if somefing 'orrible don't 'appen to one of us like.'

I tried not to feel guilty. Although I'd never tackled a crow (they were too big and had mean beaks), perhaps one or two smaller birdies had formed a meal for me in my Outling days. 'Oh, well, that's understandable,' I said.

'Yerrs,' said Henry, clearly warming to his theme. 'Take my missus. She really had a run o' bad luck with mates affore she met me. First mate she 'ad was me cousin ''Enery – 'e 'ad a disagreement wiv a farmer who 'ad a shotgun and didn't like 'im peckin' up his corn. Then there was me second cousin once removed, 'Enery. 'E was on a railway line peckin' at a nice bit o'carrion and wham! The 10.52 express from London came along, didn't it? An' then there was me mum's third cousin 'Enery…'

'Hang on, hang on,' I said, my brain reeling at these gruesome tales of corvid carnage. '*You're* 'Enery, I mean *Henry*. Your missus Cora had previous mates all called Henry?'

Henry looked at me quizzically, as though he couldn't quite work out why I was confused. 'Well, yerrs,' he said with surprise. ''S a good name, is 'Enery. Runs in th' family. Saves 'avin' the fink up new names.'

I hardly dared ask but did anyway. 'So, er – how many Henrys did she have as mates before she met you?'

'Seven,' said Henry. 'An' everyone was an 'Enery.' He puffed his chest out with pride. 'I'm 'Enery the Eighth I am, I am. Lasted longer than the others, that's fer sure.'

I didn't quite know what to say to this, but thankfully I was saved by the arrival of Red Fred who greeted us both in his usual laid-back way.

‘All set for Halloween, Henry?’ he asked.

‘Well, I might follow a few kids round the streets when they’re out Tricky Tweeting,’ replied Henry. ‘Always a chance they’ll drop some o’ the sweeties wot people gives ’em, so’s I can swoop down to peck ’em up.’ He bobbed his head, which I think must be the crow equivalent of a frown. ‘Mind you,’ he added darkly, ‘You ’ave ter be careful wot sweeties it is. Me third cousin on me Dad’s side snapped up a buggle bum sweet and then started blowin’ this big pink bubble out of ’is beak. Took ’im ages to spit it all out. Every time ’e tried ’e kept blowin’ bubbles. I remember ’e said to me, “’Enery, I’m forever blowin’ bubbles!”’

‘Was he called Henry too?’ I asked, for want of anything else to say.

‘Nah. That was ’Orace,’ said Henry. ‘Always gettin’ ’is beak into trouble.’

Thankfully, Red Fred changed the subject, or at least refocussed it, and said: ‘So… talking of Halloween, have you seen the clubhouse today, Robert?’

I had to confess that I hadn’t, although this reminded me that it must be breakfast time or at least brunch.

‘Pip’s been decorating some more,’ chuckled Fred. ‘Come and see. Do you want to come along too, Henry?’

‘Nah, it’s alright Fred,’ said Henry, suddenly giving his chest feathers a good preening. ‘One o’ the plot holders is plantin’ some seeds over on the east side. Reckon he’s about finished now, so I can swoop in and fill me beak.’

‘Well, they do say the early bird catches the worm,’ chuckled Fred.

Henry regarded him with his piercing sideways stare. ‘That so? Well, if I sees any o’ them Hurly Birds tryin’ to get worms or seeds off o’ *my* patch, there’ll be trouble!’ With that he launched himself into the air with a steady *whup-whup-whup* of his wide wings as he headed off to the east side of the allotments.

Fred winked at me. ‘Hurly Birds eh?’ he grinned. ‘Yow just can’t trust ‘em.’

We arrived at the clubhouse at the same time as Betty, who was just getting out of her car. This was good timing because she’d be giving us our meal. And, like us, Betty was quite taken aback by the strings of pumpkin-shaped orange lights along the outside of the clubhouse, (although they weren’t yet lit) and lots of spooky stickers on the windows and glass pane of the door. There were bats, jack o’lanterns, ghosts (nothing like the ghost cat – these just looked like bedsheets) and skeletons.

‘D’you like them Betty?’ said Pip, appearing at the door. ‘They glow in the dark. And don’t worry – they peel off easily enough.’

'Um... very nice,' said Betty uncertainly. She followed Pip into the clubhouse and we followed Betty. And it certainly looked as though Pip had been busy. As well as the streamers and spooky models she'd arranged the other day, there were now half a dozen carved jack o'lanterns dotted around the clubhouse on various tables, everyone with a different face.

'Hey, you'll like this one, Robert and Fred,' said Pip excitedly. She picked up a large pumpkin and plonked it down on our couch so we could see it better. The carving was of a cat's face and very intricately done. I was impressed. Fred sniffed it curiously and looked at me, conveying that it was, when all was said and done, just a carved pumpkin.

'Very nice,' said Betty, diplomatically. 'Did you carve them all?'

'A couple of them,' said Pip. 'I must admit I didn't do this brilliant cat one. My next-door neighbour knows I love Halloween and she's very artistic, so she made this one and three of the others for me. I commissioned them specially. They'll all look great when they're lit up!'

At this point we temporarily lost interest in the Halloween decorations, as Betty opened a tin of cat food and began forking some into bowls for us. Barbara strolled in at this point with impeccable timing, so the three of us settled down to eat contentedly.

Once we'd finished it was, of course, time for a wash, so we all set to on our ablutions. By the time I'd finished washing between my toes I noticed that Donna, Anji, Colin and a couple of other committee members had arrived and were arranging themselves around the big table. Betty was opening her laptop and there seemed to be a general air of excitement. Obviously, I could smell the excitement wafting off the humans, which again made me wonder how on earth they managed to communicate effectively by just using words. Smells can tell you so much more (sometimes too much).

I noticed Anji was holding the box containing the cat skull. I pretended not to notice what she was doing, as she cautiously took the skull out of the box, obviously not wishing to upset us cats, and placed it on the table. Fred and Barbara were still washing and oblivious to this. I padded closer to the table to listen to what was being said.

'So... I heard from my friend Maeve at the Uni,' Anji was saying. 'She emailed me about the bracelet the workmen found with the cat skull, so I forwarded the email to you, Betty, you should have it now.'

'Let's see,' said Betty tapping the keys of the laptop. 'Ah yes, here it is...' She looked closely at the screen. 'Oh, goodness,' she exclaimed.

'What does it say then?' queried Colin, a little impatiently.

'Perhaps you'd like to explain, Anji?' said Betty. 'After all, I expect you've read it carefully already.'

Anji beamed and looked around the table at each of the committee members. She took a deep breath. 'Well, Maeve got back from her archaeological dig and was able to sneak the bracelet in with some of the finds they brought back for analysis in the Uni lab, because they're very particular about who uses their equipment. I think it's all to do with research budgets and so on and...'

'Never mind all that now eh, love,' said Donna, gently squeezing Anji's hand. 'Just tell them what she found.'

'Oh yes, right, of course,' smiled Anji quickly. 'So, they did some tests on the bracelet and found that yes, it's made of copper and they dated it back to the mid to late seventeenth or early eighteenth century...'

'Is it valuable?' interrupted Colin.

'Sadly not, at least not in monetary terms,' replied Anji. 'Their analysis showed it was fairly basic copper, nothing fancy. But they matched dirt deposits they found on it with samples of the earth I found inside the cat skull and some that I took from the trench the workmen had dug. They match in every respect, so it does seem to have been buried for at least three hundred years.'

There was a general murmur of surprise from the committee.

'But that's not the best bit,' continued Anji excitedly. 'Can you show them the photo attachments with the email please Betty?'

Betty tapped a couple of keys and then turned the laptop round so that everyone could see it. I hopped up onto the end of the table to take a look. The committee barely acknowledged me being there as they were so intent on the screen. Bit rude, but understandable.

'What does that say on it?' said Colin, putting his glasses on and peering closely at the screen.

I inched closer. There were three photographs displayed on the screen. The top one showed the bracelet, which seemed to have been cleaned and was a lot shinier than when it had been dug up. The second photograph was a close-up of the inside of the bracelet, showing some faint scratches. The third photograph was a close-up of the scratches. Betty tapped a key and the photograph enlarged to fill the whole screen:

T I P

'Those... those are letters, aren't they?' breathed Colin.

'Absolutely!' exclaimed Anji delightedly. 'Maeve noticed the scratches inside the bracelet. They were very faded and difficult to see, so she did an enhanced electron microscope scan of the area. She said that there were definitely letters scratched into the metal but didn't appear to have been professionally done, like by an engraver or metal worker, so they were quite shallow. Added to this, over time, the metal had worn down probably by being moving up and down the wrist of the wearer. As you can see from the enhancement, the letters seem to be T, I and P.'

'*Tip*?' said Betty. 'Is that a name? Or maybe they're someone's initials?'

'It's hard to say,' said Anji, 'Of course, me and Donna being members of the Midlandtown Historical Society have access to quite a few county records, so we're going to check if the name "Tip" is significant from that time period. After all, names change over time, so "Tip" might have been a local name and…'

'What about the cat skull?' said Pip suddenly, tapping the skull to emphasise her point, the tapping making a chilly, hollow echo. 'The bracelet was buried with it – possibly even with the whole cat's body, right? Maybe "Tip" was the cat's name?'

The committee all exclaimed their surprise. I thought that was a good explanation and realised that my heart was beating faster with excitement.

'Maybe the cat's owner loved the cat so much they scratched its name on their bracelet and buried it with the cat when it died,' said Pip.

There was a general nodding of heads and murmurs of agreement from around the table. I noticed that Fred and Barbara had stopped washing and were listening intently from the floor.

'Hang on,' put in Colin. 'I thought back in those days cats were feared as being witches' familiars and people used to persecute them for it, 'cos they believed cats to be agents of the devil in cat form?'

Donna cut in; 'So-called "familiars" weren't exclusively cats, other animals could just as easily be. Anyway, we don't think that fear of cats as so-called "familiars" or as "agents of the devil" was as widespread as the history books and records would have us believe,' she said. 'After all, cats were very useful for keeping vermin down on farms and around grain stores and suchlike. Okay, maybe *some* people – usually professional witch hunters and over-zealous clergymen – thought that cats were evil, but most ordinary folk would've found cats quite useful. Although keeping cats as pets wasn't really a thing back then, I daresay some people had a favourite cat. So maybe "Tip" was a favourite cat?'

'Assuming it *is* the cat's name, of course,' added Betty.

'Well, I think it's *definitely* the cat's name!' said Pip, folding her arms decisively.

'You can trust *Pip* to work out it's *Tip*!" giggled Donna, to general murmurs of amusement.

The committee continued to discuss the skull and bracelet, but at this point my attention wandered. I was appalled at what I'd heard! I had a vague idea that witches were something to do with Halloween and I also knew that there were some very silly humans who didn't like cats. Usually these were people with posh gardens who objected to cats doing what cats do, like wandering and pooing where they please. But seeing cats as evil? Or agents of the devil? And "familiars", whatever they were?

But the more I thought about this, the more *something* seemed to be nagging away at the back of my mind. It felt like a memory from long ago, but so long ago I couldn't quite reach it. The more I thought about it, the further away it seemed to slip. This whole witch's cat thing was something I needed to talk to Janet about.

I realised that the humans were still talking and looking at the laptop again. I padded over to take a closer look myself.

'So what's this mark then?' one of the committee members was asking, pointing to another photograph which was now filling the screen.

'This was on the other side of the bracelet opposite the letters,' said Anji. 'Maeve wasn't sure if it was letters or some sort of symbol.'

'Not a pentangle is it?' whispered Colin.

'Honestly Colin, you're in a dark mood today,' said Pip, nudging him playfully. 'Must be because it's Halloween.' This brought some chuckles – slightly nervous chuckles – from the others.

Colin muttered something under his breath.

The image on the laptop showed another faint scratching:

MG

Anji was saying; 'If it's not the letters "MG", then possibly it *is* some sort of picture or symbol, maybe some kind of family crest, although it looks a bit rough for that. We're going to investigate the local records, check online and so on.'

'You know,' said Pip thoughtfully. 'Whatever you find out, Anji... well... even if you *don't* find anything out... I think we should re-bury the skull and bracelet. After all, they were buried together, so they're meant to be together.'

'Now who's coming over all spooky on Halloween?' chuckled Colin.

Pip looked slightly miffed. 'It's not that,' she said. 'Who knows? By digging it up we've disturbed a resting spirit?'

Colin snorted dismissively and a couple of the committee members gave more nervous chuckles, but I noticed that Betty, Anji, Donna and especially Pip looked quite serious.

'I'm not against reburying the skull and bracelet,' said Anji, reaching out and squeezing Pip's hand in a comforting way. 'Only thing is, Maeve's still got the bracelet and she's hoping to run some more tests on it, see if there's any other clues as to who it belonged to. In the meantime, we've got plenty to go on from our end to investigate.'

This seemed to satisfy Pip who nodded in agreement.

I jumped down to the floor and trotted over to Fred and Barbara. 'Did you hear that?' I almost hissed. '"*Disturbed a spirit*" Pip said.' Fred and Barbara both nodded their agreement. '*That's* why the ghost cat is showing itself,' I whispered breathlessly. 'We need to bury the skull and bracelet again! Maybe then the ghost cat will be at rest again!'

'I agree,' said Barbara. 'But how are *we* going to do that?'

'I don't know,' I said, somewhat deflated. 'But I'm going to find a way!'

'But can you be sure that's what the ghost cat *wants*, mate?' said Fred. 'Perhaps... well... perhaps it's *looking* for something?'

'Or some*one*,' added Barbara.

We all sat silently considering this.

'Well, it's Halloween night tonight, isn't it?' I said at length, 'Like we said, this is the ideal time to find out. And I know just who to ask for help.

Chapter Ten

All Hallows Eve

'Come on, this way – don't be shy,' said Janet, as she briskly trotted towards the slope leading to the pond in the wild area. Her coat looked silvery in the moonlight and just as pretty as it did by day. Janet seemed to have a much greater confidence when she was doing something mystical. Well, she was Tiberius' famulus, after all.

There were six of us in total – me, Red Fred, Barbara, GG and ET following in a line behind Janet. Dorothy had declined to come with us, making the excuse that she didn't want to get her paws muddy by the pond and she wasn't about to listen to a load of "mystic mog mumbo-jumbo." When Fred had told her that he understood it was okay if she was frightened, she gave him one of her Special Withering Looks but didn't give way to his gentle cajoling. I could understand how she felt. When you've been up close and personal with a ghostly cat which then runs after you, your courage does take a bit of a knock.

It was dark now, but the full moon was shining brightly, casting its silvery embrace over the allotments and enhancing the shadows into deep, inky black voids. Stars twinkled brightly and more were visible than usual. I couldn't help but stop, sit down and look up, remarking on the stars. Janet stopped too but her tail was twitching slightly showing impatience.

'Sorry to hold us up, Janet,' I said, although I was secretly glad of a slight delay in possibly confronting the ghost cat again. 'It's such a clear night, look at all those stars.'

The others looked up (ET leaning against Red Fred for balance) and also remarked on this too.

'Usually, we can't see stars clearly from cities and towns,' said GG. 'It's because of light pollution, caused by artificial lighting. I read about this on Moggle on Betty's laptop.'

'What's arty farty lighting then?' asked Fred. 'Isn't that when humans put up all those fancy little lights around their houses?'

'*Artificial* lighting,' corrected GG. 'It means it's not natural light, like you get from the sun or the moon. Human-made light, that's electric lighting in houses, factories and offices, and from streetlamps and cars. That sort of thing.'

'So, what's this light *poo loo shun*?' I asked. 'Sounds like some sort of toilet that you want to avoid. Has it got anything to do with leaf mould?'

GG sighed but explained patiently: 'Pollution means harmful stuff messing up the world. Generally, humans create pollution very easily. They don't mean to, but it's the way they live. Light *pollution* means all the artificial light shines up into the sky and blocks out natural light from the stars. There's good old-fashioned smoky pollution too, exhaust fumes from cars and suchlike. But there's a bit of a wind tonight, so maybe that's been blown away at least.'

I considered this. The wind blowing car fumes and smoke away I could understand, but either lots of humans had turned off their electric lights or there really *was* something magical in the air tonight.

'I-i-it's v-v-*veryprettythough*,' wibbled ET in an awe-struck way.

'It's *beautiful*,' I said with feeling. 'It's a shame that humans block such a wonderful view with their arty fickle lights.'

'They can't help it really,' Janet chipped in. 'It's been a long time since they lived in caves or huts, close to nature. Making fire didn't just keep them warm or cook the meat from the animals they hunted, it kept the dark away. Now they can make as much light as they like and it changes the whole way they live in the world.'

'Exactly!' added GG. 'Did you read that on Moggle too?'

'No. I just sort of knew it already,' said Janet. 'I think I remembered it from somewhere'. As usual, there was a hint of mystery to what she said. Once again, I had the impression that she knew far more than she let on. Or perhaps knew far more than she actually knew herself.

GG continued: 'They can turn off their lights, but they know they can always turn them on again. And it never gets *really* dark at night. *Real* darkness would scare the pants off them!'

'Whatever the reason, it's still a lovely clear night though,' said Barbara, still looking up. 'Those stars kind of make shapes, don't they?'

'That's the constellations,' said Janet. 'Tiberius told me about them. At least, I think he did.' She scanned the sky. 'Ah yes, that's the Plough… there's Orion's belt and oh yes! That bright one, that's Sirius.'

'Siri-who?' said Fred.

'Sirius. Also known as the Dog Star,' replied Janet.

'*Dog!!! Where?!*' we all said in unison, looking around nervously, our fur bristling automatically.

'Don't panic! It's just the name humans gave that particular star,' said Janet soothingly. 'I don't know why.'

'Huh!' muttered Fred, giving his fluffed-up tail a quick lick to flatten it down. 'They should've called it the Cat Star!'

Janet stood up purposefully. 'Come on then,' she said briskly. 'Stargazing's all very nice but it doesn't get our ghost cat mystery solved. Let's get to the pond while the gateway's still open.'

The gateway that Janet was referring to is the barrier between this world and the world of the Fae. I didn't understand it all, but the pond, or at least the place where the pond was now, used to be an ancient stone circle that had been torn down a few hundred years ago by humans in the name of religion. The pond had been dug out where the stones had been to make a private fishpond for someone called The Bishop who had a fine house built nearby.

Much as I liked the idea of a private pond full of fish to eat (and let's face it, I'd seen lots of these in people's back gardens when I was an Outling Cat), it was a terrible act of vandalism to destroy the sacred stones. I'd seen most of this happening in that strange dream I'd had while I was lying injured in the cellar of the old cottage, except that I wasn't so sure it *had* been a dream after all.

The strangest thing though was that the stone circle *still existed in the same place* but also not *here* where the pond existed. Tiberius had explained (sort of) that the world of the Fae was "the other side of the shadow," and as shadows were incredibly thin, that's how close they were to us.

I wasn't totally surprised when the mysterious white mist we'd seen at the Gathering billowed up as if from nowhere. Janet simply marched boldly into it and, after a slight hesitation, we all followed. The mist seemed to deaden all sound, every breath of wind, every rustle of leaves or skitter of vole feet in the undergrowth. We walked on in silence until suddenly the mist was behind us and we were at the edge of the slope leading down to the pond. It wasn't very far from where we'd been looking at the stars to reach the pond, but it would normally take longer to walk here – the mist somehow brought us here quickly, as it had done once before.

The water of the pond formed a perfect inky black mirror in which the moon and stars were reflected. If anything, they looked a lot brighter and closer than they did in the sky. Trails of mist were curling around the edge of the pond and as they billowed up gently in the breeze, I could just make out the shapes of the tall standing stones which formed the stone circle; ancient, pitted, dotted with lichen, standing like silent sentinels as they had done for thousands of human years. The stones didn't seem to be as solid as they had when they'd appeared at the Gathering all those moonths before. Somehow the whole area was bathed in a soft white glow, but where the light was coming from, I couldn't be sure.

As I looked around the pond, I saw other shapes forming, or at least simply coming into focus, as though they'd always been there, just like the stones, except that I was only just noticing them. They were gnomes – small people, much smaller than humans and not much taller than us cats. They had nut brown skin and wore rough, but serviceable clothes, mostly some kind of shirts with jerkins and waistcoats, and pointed hats. Sticking up from the sides of their hats were pointy ears. Not as pointed as a cat's but pointier than a human's. Most of the gnomes had beards of varying length and colour, while some didn't have beards at all but had quite long hair. These I took to be female Fae. There were some even smaller gnomes running about, dodging in between the bigger gnomes' legs and hopping over stones. These I guessed must be gnome children. The older gnomes were standing or sitting in groups chatting, drinking from rough wooden cups or chewing on what looked like strips of tree bark.

One group of six gnomes seemed to be playing some kind of game, all sitting cross-legged in a circle, looking quite serious as they took it in turns to toss stones and acorns into the centre of the circle. Suddenly, one of the gnomes jumped to his feet, waved his arms in the air and gave a shout of excitement. The others all leaned back and threw their remaining acorns and stones down in disgust. Whatever the game was about, the excited gnome had clearly won.

The more I looked, the more I realised that there were more little people than just the gnomes. There were slightly taller creatures, with long legs and arms, longer pointy ears and quite sharp noses. They wore long, trailing wisps of material and seemed to glow with some kind of inner light. Then, flitting around above the other Fae and zipping across the water of the pond were small, delicate creatures with gauzy wings, each glowing with a particular colour, leaving bright trails of light behind them. I knew these to be fairies, having met some of them before. It was hard to follow their movements as they were so fast, their coloured trails merging in a knotted rainbow which seemed to melt and drip down into the water of the pond.

'Blimey, it's busy here tonight!' observed Red Fred. He looked up as a fairy zoomed low over his head. By the tensing of his muscles, I could tell he was fighting the instinctive urge to leap up and grab the little creature. Even if he'd wanted to, he wouldn't have succeeded. The fairy flitted up into the sky out of reach, with a high-pitched little laugh which sounded like the tinkling of tiny bells and seemed to become a little ball of light.

'Ah, here's Oakroot,' said Janet brightly, as a very self-assured gnome strode up to us, his thumbs tucked into the pockets of his waistcoat. He had a long white beard and the usual pointy hat and wore a red and white spotted neckerchief.

'Greetings, feline friends!' he boomed good-naturedly. 'Welcome to our Halloween gathering!'

I'd met Oakroot previously and not always when I was Robert if my dream were to be believed. He was the leader of the gnomes and acted as a kind of spokesgnome between the world of the allotments and the world of the Fae. He and several of his fellow Fae had been present here at the Gathering some moonths ago.

'Greetings, noble Oakroot,' said Janet with a polite bow of her head. We all offered our greetings and bowed our heads respectfully. ET managed this perfectly. If anyone had a body that was designed to bow, it was ET.

The formalities over, Oakroot turned slightly and gestured to the Fae ranged around the pond. 'Come an' join us,' he said. 'All be welcome on this night. Old Brock an' his clan were here just now an' I daresay Ruby and her foxy family'll be along soon an' all.'

We followed Oakroot to the other side of the pond. As we passed one of the tall standing stones, I felt my tail brush against it. It felt solid enough, even though it seemed to be a shape in the air rather than an actual physical object. Suddenly I felt a rush of warm air, whilst the smell of summer flowers wafted past my nose. It put me in mind of one of those long, hot summer afternoons, when I would doze under a bush, enjoying the cool of the shade but also soaking up the warmth of the sun. It felt so… peaceful, so relaxing.

'Wow! Did you smell that and feel that warmth?' I exclaimed.

Oakroot looked round and smiled broadly. 'Ah. Ye've caught a whiff o' our world an t'other side o' the shadow,' he said. 'If ye touched the stone ye opened a hole.'

'Oh! Sorry!' I blurted. 'I didn't mean to!'

'Don't ye worry Robert me lad!' chuckled Oakroot. 'The hole closed when ye stop touchin' the stone. The shadow's thin tonight, so 'tis easy to reach 'twixt the worlds.'

Oakroot led us to a semi-circle of five round stones set back a little way from the pond. He sat on the middle stone and called out something that sounded like '*Ruuugleharrgah*!'

'He's talking in gnomish,' Janet whispered to me.

'Sounds like he needs to clear his throat,' observed Fred drily, which earned him a hissed '*Shhh!*' from Janet.

Two gnomes, a male and a female walked up and sat on the stones either side of Oakroot's stone. The male gnome had a bushy ginger beard streaked with silver. The female had long white hair and wore a long skirt which reached almost to her feet. Both looked old and wise, but their eyes were bright and clear, shining with wisdom.

Then, almost too fast to see clearly, one of the long, thin creatures arrived, as though it appeared from thin air. It sat, somewhat awkwardly, on one of the other stones, stretching its long legs out in front of it. It had a faint glow around it, which Janet later told me was its natural *aura*. I noticed that it was barefoot and that it had three human-type toes on each foot. On closer inspection its wispy clothes were a very pale blue colour but looked white under the glow of its aura which pulsed brighter, then dimmer, every few seconds.

Finally, a small ball of glowing bright pinky-green light dipped down from the sky above the opposite outer stone. Gradually the glow faded to reveal a fairy, looking just like a miniature human girl, wearing a glittery pinky-green dress, the gauzy wings on her back fluttering so fast they were just a blur. This reminded me of the dragonflies and damselflies that flitted across the pond in the warmer weather. The fairy hovered briefly, then flew down to perch delicately on the stone.

Oakroot indicated that we should all sit in front of the stones. 'Make yourselves comfortable, my friends,' he said. 'I'm guessing ye have a tale to tell us.'

'We do,' said Janet. 'Or rather Robert does, as he's been involved the most.'

Oakroot nodded gravely. 'Aye, but affore ye tell us, young Robert, allow me to introduce the elders here assembled.' He gestured to the female gnome on his right. 'This is Hollybough,' he said, nodding to the lady gnome. 'She's one of the wise wood gnomes.' He turned to the male gnome on his right. 'And this is Brod Tanglewood, Keeper of the

Mushrooms.' He leant forward slightly and gestured to the tall thin creature. 'This is Snorri, an elder of the Elves.' The tall elf creature nodded gravely to Oakroot, who then gestured towards the fairy. 'And this is Tallia, honoured Ambassador for the Fae of the Stone Circle.' The little fairy held the hem of her dress in both hands, hovered briefly in the air and dropped a curtsy, flashing a cheeky smile at Oakroot.

We all nodded respectfully at the assembled Fae elders. I felt rather embarrassed, as though I was a kitten caught by his mother doing something that a kitten shouldn't and getting carried off by the scruff of his neck. Not that I could remember what my mother looked like, I reflected sadly.

'Ye picked the best night to be askin' of us,' said Oakroot, rummaging in his waistcoat pocket and pulling out a surprisingly long clay pipe. 'T'ain't often ye get us all assembled on this side o' the shadow. Oakroot clicked his finger and thumb (as I'd seen humans do) causing a spark to appear in the air (as I hadn't seen humans do) which then dropped into the bowl of his pipe. I caught a whiff of something like warm compost as a thin trail of smoke trickled into the air from the pipe. He leaned back and took the pipe from his mouth, then leaned forward intently and said, 'So Robert me lad – tell us your story.'

The Fae elders were conferring together while we waited a little way off. I'd told them all about the ghost cat, the skull, the bracelet, the strange markings on the bracelet, everything in fact. Barbara and ET had added details of their sightings of the ghost cats, while GG had explained about searching online and about seeing the ghost cat in one of the newspaper photographs ('So it's definitely *something*!' she'd said). Red Fred, of course, hadn't seen the ghost cat (at least not yet), but stoically vouched for our veracity. (GG explained to me what that meant later). Janet had simply quietly said that she'd felt something 'adrift in the ether,' which the Fae agreed with. (GG couldn't explain that to me, but I took it to mean that Janet had an odd feeling about things around the Allotments).

'Do you think they might know who the ghost cat is?' pondered Barbara.

'If anyone does, they should,' said Janet.

'I-I-I h-h-*hopetheydo*,' wibbled ET nervously. 'I-I-It's a-a-a *bitoffputting* h-h-having a g-g-*ghostcataround* the a-a-allotments.

'It's a pity Tiberius is hibernating right now,' I said. 'He seems to know everything that's going on around the Allotments. But I thought the Fae might be a good bet for answers.'

'That was a good idea,' agreed Janet. She nodded towards the Fae where Oakroot was gesturing to us to come back over. As we approached, I noticed that the Tallia the fairy wasn't there.

'Well now, Robert and friends,' said Oakroot, sitting up straight with his hands on his knees and his pipe tucked behind one ear. 'We've conferred and we think you've got a genuine cat's ghost here.'

'We *know* that!' muttered Fred under his breath.

Oakroot smiled and nodded towards Fred. His pointy ears were obviously exceptionally good at picking up the smallest of sounds. 'Aye, but there's all sorts o'things that can be called ghosts, young Fred. And to be honest with ye, we have no idea who the unfortunate creature may be.'

My face fell, my hopes dashed. 'Oh, we were hoping you might have… well… seen it,' I said. 'Or better still know who the cat was when he was alive and maybe what he wants now.'

'T'ain't that often we's this side o' the shadow,' said Oakroot. 'This time o'the year, like Halloween, 'tis easier for us to come through, as the shadow between the worlds is thinner. So, we think ye best talk to someone as knows about ghosts an' the like.'

'Lots of your people came through to the Gathering,' said Barbara, looking puzzled. 'That wasn't at this time of year.'

'Aye, some of us did at that,' conceded Oakroot. 'An' I can hop through on me own now an' again. But it requires powerful magic, so we can't do it often. So, however that poor creature met his fate, none of us saw it happen.' He smiled and added, 'So we think ye'd be best talkin' to someone as knows more about such things and sees more on this side than we do. Tallia's gone to fetch him.'

At that moment, the little fairy reappeared, twinkling brightly and lowered herself to her stone. 'He's coming Oakroot,' Tallia said in her high-pitched little voice. 'I think his fellow players will be glad of the chance to win.' She put a hand to her mouth and giggled.

Following her into the semi-circle came a gnome. I realised he was the one I'd seen playing the odd game of stones and acorns with the five other gnomes beside the pond and winning.

Now, as you know, I'm a cat and we don't pay a lot of attention to clothes, mainly because we don't wear them, but this gnome was so positively flamboyant in the way he dressed, you couldn't help *but* notice his clothes. I realised that under the soft glow of light around the pond I hadn't seen how colourful his clothes actually were. He wore a bright red waistcoat, a green neckerchief, blue trousers and a hat to match. He wore long black boots which positively shined. His white beard was much shorter than the other gnomes, trimmed to a neat point. His skin seemed to be paler than the other gnomes, almost shiny. He had rosy round cheeks and sparkling green eyes. Even the tip of his snubby little nose looked as rosy as his cheeks. He looked somehow familiar, although the only gnomes I'd seen before had been made of plastic or stone and were placed in people's gardens, invariably sitting by a pond holding a fishing rod. And yet…

'You sent for me, elders?' he said, bowing and doffing his cap to reveal some rather splendid wavy white hair. He had a rich, melodious voice which sounded less woody than Oakroot's and more… *human*.

'Yes, thank you for coming,' said Oakroot. 'Has Tallia told ye of our feline friends' concern?'

'She has,' said the gnome, replacing his hat and turning to us. 'Pleased to meet you all. My name's Alan Titchbark. I'm a garden gnome.'

'Er – young Alan here spends a lot o' time close to humans,' explained Oakroot. 'He's our kind o'… well… eyes 'n' ears on the human world, aren't ye, Alan?'

'I certainly am!' exclaimed the gnome cheerfully. 'I gather you've got ghost trouble?'

'Er… well, yes. *Sort of* trouble,' I said uncertainly. 'I can't be sure this ghost cat means us any harm as such, it just kind of acts…'

'Lost?' Alan finished for me.

'Exactly.' I said, 'Sort of…'

'Confused?'

'Yes! Confused!'

'Like we are,' chuckled Fred.

'Ah, you must be Red Fred,' beamed Alan. 'Your sister Ginger sends her love. She's very happy as a Home Cat in her various human homes. She says she'll pop over to the Allotments to visit you soon.'

Fred looked taken aback. 'Oh, I haven't seen Ginger since we were kittens and she was rehomed,' he said. 'Does she live close by then?'

'Not far, she lives in quite a few different places and…' began Alan, but he was interrupted in a friendly way by Oakroot.

'I think if ye all go an' talk, Alan here may be o' help,' he said. 'We elders'd best get back to our Halloween celebrations.'

'Yes of course,' said Janet. 'Thank you all for your help.' She bowed politely to the elders who had stood up (or in Tallia's case flown up). The rest of us quickly followed suit. The elders all bowed back and then, in the blink of an eye, they simply weren't there any longer.

Oakroot was still there, however, and sidled up to me, holding one hand against his cheek. He whispered into my ear. 'Alan's a good lad,' he said. 'But spendin' a lot o'time with humans makes 'im, well… a bit… *human*. Like the way he talks and acts. Best bear it in mind.'

'Oh, I will. I'm quite used to humans now,' I whispered back.

'His name's not really *Alan*,' added Oakroot. 'That's just his human alias. His real name's Blithesome Beechbark, but don't let on.' He winked at me. 'Anyways,' he said in a louder voice, 'I'll go see if I can have a game of Squirrel Stones with the lads. Now Blithe – I mean *Alan* – ain't playin', I might stand a chance o' winnin'.' With that, he gave me a quick bow and hurried off.

I turned back to Alan who was rubbing has hands together as though in anticipation for some pleasurable task.

'So, Robert…' he beamed, 'You've got ghost trouble?'

Chapter Eleven

Talking of Ghosts…

Alan led us a little way from the hubbub of the Fae festivities.

'Let's just go up the slope a bit where it's quieter,' he suggested.

'Good idea!' exclaimed Red Fred crossly, as a couple of tiny gnome children barrelled past, one running under him and the other leaping onto his back. Before he could react, the gnome child sprang off his back, landing on its friend (or possible sibling) and they both rolled off down the slope, giggling the whole time.

Once we were at the top of the slope, Alan sat cross-legged and motioned to us to sit down. He'd been handed a wooden cup by a fellow gnome as we'd headed off to the slope and now he took a long drink from it. 'Ahh!' he said in obvious satisfaction. 'Pumpkin ale. You can't beat it for a Halloween treat!'

'Is it always this… *frantic* on Halloween?' I asked.

'You should see it on the other side of the shadow,' said Alan. 'These folks have come this side for a bit of a break from all the partying.'

'Aren't your people afraid of being seen or heard by humans?' I asked. 'I mean, okay, it's night-time and there's no plot holders about but even so…'

'Oh, no worries about that,' said Alan airily. 'The magic mist acts as a protection. If humans come along here, they'll see us at first of course, but then the magic'll make them see what they *expect* to see. They expect to see the pond, they'll see the pond. They'll simply forget they saw us. It's the way human brains work. Their senses tell them what's there and their brain doesn't believe it.'

'That's clever,' I said, wondering how many times the various Fae might have been flitting around the allotments in broad daylight, unseen or at least unnoticed by the plot holders.

'Mind you,' chuckled Alan, 'It doesn't always work. Little children can see us, so if we see a small child, we just make ourselves scarce very quickly. And sometimes you get a particularly strong-minded human whose brain just won't blot out that they're seeing us. But then their brain substitutes something in our place, usually something the human doesn't like. I remember this one time when this bloke came on a group of us playing squirrel stones in the woods. He babbles 'Oh my God!' and runs off shouting that he's seen a hippopotamus.' He frowned. 'Or was it his mother-in-law? One of the two anyway, possibly both.'

'S-s-so w-w-what d-d-does a *gardennomedo*?' asked ET. 'D-d-do all g-g-*gardenshavethem*?'

'ET was born on the allotments, Alan,' explained GG. 'She hasn't seen a human garden.'

'Some do, some don't, ET,' said Alan kindly. 'Nowadays, most humans think garden gnomes are *tacky*. Blooming cheek if you ask me. But there's still enough people who like them to let us sneak into their gardens. A garden is one of the best places to observe humans.'

'I don't understand,' I said, feeling, yet again, that the world was a lot more complicated than I thought it was. 'I thought garden gnomes weren't real. Well, I mean, they *are* real, I saw plenty of them when I was an Outling, but they're made of stone or plastic.'

'Like little statues,' added GG.

'Ah, well now,' chuckled Alan, taking another sip of pumpkin ale before continuing. '*Most* of them *are* made of stone or plastic. Others just *look* that way. See how smooth and shiny my skin is? A quick dunk in *Gnome-Glo™* does that... made entirely from natural products including fresh beech nut oil. Shiny skin, rosy cheeks, bright clothes, a big grin and the ability to stay really still, that's all you need to fool humans. It's called hiding in plain sight.'

'Amazing!' we pretty much all exclaimed at once.

'I remember seeing *you* in a few gardens a while back, Robert,' said Alan. 'When you were an Outling. Very fond of nicking Home Cats' food and dibbling in fishponds as I recall.' He winked mischievously. 'I bet you didn't pay any attention to the grinning garden gnome with the fishing rod, did you?'

'Impressive!' I agreed. 'But why do you need to observe humans?'

'Well, it pays to keep an eye on what they're doing this side of the shadow,' said Alan, looking serious for a moment. 'You never know what bright ideas they might be coming up with to spoil the environment. Oh, I know *some* humans are pretty decent folk, just want to get on with their lives, but it's the ones with lots of money and power you've got to watch. The ones that want to bulldoze ancient woodlands to build office blocks that no-one will work in or houses that ordinary folk can't afford. Or put blooming great long railway lines which no-one really needs through meadows and valleys. *And* they don't mind if they knock down a few folks' houses on the way. Thing is, they don't just upset the balance of nature and the order of things on this side of the shadow. It affects our side too, especially all that iron they use. It affects *all* sides in fact.'

'So how do you find things out by sitting in gardens?' said GG, looking puzzled.

'We listen. We watch. We read the newspapers when they're delivered or thrown away. We sneak into houses and watch televisions, log onto their computers and scan the Internet.' (GG nodded knowingly at this point). 'When humans are working in their gardens, they often have the radio switched on. There are always news bulletins to listen out for and sometimes there's even some good pop songs. I prefer the early eighties stuff myself, but that's probably because I was *in* my early eighties when those songs came out.' [10]

'And can you *do* anything about the damage humans cause?' I asked.

'Oh yes, if we need to intervene, we will,' said Alan. 'You'd be surprised at how many Fae get themselves elected to government by humans or form pressure groups. It's easy enough for us to use a bit of magic to appear human.' I must have looked concerned because he added: 'Oh, don't worry, it's nothing sinister. We just do our best to keep the world safe.' He grinned broadly and winked. 'You could say it's all a case of *elfin safety*.'

We must have looked blank because Alan's face fell. 'Tough crowd,' he muttered.

'But *anyway*,' said Red Fred in his usual laid-back tone of voice, but as always coming straight to the point. 'What about this ghost cat that's popped up on the Allotments? What can you tell us about *that*? It's got everybody all jittery and Dorothy's been extra grumpy about it, so it's causing quite a few problems.'

'That's right,' added Barbara, with feeling. 'A ghost cat is bad enough, but a really grumpy Dorothy is… well, *unbearable*!'

'I just wonder if we can help it – *him* rather – in some way,' I said. 'I think his name is Tip. He seems to want something but can't *tell* us what.'

'Looks like we're going to have to explain everything again,' sighed Barbara.

'No need,' said Alan brightly. 'Little Tallia magicked your conversation with the elders into my head when she came to fetch me, it saves a lot of time repeating things.[11] So, I've been giving the matter some serious thought.'

'I wish someone would magic some of *this* out of my head,' I sighed. 'It's really hard keeping up with it all. I'm getting a headache.'

'Never mind, mate,' said Fred, nudging me playfully. 'If Dorothy was here, she'd tell you not to worry because it'll all dribble out of your ears because your brain's too tiny to take it all in.'

'I didn't realise you were Dorothy's copycat, Fred,' I said drily. 'Next you'll be telling me that's she's your Darling Dorothy Dumpling!'

The others all laughed. Fred grinned good-naturedly. 'Well, *I* wasn't the one she told how *handsome* she thought he was, eh?' he smirked.

---

[10] I had no idea what the early eighties were, but GG looked it up online later and told me that it had something to do with humans having big hair and wearing lots of make-up.

[11] Nawthors find this kind of magic very useful too.

If cats could blush, I would have done. Instead, I had a hasty wash and declined to answer. I sneaked a look across at Janet to see her reaction to this, but she didn't seem to have noticed and was closely inspecting a bug or something in a tuft of grass.

Thankfully, Barbara came to my rescue again. 'So Alan, what do you know about ghosts?'

The gnome sipped his pumpkin ale thoughtfully, then lay back on the grass, supported by his elbows. 'I've seen a fair few ghosts over the years I've been watching humans', he said. 'Thing about ghosts is, there's lots of different sorts. What humans tend to call "ghosts" cover a wide range of phenomena.'

'What's a *fenommeena* when it's at home?' asked Fred.

'*Phenomena*,' corrected Alan. 'It means… well... odd things, odd happenings. Ghosts are a case in point.' He took a deep breath, then sat up. 'Right, so… *most* ghosts aren't actually *real*. They're sort of echoes of things that have happened. They're usually found in buildings like really old houses or castles. The buildings absorb energy. You know, like on a hot day, the ground warms up and holds the sun's heat? Same thing with psychic energy. One of the most powerful energies is emotion, and that's generated by the brain, although some folks reckon it can be generated by the heart.

Humans can be *very* emotional at times. Well, the stones absorb all that emotional energy over the years and store it. If it's a *really* emotional event, like if someone gets killed – and humans kill each other quite a lot – then there's a *lot* of emotional energy stored up.

'So later – and it can be years and years later, another human comes along and if the conditions are right and their brain is receptive enough, the stones will release that emotional energy and the living human will see those events played out again. So they'll see the human who died, or was murdered or whatever, doing the same actions over and over again. It's like a film or, you know, a TV programme or something on the Internet. The "ghost" can't see you or react to you any more than someone on the telly can – it's just an image.'

'Ah, I've got it,' said GG brightly. 'So films are like moving photographs of things that really happened, but they themselves aren't actually *real*.'

'Give GG a cigar!' exclaimed Alan happily, then quickly added, 'Or maybe some cat treats. Bit healthier. But yes, that's it *exactly* GG.'

'What about *Skalpe* or *Mooz* on the Internet?' said Barbara. 'I've seen humans talking to each other on that and…'

'That's a different thing,' said GG. 'It's like a telephone where humans can *see* each other as well as *talk* to each other. But you couldn't have a conversation with someone in a film, could you? Well… *maybe* you could but they wouldn't answer back. Not usually, anyway.'

I was doing my best to keep up with this discussion. 'But Tip – the ghost cat – doesn't do the same things over and over again,' I said. 'He seems to *know* what he's doing.'

'And that's the other sort of ghost,' said Alan. 'These are *spirit*s. There's not many of them compared to the "Replay Ghosts", but there's enough so's you'd notice them if you were in the right state of mind. Well, if you're a human anyway. Fae and animals are really receptive to them 'cos we see the *whole* world, not just the bits that humans *choose* to see. They can't help it. It's because they've evolved and got technology and civilization and all that. It moves them further away from the real world, from nature. Oh, as I said, there's a few humans who can connect better with the natural world and see the Fae and communicate with spirits, but hardly any of the other humans believe them.'

'Like I've always said, humans are strange,' I said. 'So… Tip is a *spirit* then? A *real* ghost? I've seen him walk through solid objects.'

'I'd say he definitely is,' said Alan. 'The thing about most sprit-ghosts is, they're usually troubled by something. They've left some important business in life unfinished and they're trying to complete it. Or they're looking for something or someone. And the saddest thing about most spirits is they're not even aware that they're spirit-ghosts and they keep trying to make the living see them. That's how people get haunted.'

'And animals too!' I added.

'Absolutely,' agreed Alan. 'It's trying to convince them that they are ghosts and that they can move onto the next realm, maybe choose to have another turn at life in a different body. I know you know about *that* Robert. But animal ghosts aren't as common as human ghosts because most animals' spirits move on quite easily. Seems to me that Tip is connected to something here.'

'Could it be his skull? Or the bracelet?' I asked.

'The skull maybe not so much,' said Alan carefully. 'After all, that's just what's left of his physical body and he doesn't need that. The *bracelet* I'm not sure about. It's obviously a human bracelet, so maybe it was worn by someone close to him.'

'Like an owner?'[12] said GG.

'Very likely, GG. That's what happens with most animal spirits that don't move on,' said Alan, nodding. 'They're still looking for the human owners they knew and loved when they were alive. So Tip wanted to be with his owner again so his spirit waited for them and kind of slept, waiting.'

'Like hibernating?' asked Janet.

'Like that, yes,' said Alan. 'Good comparison there, Janet. So when the skull and bracelet were dug up, his spirit woke up.'

'That makes sense,' I agreed. 'But if he's looking for his owner, well… surely they've been dead an awfully long time too? After all, Maeve at the Uni said the bracelet was really old.'

'That could be a problem of course,' said Alan thoughtfully. 'Mind you, the owner could be buried somewhere nearby for all we know. This land wasn't always the Allotments of course. Doesn't mean their spirit's still there though. In a case like this, the trouble is convincing the ghost that so much time has gone by, the thing they want to do or the person they want to find isn't around any longer. Sometimes you can manage to get through to them and they come to accept it. Then they find peace of mind and move on.'

'So… I just need to *talk* to the ghost cat then?' I said, cautiously.

'Yes. He seems to have latched onto you Robert,' said Alan. 'Probably because you're the first living thing he saw when came back to this world.'

'W-w-won't th-that b-b-be *abitdangerous*?' wibbled ET with concern.

'No, not at all ET,' said Alan reassuringly. 'Ghosts can't harm you. Even if they wanted to, they'd walk right through you. At best you'd feel a bit of cold draught.'

'Okay…' I said slowly. 'I'll do that. I'll talk to him. Ask him what he wants, what he's looking for.'

Alan nodded approvingly.

---

[12] GG used the cat word for "owner" of course, as no-one *owns* a cat. It translates from the Kittish as: *"The human who dwells with the feline and serves the feline's needs"*, but for ease of the reader's understanding, I've used the simplest human word.

'What if one of *us* sees him before Robert does?' asked Janet.

'Oh, you can try talking to him too, of course,' said Alan. 'But my guess is it'll only be Robert he'll engage with.'

'That's good, because Robert's a really friendly fella,' said Barbara. I felt a glow of pride at that.

'Bloomin' good job he didn't see Dorothy first then, wasn't it?' observed Fred.

'Am I more likely to see him tonight?' I asked. 'What with it being Halloween and all?'

Alan rubbed his bearded chin thoughtfully. 'Not really,' he said at length. 'You see, although the shadow between the worlds wears thin at the year's end, between now and the Winter Solstice, it doesn't necessarily mean ghosts are about any more than usual. They can be about anytime. Oh, we get all sorts coming through from other worlds at this time of the year, that's how the idea of Halloween came about in the first place. I just think Tip might find it all a bit busy round here tonight to make an appearance.'

'All sorts of *what* come through?' I asked.

'Ah, you don't really want to be bothered about that,' said Alan airily. 'If any of them are troublesome, us Fae send them back.'

I pondered this for a moment. I knew that the Allotments – or rather the land the Allotments were on – was a magical place, not least because of the phantom stone circle, However, there was clearly a lot more going on around here than I realised.

Alan stood up. 'Well, I hope I've been of some help Robert and friends,' he said brightly. 'If you need any help or need to tell me something – and I'd certainly be interested to hear how you get on – just ask Oakroot to pass a message onto me. I've got to get back to work tomorrow. I'm watching some government minister at the moment. And he's got a really big garden.'

'Thanks Alan,' I said, standing up too, rubbing my head against his body in a friendly fashion. Alain stroked my fur and tickled my cheek in an equally friendly way.

'You're a remarkable one, you are, Robert,' he said. 'Then again, you always were.'

Before I could query this, the other cats all bundled around the little gnome and rubbed their heads against him, much to Alan's delight, even though Fred's affectionate head butt nearly knocked him over.

'I'll be back this way for the Winter Solstice,' said Alan cheerfully. 'So... if I haven't heard from you before, we'll catch up then.' He adjusted his hat and squared his shoulders. 'Right, time for another game or two of squirrel stones,' he said. 'Got to give the lads and lasses a chance to win something back. I mean, I can't help it if I'm such a good player, can I? I'm one hundred and fifty acorns, fifty-five chestnuts and three walnuts up already!'

With that, he set off down the slope with a cheery 'Goodbye!' to us all.

We watched him reach the pond and nip round to the other side, past Tiberius' flowerpot and back to the huddle of gnomes playing, we assumed, squirrel stones. Quite a crowd had gathered around them, so the game must have been getting remarkably interesting.

The magical mist began to waft around us, as though on cue for us to leave.

'We'd best be getting back to the Allotments,' said Janet. 'Just in case Tip's ghost turns up again.' The others began to walk into the mist and disappeared from view, no doubt being transported swiftly back to the allotments.

I waited for a moment and looked back down the slope to the pond. The Fae's voices seemed further away now as the mist was blurring everything. A couple of little glowing fairy lights dancing above the water seemed muted and less bright. I caught a last glimpse of the stone circle, fading out of view. Something was nagging away at the back of my mind.

'Are you okay, Robert?' asked Janet, appearing bedside me, a concerned look on her face.

'Yes, yes, I'm okay,' I said, looking away from the pond. 'I just thought I... remembered something. Something… *familiar*. But it's gone now.'

'Maybe it will come back to you,' said Janet kindly. 'Shall we get back now? You never know, the ghost cat may show himself tonight after all.'

'Yes, yes, let's go,' I said. 'It's been an interesting evening.'

With that, we both walked into the mist. Within a few steps, we found ourselves back on the Allotments in our world, leaving the Fae to their Halloween celebrations, just a shadow away.

Chapter Twelve

Rockets, Rackets and Rescue

'What was *that?!*' exclaimed Barbara, his ears flattening and tail twitching madly as a series of loud bangs echoed around the allotments.

'Fireworks!' muttered Red Fred darkly. 'Always this time of year. Sounds like someone's setting them off nearby. And it's not even Bonfire Night for a couple of days yet!'

'Oh, of course,' said Barbara, having a quick wash to settle his nerves. 'I always forget until they start up again.'

'Yes, I know all about *fireworks*!' I added with feeling. 'When I was an Outling Cat, this time of year was awful. Not just for us Outlings either – the Home Cats and dogs didn't like it much either. Nor the birds. In fact, I don't think *any* animal liked all the bangs going off!'

Fred, Barbara, ET and I were sitting quietly by a big compost heap next to one of the freshly dug over plots, enjoying the warmth radiating out from it. This was caused by the plants decaying and releasing heat (GG had explained this to us), and very nice to sit around on a cold, overcast November day.

'Reckon we must be lucky being here on the allotments,' observed Fred. 'No-one lets off fireworks here. Have to say though, some of them racket ones that make nice patterns in the sky are good to watch… at least from indoors. Just wish they were all a bit… *quieter* really.'

'Rackets?' I said, puzzled. 'I think you mean *rockets*, Fred.'

'I thought rocket was one of those lettuce-y plants that some people grow on the allotments,' said Fred.

'Same word, different thing,' I said, pleased to be able to speak with some knowledge for a change. 'Although "rackets" sounds better because they do.'

'Do what?'

'Make a racket!'

'H-h-hang on,' interjected ET, with a puzzled expression on her face. 'I-I-I th-th-thought r-r-r-rackets w-w-were u-u-used *inttennismatches*. I-I-I've s-s-seen t-t-tennis g-ggames *onBetty'slaptop*. Th-Th- the h-h-humans wh-wh-who t-t-talk *aboutthegame* a-a-always s-s-say th-th-the p-p-players *haverackets*.'

'That's true, said Barbara. 'I've never seen 'em fly into the air and explode into coloured stars. Mind you, I've seen some of the tennis players throw their rackets down if they hit the ball wrong.'

'And they swear a lot and shout out things like "*You Cannot Be Serious*!" when they do that,' I added, having also watched the curious backwards and forwards game on Betty's laptop. 'Maybe that's why they're called rackets[13], 'cos the players make a racket?'

'Like those rockets?' said Fred.

'Umm… I've kind of lost the thread here,' I said, feeling my brain begin to protest at all the exercise I was forcing it to take. It was time to get back onto the original subject.

'It's worse when you're out there sure enough,' I said, nodding in the general direction of the allotment gates. 'The number of times I had to run from stupid little humans who threw fireworks at me in the street. And some not-so-little humans, come to that.'

We all considered this with serious nods.

'Betty usually makes sure we're all safely in our sheds on Bonfire Night,' said Fred. 'Apart from the burnt-out rockety-rackety things landing on one of the plots, we're well away from it.'

'That's good to hear,' I said happily. 'This'll be the first year I feel safe around Bonfire Night.'

'I th-th-thought i-i-it w-w-was c-c-called *GuideForksNight*,' said ET.

'I heard that too,' I said. 'I've seen humans cooking things like potatoes and sausages in their bonfires on Bonfire Night. Maybe they have to *guide their forks* onto the food because it's so smoky and they can't see it properly.'

'Actually, it's *Guy Fawkes* night!' snorted Dorothy, appearing from behind a coldframe. 'I learned this at the bookshop. Guy Fawkes was the name of a human who tried to blow up another lot of humans he and his friends didn't like. But he was caught before he could do it.'

'Oh, that's humans for you,' I muttered. 'Always disagreeing with each other about something.'

'Honestly,' grumbled Dorothy, rudely pushing between Barbara and me so she could warm her bottom against the compost heap. 'The things you lot ramble on about. Don't you know *anything*?'

---

[13] Of course, the real spelling is *racquets*, but when you're a cat, Humanese is hard enough to understand as it is without different spellings that sound the same and mean different things. I'd heard something somewhere about racquets used to made with catgut, but I'm sure that's just a rumour… At least, I hope so!

'Well, we know where you can see a cat skull,' chuckled Fred, winking at me. 'Oh, I forgot, it *frightened* you, didn't it?'

Dorothy gave him a Look and pretended she hadn't heard.

'Anyway,' said Barbara brightly, trying to prevent an argument. 'We haven't seen the ghost cat for ages. I thought we might see it after we went to the Fae's Halloween party.'

'Alan said we might not see him at Halloween,' I reminded him. 'Maybe it was too busy for him to show himself after all?'

'Huh! What do you expect?' snorted Dorothy. 'As if you'd find out anything useful from a *garden gnome*! I always thought you lot were away with the fairies and this just confirms it!'

I was beginning to regret telling Dorothy about what Alan and the other Fae had told us.

'If you hadn't been so bothered about getting your paws muddy and had come with us that night, you might have learned something, Dorothy!' snapped Barbara, crossly. This earned him a Very Hard Look.

I could see one of Dorothy's front paws twitching ready to administer a bop round the ear to Barbara.

'Look, whether you believe what Alan told us or not,' I said reasonably, '*You've* seen the ghost cat yourself. I honestly don't think Tip means us any harm.'

'And that's another thing,' added Dorothy dismissively. 'What sort of name is "*Tip*" for a respectable cat? You don't know that's its name, if indeed it ever had one. It was probably a Stray anyway. I wish you'd never brought the wretched thing onto the allotments!'

'*I* didn't bring it – *him* – here!' I protested. 'He appeared by himself! *I* can't help it if he needs to tell me something! I didn't ask for all this, you know! Why don't *you* come up with a plan how to deal with a ghost cat if you're so clever? *Ow!*'

I'd been bopped round the ear.

Things kind of went downhill after that. I'd hissed at Dorothy, Barbara had joined in, fluffing himself up angrily. ET had tried to fluff herself up and stand on her toes but had fallen over, and Red Fred had prodded Dorothy warningly with one of his big paws and told her to calm down. After this, Dorothy had stalked off, tail in the air, calling us all a Bunch of Ignorant Strays as she departed.

'Honestly, she gets worse!' muttered Red Fred, helping ET to her feet by nudging her up with his head. ET gave him a wobbly nose kiss of thanks. It struck me that ET and Red Fred seemed to be a lot closer to each other these days, which set me thinking of Janet.

'I think we're all a bit on edge,' I said, a little more charitably towards Dorothy than I felt (especially around the ear she'd bopped). 'The fireworks don't help.'

'Look, why don't we go and see if there's any mice around to be hunted?' said Fred. 'That'll take our minds off fireworks and ghost cats for a while.'

We all agreed that this was a Good Idea and strolled off, taking great care to sniff around any interesting objects, like watering cans or seed trays. After all, you never know what you might find.

Our wanderings led us through several plots, across the paths between plots and through more plots again. There were plenty of interesting things to sniff and one plot holder had been a bit careless with their cheese sandwiches, so there were pieces of grated cheese scattered around the plot, so we were all able to vacuum up a few. Unfortunately, there were no mice to be found, not even nesting in the scarecrows, as far as we could tell. I suspected they were watching us, keeping well out of our way, the unsporting little scamps.

We pushed our way through a thicket of slowly dying-off dahlias to bring us out onto another path, when we saw GG and Janet sitting either side of what looked like a small brown football. We trotted over to them. As we drew nearer, we realised that they weren't looking at a football at all, but a small hedgehog, which was rolled up in a ball shape. This was rather an unusual sight, given the fact that it was daytime and also November, when hedgehogs would usually have been hibernating.

We greeted the girls and I asked what was wrong with the hedgehog.

'From what we can make out, he's not feeling very well,' said Janet, looking concerned. 'I think it's dangerous for him to be out and about at this time of year.'

'And in the daytime, too,' added GG.

I lay down on the path and shuffled closer to the Hedgehog, going as close as I dared with my sensitive nose so close to its prickly spines. I realised that it must have been a very young hedgehog, not just because it was small but also as its spines were very light brown.

I'd had plenty of experience of hedgehogs in the many human gardens I'd visited as an Outling. Some kind humans put out cat food for them to eat of a night and those hedgehogs who did particularly well for slugs, snails and worms in the gardens usually wouldn't eat all of the cat food. On several occasions they'd been quite affable and let me share the cat food.

Most hedgehogs had a cheerful nature, mainly because there weren't many animals that could bother them, because at the first sign of danger they'd simply roll up into a ball and wait until the danger had passed. It had been very amusing to see any number of daft dogs – especially the small yappy ones – bark and snap at a hedgehog and then get a nose full of prickles for their trouble. Cars, however, were a different matter and I'd had several conversations with hedgehogs about the dangers presented when crossing a road, even in a relatively quiet street, because cars could move faster than animals. Rolling up into a ball wasn't going to protect them from a car's wheels.

'Hello, Little Hoglet,' I said. 'What's your name?'

'Oo wansa no?' came a muffled, snuffly voice.

'I'm Robert,' I said. 'I live on the allotments. These are my friends. We wondered why you were out in the daytime and in the cold.'

'Oo wanna eet muh?' came the snuffly-wuffly reply. 'I don tase nise an 'm prikrly.'

'No, we don't want to eat you,' I said, as reassuringly as I could. 'Can you – er – unroll so we can talk a bit better? I promise we won't try to eat you.'

Very slowly and with painful sounding grunts, the little hedgehog raised its head and began to unroll itself. I could see even more clearly how young it was.

'What's your name, Little Hoglet?' asked Janet kindly.

The hedgehog's little black nose twitched as he turned his head towards her. His bead-like dark eyes looked dull and tired. 'Hotchi,' he said, somewhat more clearly now that his snout wasn't tucked into his tummy.

'Why aren't you hibernating, Hotchi?' I asked.

'Tried to, didn't I?' snuffled Hotchi. 'Couldn't get into a deep enough sleep. I was still hungry, see? Didn't get enough to eat affore I needed to sleep. I was the smallest of my litter, last little nailbrush to go out inter the big wide world. Ate as much as I could find a' course, but then it got colder, so I reckoned I should hibernate. Found a bit of sacking inna shed to curl up in. But like I said… couldn't sleep prop'ly 'cos I was hungry, so, I come out las' night to find some food, no luck. Then it got really cold, so I rolled up inna ball to wait 'til it got warmer. But it didn't, an' now it's daytime an' it's even colder and... and… I fink I'm gonna *die*.'

He gave a snuffly sob and tried to curl up into a ball again, but seemed too worn out to do so. I'd seen this kind of thing all too often when I was an Outling. When an animal gives up like this, it's not going to end well.

I looked at the others helplessly.

'Should we go and tell one of the plot holders?' asked GG. 'I know some kind humans rescue poorly hedgehogs and…'

Hotchi raised his snout, suddenly alert. 'You mean *hoomins*?' he snapped. 'Them big, noisy ape fings that dig ever'thin' up? No fanks!' He gave a long wheezing snuffle, then curled up again, his outburst clearly having exhausted him.

For the next few minutes each of us tried to reason with the little hedgehog that most of the plot holders were very nice and kind, but he flatly refused to answer. Or couldn't muster the strength to argue.

The wind was getting up and ruffled my fur. It certainly felt colder now. Then I had an idea.

'Hang on,' I said. 'There's that empty plot at the end of the next row, isn't there? I've seen some of the plot holders dumping grass cuttings and leaves on there in a pile. I heard Colin talking about it. He said it'd make good compost, but it won't be touched until Spring. Maybe Hotchi could hibernate there?'

'Good idea, Robert!' exclaimed Janet. 'That's a *very* clever idea!' I felt my heart beat a little faster as she said this. 'I bet there's plenty of worms and slugs in that pile too, so Hotchi could get a good meal before he hibernates.'

'What about it, Hotchi?' I said bending down to him again. 'We can show you where the plot is. You'd be warm and safe and you could hibernate.'

'Don'… fink… I c'n… walk,' mumbled Hotchi. ''oo cold…. feel… cold.'

We all looked at each other despairingly.

'Wait a moment,' said Barbara. 'We should use our heads.'

'Well, we're *tryin'* to think of something, mate,' said Fred.

'No, no,' said Barbara impatiently. 'I mean, *really* use our heads! We could *roll* him to the plot. We can't really use our paws, too prickly for one thing…'

'We'd get prickles in our noses!' protested Fred.

'No, we won't, not if we bend our heads down like *this*,' said Barbara excitedly, ducking his head down. 'Then we lean our heads against him and push up a bit, and he rolls. Okay, we might feel a *bit* of prickling, but it won't be on our faces or our noses.'

'Y-y-you m-m-mean l-l-like w-w-when I f-f-fall over a-a-and Y-y-you a-a-and *F-F-Fredhelpsmeup*?' wibbled ET, equally excitedly.

'That's right, ET!' replied Barbara. 'If we all take turns and roll Hotchi here along the path, cross over at the end of this one, then go down the next path just a bit, the empty plot's just there, isn't it?'

We all agreed that it was a great idea. I asked Hotchi if he could roll up as tight as possible. He didn't reply, being obviously even colder and weaker, but made a valiant effort to roll himself tighter. I hoped he'd heard what we'd said and didn't think we were trying to eat him after all.

'Okay guys,' said Barbara, with determination. 'Heads down! *Hoglets roll!*'

About half an hour later, we arrived at the vacant plot. It had been a team effort from the start. ET couldn't risk trying to use her head to roll Hotchi along for fear of falling over, so she proudly led the way for us, in her distinctive wobbly fashion, weaving from one side of the path to the other (and occasionally falling over). We others took turns using our heads to roll Hotchi along the middle of the path. This was fine until we encountered the many potholes and dips in the old pathway, which meant that Hotchi rolled into them and it took two or three of us to headbutt him out of it. Luckily, it hadn't rained for a few days so none of the holes had rainwater in them. In a way, the dips and potholes were quite useful, because the jolting kept Hotchi awake and focussed. Judging by the snuffly swearing that we heard from time to time, it seemed that he was *very* focussed indeed.

'We're here, Hotchi,' I said, trying to sound as cheerful as I could. 'Look at this lovely big pile of leaves and grass and stuff.'

The little hedgehog began to slowly uncurl, with a series of grunts. 'I feel dizzy!' he grumbled. 'And sick! And this is you lot tryin' to *help* me, right?'

'Oh, don't be like that!' said GG brightly, trying to cajole Hotchi along. She pushed her head onto the big pile of leaves for a second or two then pulled it back out and sneezed. 'Look, all the leaves are lovely and dry, Lots of nice dry grass in there too.'

'You'll be really snug in there!' added Fred.

'Warm as toast!' continued GG.

'What's toast when it's at 'ome?' snuffled Hotchi suspiciously.

Much as I felt sorry for the little hedgehog, his grumbling was beginning to get on my nerves somewhat. After all, we'd all got achey heads from rolling him along the path, as well as a few unavoidable prickles. No doubt we'd picked up a few fleas too if the itching on my face fur was anything to go by. I sat down and scratched my cheeks and chin vigorously with my back leg.

There were various pieces of broken concrete paving slab at one end of the plot and Janet started to dig under one of them. 'Let's see if we can find you something to eat,' she said. 'Help me turn these stones over, Fred.'

With a heave of exertion, Fred turned one of the stones over with his back legs.

'*Bingo!*' exclaimed Janet, as the exposed underside of the broken piece of slab revealed three fat slugs clinging to it.

Hotchi's nose twitched madly and, with a great deal of effort, he hauled himself over to the upended stone. '*Mmmm!* That's more like it!' he snuffled and fell upon the unfortunate slugs, chomping each one down in rapid succession. I winced at the little popping sound each made as Hotchi's sharp little teeth and powerful jaws did their work. I know us cats can be a bit messy when it comes to eating our prey, but at least our prey mostly has fur and bones and doesn't go "pop" when you eat it.[14]

'Over here, Hotchi, mate!' chuckled Fred indicating the hollow left by another overturned piece of slab. 'Worms!'

With a surprising turn of speed, Hotchi barrelled over to the hollow and snapped up the worms one by one, chomping vigorously. At this point I felt rather sick. It was one thing watching Tiberius eat worms and bugs – they tended to pretty much disappear into his wide mouth via his sticky tongue in one or two gulps with no chewing involved – but hedgehogs are somewhat noisier about it. And definitely messier.

After three more stones had been turned over to reveal more invertebrate cuisine, Hotchi seemed satisfied, his pink tongue running across his snout to lick it clean of slime and bits of… whatever. His eyes seemed brighter and his prickles seemed more erect.

'Thanks kitties,' he said, gratefully. 'I really needed that. I feel a lot better now.' He yawned expansively, treating us all to the sight of his rows of sharp teeth. 'I think… I think I'm ready to hibernate now.'

With that, he barged his way into the pile of leaves, snuffling and muttering all the time. The little tunnel he left behind him soon closed up as leaves and grass cuttings fell down behind him.

I walked over to the pile. 'You okay in there, Hotchi?' I called.

---

[14] It usually goes "crunch".

'Ys fanks!' came the muffled, snuffy reply. 'Jus' getting' comftble. Ahh, s'nice.' I heard a yawn, then Hotchi snuffled sleepily: 'Fnks agin kitush. G'nite.'

We all listened intently, our heads cocked sideways against the pile. We could hear little snuffly snores and very light breathing.

'Sounds like he's slipping into his hibernation sleep,' said Janet.

'Well, I think we did some good there,' I said. I suddenly felt a terrible itch on my cheek and scratched vigorously. Barbara started to do the same, followed by Fred, then GG and finally Janet.

'O-o-oh d-d-dear,' wibbled ET. 'H-h-*hedgehogfleas*!'

'It's alright for you, ET, you didn't have to roll him with your head!' muttered Fred.

'Let's go to the clubhouse,' I suggested. 'If Betty sees us scratching, she might put some of that magic flea treatment on our necks.'

'Ooh! That flea stuff feels so *cold*!' moaned Barbara.

'Better than scratching all winter,' I chuckled.

As we set off down the path in the direction of the clubhouse it suddenly occurred to me that I hadn't thought about Tip the ghost cat for quite a long time since we'd come across Hotchi. It had felt good to help the little hedgehog to survive. Now, if I could just help Tip to find peace…

‘Good work eh, mate?’ said Fred walking alongside me. ‘Don’t suppose we’ll see young Hotchi ’til Springtime now.’

I looked back to the vacant plot and the pile of leaves. ‘I expect so,’ I agreed.

Little did I know how wrong we both were…

Chapter Thirteen

Fireworks!

'What the heck are *they* doing here?'

Barbara and I stared in disbelief when we saw Floggitt and Leggitt climbing out of a grubby van which they'd parked on the grassed area by the clubhouse. The van proclaimed *Floggitt & Leggitt: Antique Sales and House Clearances*, followed by a telephone number and website address.

'I don't know, Barb,' I muttered, 'But whatever it is, it can't be good.'

'I didn't think they'd be welcome *here*,' said Barbara, narrowing his eyes. 'Not after all that business with their giant pumpkin!'

Floggitt and Leggitt were today dressed in overalls and were wearing boots. Leggitt still had his trilby hat perched on the back of his head. I wondered if the grease on his hair somehow acted like a kind of glue to keep the hat on. The two of them slid the side door of the van open and began to unpack gardening tools; two rakes, a spade and a fork. It made me think that humans put an awful lot of effort into digging with all these different tools. Us cats can dig, fork and rake the earth, all without tools. Admittedly, that's usually to do our toilet, but it's much easier with claws.

'*Hello?* Mr Floggitt? Mr Leggitt?' Betty came to the door of the clubhouse and called out to them, waving. 'Could you come over for a moment please?'

'What does *she* want?' muttered Leggitt irritably under his breath.

'I think we can guess,' muttered back Floggitt. He waved back to Betty. 'Certainly Mrs DeGatto!' he called out cheerfully. Then, speaking quietly out of the corner of his mouth to Leggitt, he whispered: 'Remember what we agreed? Keep smiling, keep it friendly, don't give 'em any excuse to object.'

Leggitt nodded and fixed a broad, sickly and above all, *false* smile onto his sharp little face as they both ambled towards the clubhouse, deliberately not hurrying.

As they approached, a group of plot holders gathered behind Betty in the doorway of the clubhouse, jostled for space, then spilled out onto the paved area. I noticed Donna and Anji, Digby, Old Ted, Pip and Colin. They were all frowning and did not look at all happy.

'This might be interesting,' Barbara said. We trotted after Floggitt and Leggitt, then sat a short distance away by the edge of the plots to watch proceedings, as they reached the group of plot holders.

Leggitt tipped the brim of his trilby to Betty. Us cats are good at reading human body language and I knew he wasn't sincere in this outward show of respect.

'Good day to you all,' beamed Floggitt, flashing his equally false smile to the assembled party. 'How can we help you on this fine Bonfire Night – er - afternoon?'

I saw Donna mutter something under her breath and guessed it wasn't a reply to them which could be spoken outright.

I sniffed the air. I could smell smoke from somewhere beyond the allotments. Although it was only early afternoon, it seemed that some people had already lit a bonfire. No doubt there'd be the bangs of fireworks soon. Of course, tonight all us cats would be safely in our sheds, away from the bangs and flashes of hundreds of fireworks. At the sound of raised voices, I turned my attention to the group outside the clubhouse. It looked like there would be fireworks there too…

'You bloomin' well cheated your way onto these Allotments, so yer did!' exclaimed Digby, waving his walking stick in agitation.

'Are you suggesting we are *liars*, Mr Dogbert?' said Floggitt smoothly, holding his hand over his chest as though he was deeply shocked. 'I'd say that was something of a slanderous statement, wouldn't you, Mr Leggitt?'

'I certainly would!' snapped Leggitt, his smile now gone, his beady little eyes flitting from plot holder to plot holder.

Betty held up a placating hand. 'It's just that – um – your application…' she rummaged in her coat pocket and pulled out a square of paper which, when unfolded, revealed itself to be an application form for a plot on Sunnyside Allotments. 'Well, it wasn't made in your name, you see. It was registered under a Mrs… um…' she pushed her spectacles up her nose and looked at the form. '… A Mrs Lottie Moolah.'

'That's right,' said Leggitt tersely. 'She's my grown-up daughter. What's the problem?'

'Well, it's just that…'

'Just that it isn't a plot for your daughter at all, is it?' snapped Colin crossly. 'I happen to know, being reliably informed by my sister's husband's cousin's wife that your daughter lives in Spain where she runs a villa timeshare business.'

'And?' said Leggitt flatly, folding his arms.

'It's a fraudulent application!' shouted Colin, going red in the face. 'Anyway, I've heard about Lottie Moolah's husband Spenser Moolah. Wasn't he in the papers a while back for some tax scam? Decamped to sunny Costa Pacquet in Spain to escape the law!'

'That was never proven in a court of law!' shouted Leggitt turning even more red in the face. 'And my little girl runs a *respectable* business!'

Betty started to frantically shush Colin. Floggitt held up a hand in a placatory gesture. 'I think you'll find that my colleague Mr Leggitt is perfectly entitled to act in proxy for his daughter. It is stated in the Sunnyside Allotments rules – which we have read *very* carefully on your own website – that a relative, or indeed friend or sundry other acquaintance, may act on behalf of a plot holder by maintaining their allotted plot in the plot holder's unavoidable absence. Indeed, is it also not in those *very same rules* that it is the duty of all plot holders to keep their plots in good order?'

'Well, yes, it is,' conceded Betty.

'But your daughter hasn't even *been* here!' snarled Colin.

'Doesn't mean she won't be next time she's in the UK,' said Leggitt, arms folded, head held high in defiance. 'And that's why we're here, to maintain her plot in good order and…'

'… plant some vegetables,' added Floggitt smoothly.

'Yeah, and keep an eye on *our* vegetables too!' hollered Digby, waving his stick angrily. 'Stealin' all our growin' secrets too no doubt! You blaggards!' He was so agitated that he would have fallen over if Old Ted hadn't caught him and held him upright. 'It's all so's you can cheat and win the Pumpkin competition next year!'

'Are you suggesting that we would somehow wish to *sabotage* your pumpkins?' asked Floggitt innocently. 'That really *is* a serious accusation! After all, we are merely acting on behalf of Mr Leggitt's daughter. I believe she may well have sent an email *this very day* advising Mrs DeGatto that we would be acting on her behalf and…'

'Hang on, *hang on*,' said Donna pushing her way to the front of the group and striding over to stand in front of them both, hands on her hips, chin jutting out defiantly. Donna could look quite intimidating, especially with her shocking red hair and numerous tattoos and piercings. Leggitt took a nervous step backwards but Floggitt, with commendable bravery (or stupidity) stood his ground as Donna continued: '*Why* does she *want* a plot? Can you tell us that? I mean, she lives in Spain. How's she going to do anything with it?'

'She's *always* wanted an allotment plot, see?' said Leggitt in an innocent, almost sing-song voice. 'Ever since she was a little girl. She'd say to me: "Daddy", she'd say – she used to call me Daddy you know – "Daddy, I *wish* I could have an allotment plot of my very own, just like you and Uncle Floggy!" But we couldn't ever get another plot on the allotments we rented. But I've never forgotten what she asked and nor has she. So, when I saw that there were vacant plots on Sunnyside Allotments, well, I emailed her straight away and she asked me to send an application for one on her behalf.'

'How's she going to get the benefit of it then?' demanded Donna.

'Easy!' retorted Leggitt. 'We'll take lots of photographs of the plot to show what we've planted and how well it's all growing, then email them to her in Spain.'

'A likely story!' Donna and I said at the same time. Floggitt and Leggitt looked round at me. Obviously, they would have only heard a loud *meow* from me.

'Ah, it's the cute kitty who was being chased by the naughty doggy who knocked our pumpkin over,' beamed Floggitt. 'Saying hello are you puss? *Meow! Meow*!'

‘The guy’s such a twonk,’ muttered Barbara. ‘Can’t talk Kittish to save his life!’

‘Well, I’m sorry you choose not to believe us,’ said Floggitt briskly. ‘However, as I said, the application is all in order and I also believe that Mr Leg… that *Mrs Moolah* paid the required deposit and three months’ rent in advance by e-bank transfer, is that not correct, Mrs DeGatto?’

‘Yes, that’s true,’ said Betty, looking helplessly at the other plot holders. ‘It’s all above board.’

‘Then I can see no problem with our being here,’ said Floggitt smoothly. ‘Come, Mr Leggitt, let us go and tidy Lottie’s plot for her. I saw from the photos online that it’s in something of a sorry state, being covered with broken paving slabs and leaves.’

‘S’right, Mr Floggitt,’ said Leggitt. He cheekily tipped his hat again to Betty and hoisted both rakes onto his shoulder, whilst Floggitt hefted the spade and fork. ‘If you’ll excuse us folks, we’ve got work to do. We’re going to rake all those leaves up and burn them, it being Bonfire Night after all.’

‘You could use them for leaf mould!’ exclaimed Colin angrily. ‘Or you could give them to *me* to make leaf mould compost!’

‘Now *why* would we want to do that?’ said Floggitt smugly. ‘In any event, we think the ashes will be better for the soil. We each have our own recipes for horticultural success, Colin. Oh, and don’t worry,’ he added, smiling at everyone. ‘We’ll make sure our bonfire is nice and safe and within the rules of the Allotments.’

‘Best keep an eye out on your own plots though. Just in case there’s *saboteurs* about.’ Leggitt sniggered, with a burping sort of *hyuk-hyuk-hyuk* sound.

With that parting shot, they set off. The disgruntled group of plot holders watched them go, frowning and muttering.

‘I’m sorry!’ exclaimed Betty to the others. ‘I didn’t know Lottie Moolah was his daughter. And there really are no grounds to refuse her application or for them both to be here on her behalf.’

‘That’s as maybe,’ growled Colin. ‘But I’ll be watching them! I know they’re up to no good!’

‘They’ll be spyin’ on us, mark my words!’ grumbled Digby, ominously.

‘They cannot be trusted!’ agreed Old Ted in his deep, baritone voice.

The others all nodded and added their agreement.

Barbara and I watched the little group go back into the clubhouse, still complaining. Then we turned to watch Floggitt and Leggitt walking down one of the paths between the plots. I knew there was an empty plot about halfway down, so I didn't give the matter any further thought….

… That is, until about half an hour later when Barbara and I, now joined by Red Fred, happened to be wandering through the dry, dead foliage next to the empty plot where Hotchi was hibernating in the pile of leaves. To my absolute horror, I saw that Floggitt and Leggitt were working on that exact same plot!

'Oh no!' I exclaimed. 'That's Hotchi's pile of leaves! They've rented *that* plot!'

'What are they saying?' whispered Barbara as he inched a little closer, still hidden by the yellowing leaves of whatever plants had been growing on the adjacent plot. We all listened carefully.

'… so I reckon we could set up a couple of them little spy cameras near their plots,' Leggitt was saying as he raked a few more dry leaves onto the pile. 'Soon see what they're growing, eh?'

'Maybe even manage to get cameras in their sheds,' chuckled Floggitt as he tossed a chunk of broken paving slab onto a pile at the end of the plot. So, they *were* planning to spy on the other plot holders! Colin was right, vegetable competitions were *very* serious!

It was obvious they'd been tidying the plot up, as the two rakes were lying on the freshly forked up earth (even I knew it was dangerous to leave rakes lying around like that). Just then, both men straightened up, stretching and rubbing their backs, making groaning noises in the way that I'd seen several plot holders do after working on their plots. Then a horrible thought struck me.

'Leggitt had mentioned something about a bonfire, hadn't he?' I exclaimed.

'Oh no! *That* pile of leaves!' gasped Barbara.

'But Hotchi's hibernating in there!' Fred added.

'Yes, but *they* don't know that do they?' I said. 'And they probably don't care anyway!'

'Right Floggy,' said Leggitt, rubbing his hands together in a business-like way. 'Time for our Bonfire!' As if to prove me right, he rummaged in his overall pocket and pulled out a box of matches. 'The leaves are nice 'n' dry, should burn nicely.'

'Pity we haven't got any fireworks to go with it, eh?' chuckled Floggitt. 'Not that we'd be allowed to have them on the precious Sunnyside Allotments, of course!'

'*Oh no,*' said Leggitt in his innocent, insincere voice, as he extracted a match from the box and prepared to strike it. 'Not us bein' nice, respectable poxy plot holders, of course.'

'Eh?' said Floggitt.

'What?' snapped Leggitt, pausing in the process of striking the match.

'You said "poxy" plot holders.'

'So?'

'It's *proxy* plot holders, you dimwit! *Proxy!'*

'Who you callin' a dimwit?'

As the unpleasant pair began arguing about the correct use of humanese words, I took advantage of their delay in setting light to the leaves. 'Quick Barbara!' I whispered urgently. 'We've got to stop them! Go and round up as many of the others as you can! Try to get the humans to take notice too!'

'Right!' said Barbara, running back through the undergrowth in the general direction of the clubhouse.

'What are *we* gonna do, mate?' asked Fred.

'We're going to do all we can to stop them lighting that bonfire!' I replied grimly.

'Hey, this is just like back in the summer when those blokes working for Grasper were going to burn the allotments, isn't it?' chuckled Fred, as he crouched down and raised his bottom in the air, tail thrashing, back legs poised, ready to spring.

'Yes,' I agreed. 'Except we haven't got all the Allotment animals and the Fae to back us up this time.'

'So... just you 'n' me then?' said Fred, winking at me, extending his claws ready for action.

'Just you 'n' me'!' I replied. If cats could high-five each other easily, we would have done.

The two men had stopped arguing now. Leggitt bent down to the pile of leaves, his back to us. We heard the noise of the match being struck, saw a little puff of smoke go up... at which point we burst out of the foliage yowling a blood-curdling feline battle cry which would strike fear into the heart of any creature within earshot.[15] I landed on Leggitt's shoulder while Red Fred landed in the middle of his back with a bone-jarring thump, the combined force of which sent him sprawling face down in the dirt with a yell of surprise and a fair bit of pain, as our claws were very sharp.

The fall knocked Leggitt's trilby hat off revealing a large bald patch on the back of his head, over which a few pathetic strands of greasy hair were combed. This explained why he wore his trilby like that. Leggitt grabbed his hat as though his life depended on it and jammed it back onto his head. *More* strange human behaviour!

---

[15] The feline battle cry in question roughly translates as: *"Cower in terror before our feline might, you small creatures who are about to die horribly*". To human ears though it sounds like: "*Meowoowwwaaarrraaaa!*"

I disentangled my claws from Leggitt's overalls and turned to the pile of leaves. To my horror, a crackling, orange tongue of fire was running swiftly over the leaves, causing them to curl, blacken and burst into flame, spreading out across the pile. It was only the outer layer of leaves burning, but I could see the leaves and dry grass underneath beginning to smoulder, sending up thick plumes of smoke. It wouldn't take long until the whole pile was ablaze and the flames would reach into the middle of the pile where Hotchi lay asleep!

Floggitt and Leggitt were struggling to their feet, swearing loudly. Fred arched his back, standing on his toes, his fur fluffed up, making himself three times larger than usual, which was quite a formidable sight, hissing and spitting, causing both men to back away cautiously. Meanwhile, despite my fear of the fire I tried desperately to dig into the pile of leaves, but only succeeded in raking more dry leaves down onto the flames.

"*Geeercha!"* snarled Leggitt, grabbing the rake and jabbing it towards Fred, who backed away slightly but then bravely inched forward again. Floggitt picked up the other rake and hefted it menacingly above Fred. He raised the rake higher, ready to bring it downwards…

… But he dropped the rake with a howl of pain as a Tortoiseshell blur burst through the undergrowth and slammed into him, resolving itself into the shape of Dorothy, all of her claws extended and dug very firmly into his left leg. Clearly his overalls weren't sufficiently robust enough to stop her claws penetrating the material and into the flesh underneath.

'*That'll* teach you to splatter me with pumpkin pith!' snarled Dorothy, just before she sank her teeth into Floggitt's leg, just to be sure. I almost felt sorry for him as he tried to hop around, hollering blue murder, but was only able to revolve on the spot, thanks to the weighty Tortoiseshell killing machine clamped firmly to him.

Suddenly GG and Barbara joined the fray, leaping onto Floggitt's back, before falling neatly to the ground on all fours. A few seconds after them, ET wobbled up the path, weaving from side to side, her fluffy tail even more fluffed up. All of them were yowling in a menacing manner.

I heard barking and the skittering of claws. Rosie thundered up the path, nearly missing the plot before skidding to a halt and colliding with poor ET who rolled off the path into a neighbouring plot. Rosie quickly recovered her sense of direction and leapt onto the vacant plot. She ran around Floggitt and Leggitt, barking madly.

'It's that ruddy mutt again!' snarled Leggitt. 'The one who knocked our pumpkin off the table! Bark at me would yer? I'll show yer!'

Leggitt tried prodding at Rosie with the rake, which prompted her to grab the rake's handle in her jaws, before she yanked it out of Leggitt's hand pulling him forward and causing him to drop to his knees.

'Rosie!' I shouted. 'There's a hedgehog in that pile of leaves! Can you dig him out?'

'What's he doing in there, Robert?' yapped Rosie excitedly. 'Doesn't he know it's on fire?'

'Probably not! Never mind that now!' I snapped. '*Just save him!*'

Without a moment's hesitation, Rosie ran to the side of the pile of leaves which was just beginning to smoulder, then began to dig furiously, as only a dog can. As she dug, she kicked leaves, grass and earth behind her, straight into Leggitt's face, prompting outraged splutters from him.

Floggitt meanwhile had somehow managed to shake Dorothy off his leg. Dorothy, GG and Barbara were all facing him, ears flat, fur and tails fluffed up, yowling and hissing. I could see that Floggitt didn't want to face another run-in with Dorothy. He suddenly bent down, grabbed his rake again and straightened up, holding the rake in front of him to fend them off.

It was at this point that I heard footsteps running up the path and human voices shouting. I was relieved to see Bex and young Tom appear, followed shortly after by Donna, Anji and Pip. I could hear more people some way behind them, but I felt a massive sense of relief at their arrival. I guessed they must have seen Rosie and the other cats running towards the plot and heard all the barking and yowling and come to see what the matter was.

Looking back, I think they were shocked into silence by the scene in front of them, because they all stood stock still, mouths open for what seemed like an eternity, right up until Hotchi, dislodged by Rosie's frantic digging, came flying out of the rapidly collapsing pile of leaves and collided with Leggitt's sharp nose, prompting him to howl with pain.

Hotchi rebounded and rolled across the earth to stop a few inches in front of Pip's feet. Thankfully, Hotchi was rolled up into a tight ball, his spines cushioning him from the impact with Leggitt and the ground. Even so, I was fearful that he might have been injured and ran over to him.

‘Hotchi!’ I hissed urgently. ‘Are you alright?’

‘S’up?’ mumbled the little hedgehog, slowly unfolding himself. ‘’S’not Spring yet is it? I felt warm an’…’

He rolled up into a ball again abruptly, as Donna bellowed: ‘What the *hell* is going on here?’ I didn’t blame Hotchi for being frightened by that – *I’d* have rolled up into a ball at that shout too!

All us cats froze on the spot. Rosie stopped digging and looked up in surprise from the smouldering, scattered leaves, the fire now extinguished as the pile had collapsed and mixed with the damp earth. Leggitt had struggled to his feet, furiously brushing leaves and mud from his face and trying to extract a hedgehog spine from the end of his nose. Floggitt snapped to attention and guiltily tried to hide the rake behind his back.

‘*This hedgehog was in that pile of leaves*!’ exclaimed Pip, dropping to her knees and looking at Hotchi with concern. She looked up and glared at Floggitt and Leggitt. ‘*And you were going to burn the leaves?!*’

Donna advanced on the two men menacingly, a murderous expression on her face, rolling her sleeves up, revealing her tattooed arms. It may have just been a trick of the light or my imagination, but her hair seemed to be turning redder to match her face. ‘You are supposed to check all piles of leaves for hedgehogs and other hibernating animals!’ she growled.

Floggitt and Leggitt backed away nervously. Floggitt brought his rake round in a defensive position, but it was yanked from his grasp by Anji, who lined up beside Donna, along with Bex. Tom, I noticed, had hurried over to restrain Rosie.

‘Look, we didn’t know there was a ruddy *hedgehog* in the pile!’ babbled Leggitt. By now the two men had retreated off the plot and were backing away across the path.

‘That’s right!’ added Floggitt, swallowing frantically. ‘It had no business to be there after all. That’s *our* plot and…’

'What do you mean "No business to be there"?' roared Donna furiously. '*No business to be there? It's a wild animal you utter dipsticks! You should have checked!*'

By now Floggitt and Leggitt had reached the edge of the path bordering the plot opposite theirs. The plot had been neatly dug over and tidied for the winter, but there was a large black plastic sack lying on the edge of the plot, the plastic bulging tightly over whatever it contained, giving it the appearance of a giant cushion. Floggitt's heel caught on the raised wooden edge of the plot and he began to fall backwards. He grabbed onto Leggitt for support but only succeeded in dragging him backwards with him. Both men gave a yell of surprise as they fell, landing on the plastic sack. Although it gave them a soft landing, the sack burst open underneath them with a loud *ploop!* revealing a mass of oozing brown, smelly, well-rotted leaf mould compost into which they swiftly sank.

'That's my plot! What arc you doin' with my compost?' shouted Old Ted, who had just puffed his way up the path with Colin beside him.

'What a waste of prime leaf mould!' added Colin with feeling. 'I bagged that up myself last year!'

Floggitt and Leggitt scrambled, slipped and, well, *slurried* to their feet, looking like two nightmarish creatures emerging from the bowels of the earth (and they certainly smelled like they'd come from *something's* bowels). To add to the awful sight and smell, I could see wisps of steam rising from their compost covered overalls. They clawed and rubbed leaf mould from their faces, sneezing and spluttering out a good deal more.

Donna was obviously still angry, but I noticed her mouth begin to curl up at the edges as she regarded the two pathetic specimens in front of her. Before she could say or do anything however, Betty bustled up, puffing and red in the face from hurrying.

'What… is going… on?' she gasped, trying to catch her breath.

The plot holders all started explaining at the same time, while Floggitt and Leggitt tried to argue back. Finally, Betty held up her hand for silence. Us cats had all lined up alongside the plot holders, watching and listening intently. Rosie, now on her lead, was sitting obediently next to Tom, her head cocked on one side, one ear raised, obviously curious as to what was going to happen. Pip was kneeling by the scattered leaves, cradling Hotchi – still curled into a ball - on her lap, having wrapped him in her jacket to keep him warm.

I'd never seen Betty really lose her temper before. If she'd jumped up and down and shouted, it would have been a worrying and unusual sight to be sure. But the fact that she spoke very calmly and deliberately to Floggitt and Leggitt made it clear that, whilst she might appear outwardly calm, she was seething with fury inside.

'Mr Floggitt, Mr Leggitt, the rules of Sunnyside Allotments are very clear,' she said firmly and quietly. 'All bonfires must be carefully controlled and… *Let me finish, if you please!*'

This last comment was hissed at Leggitt who had just started to protest. He immediately shut his mouth and put his hands behind his back like a naughty child being scolded.

'As I was saying, continued Betty in the same calm, firm and icy voice. 'All bonfires must be carefully controlled. Plot holders must check any piles of leaves or other garden waste for hedgehogs or other hibernating and hiding animals before burning. Failure to do so will result in a serious breach of the rules. You have clearly failed to do so in this case, and it was only thanks to the valiant efforts of Rosie here (Rosie's chest swelled with pride at this point), and our brave allotment cats (we all tried to look nonchalant in an *all-in-a-day's-work-ma'am* kind of way), that this poor hedgehog wasn't burned to death.'

She took a deep breath and then continued. 'Also, you were seen to be threatening the animals with your garden tools, which is also contrary to the Allotment rules and indeed is a clear case of animal cruelty and so against the law. Therefore, as Secretary of the Sunnyside Plot Holders Committee and Board of Trustees I am exercising my executive powers and revoking the membership of Mrs Lottie Moolah on the grounds of your appalling behaviour as her representatives. I will be making a full refund of her membership fee to her, although somehow, I don't think she will be particularly bothered to lose this plot. *Do I make myself clear?*'

Floggitt and Leggitt looked from Betty to Donna, who was standing with her arms folded, staring hard at them. They both nodded mutely.

'Good,' said Betty. 'You are both no longer welcome on the Sunnyside Allotments or at any event hosted here. So, if you will kindly pick up your tools, get in your van and leave, I would be most obliged.' She narrowed her eyes and added: 'In short, Mr Floggitt and Mr Leggitt, *get the hell off our allotments now*!'

The two thoroughly chastened miscreants gathered up their tools without a word and hurried off down the path to their van, shedding clumps of leaf mould as they went. They passed Digby on the way, who, having heard what had happened, waved his walking stick at them and shouted something rude.

'Good riddance to bad rubbish!' muttered Donna. 'Well done, Betty!' Her congratulations to Betty were echoed by everybody else.

'I think it's time we all headed back to the clubhouse,' said Betty. 'A nice hot cuppa is in order, I think.'

'Yes, and I'd better phone my friends Barry Eagle and Mary Cotter who run the Eagle-Cotter hedgehog sanctuary,' added Pip, carefully standing up and hugging her Hotchi-filled jacket against her. 'They can come and collect this poor little fella. They'll soon make him better. Let's find a cardboard box to put him in to keep him warm in the meantime.'

'We'd better get off home,' said Bex. 'We only came to tidy up our plot for half an hour, as Tom's on half-term this week. We need to get Rosie back indoors before the fireworks all start up.' As if to emphasise her words, we heard a series of distant bangs.

'Well done, Rosie,' said Betty, patting Rosie on the head and ruffling her fur. 'You obviously smelled that hedgehog in there. You were very brave, what with the leaves being on fire as well. Next time you come to the allotments, there'll be a special treat for you!'

Rosie panted happily, her tail wagging so fast that it was a blur.

'We'd better make sure the cats are all in their sheds as well,' added Anji. 'They don't like fireworks either.'

'I think some cat treats will help get them into the sheds,' smiled Betty. 'They deserve them after holding those terrible men at bay!'

'I've always said that animals know a lot more than we think they do,' said Pip. 'They knew the hedgehog was there and they were trying to save him. They're all so brave.'

Anji wrinkled her nose and sniffed. 'Can anyone smell cat poo?' she said, to much laughter from all present.

We followed the humans as they walked down the path, Red Fred supporting ET with his solid body.

'Hear that?' said Barbara. 'They said we're *brave.*'

'Quite right, too,' said Dorothy. 'I came running as soon as you told me what was going on.'

'Well, to be fair, Dorothy, *we* all came running when Barbara told us' said GG. '*You* were having a wash and said it wasn't any of your business. It wasn't until Barbara told you it was the men with the giant pumpkin which had splattered all over you at the Fayre that you decided to come.'

'Huh! Mere details!' snorted Dorothy, putting her nose and tail in the air and stalking ahead of us. 'I came, didn't I? I showed *them*! And anyway, hedgehogs may be all prickly and full of fleas but I wouldn't want to see them hurt.'

I smiled. Dorothy could appear very mean at times, but deep beneath that hard exterior there beat a heart of … well… there beat a heart anyway.

'Well done on rounding them all up, Barbara,' I said to my tabby friend, nudging him in a companionable way. 'And you got Rosie to come too. I didn't even know she and her family were on the allotments today.'

'I didn't know she was here either,' said Barbara looking confused. 'I don't know how she knew to come and help.'

I felt the fur on my back begin to rise slightly and my whiskers began to tingle, the familiar sensation when I sensed something strange. I trotted up to Rosie who was sniffing at some grass, ready to have a quick widdle before leaving with Bex and Tom.

'Well done again for saving Hotchi, Rosie,' I said. 'But I need to ask you something.'

'Oh, what's that Robert? Do you need more hedgehogs digging out?' said Rosie excitedly, jumping up mid-pee and causing me to take a step back for fear of getting splashed.

'No, um… I just wondered…,' I said. 'How did you know we needed help?'

'Oh, I didn't know!' said Rosie, kicking her back legs and scuffing up the grass she'd just pee'd on in the messy way that dogs do. 'It's a funny thing. I saw that white cat that was chasing you the other day. It ran right by me, so I chased after it. I just wanted to tell it off for chasing you and Dorothy.' She frowned. 'But it ran along the path and just, well, sort of *vanished* near the plot you were all on. I didn't notice where it went. Good job it led me there though, eh? We *really* saw some fireworks here today, didn't we? Got to go now – ta-ta!'

She trotted off alongside Tom and Bex. I sat down on the path. Barbara turned back and sat next to me. We looked at each other.

'Maybe it was just a connysidence?' said Barbara. He didn't sound convinced, however.

'No,' I said thoughtfully. 'I think our ghost cat Tip is looking out for us.'

Chapter Fourteen

The Return of the Sun

I watched my breath coil into the cold air before fading from view, just like the steam from the clubhouse kettle. I stretched, lifting each of my legs in turn, allowing the stretch to reach down to the tips of my toes, every muscle working in tune with those connecting it. I completed my stretch by arching my back, standing on my toes, then gently relaxing into a sit. I quickly stood up again, because, despite having fur, the ground was very cold on my bottom.

I briefly considered going back through the cat flap into my shed[16] and curling up in my nice, snug cat bed. But nature called, and my litter tray needed emptying, so it was necessary to go outdoors and find a suitable place to do my business. I surveyed the allotments, now transformed from their drab winter browns and greys into a dazzling vista of white. Frost covered the ground, clung to the bare branches of trees and seemed to grow from the brittle stems of died-off plants. The winter sun was low in the sky, its warmth barely noticeable this late in the year. What it lacked in warmth it made up for in brilliance, reflected in the millions of tiny ice crystals, which created a twinkling vista to rival the starriest night. The sky was the deepest blue, this too being reflected in frozen puddles from recent rain. It looked almost as if the sky's own colour had fallen in drops to form puddles of pure blue. It was still quite early in the morning, but any trace of mist had disappeared, leaving the air crisp and clean and cold.

I set off down the path, the pads of my feet tingling at first from the frost until they warmed up along with the rest of me. Of course, I'd seen – *experienced* – frost before when I was an Outling Cat, along with snow, rain, hail, fog, wind and sometimes sunshine. The difference now was I could appreciate the beauty of it, rather than trying to find food and shelter and hoping that I'd survive. Here in the allotments, food and shelter weren't a problem and I knew just how lucky I was to have found my way here those many moonths before.

I stopped briefly by Colin's plot, which had recently been dug over into neat furrows, now all topped with frost and hard as rock. Even the leaves (including those unburnt ones which he'd taken from Floggitt and Leggitt's now abandoned plot), piled up to make leaf mould compost were frozen solid, so there was no point having a poo there. Even if I had done so, I wouldn't have been able to rake any leaves over the poo, being the clean and fastidious cat that I was. Also, it would have been very cold on my bottom!

Feeling somewhat more desperate to answer the call of nature, I trotted off to the wild area. I pushed my way through the thick undergrowth, causing showers of ice crystals dislodged from the topmost branches to fall down onto me. Those that stuck to me quickly

---

[16] Plot holders referred to the shed as *Betty's* shed. But I allowed her to keep her garden tools and other odds and ends in there too. I even kept an eye on them for her. It only seemed fair after all the food and treats she gave me.

melted, making my fur rather damp. Eventually, at the heart of a thick bramble bush I found a path of soft, warmish earth, untouched by the frost. I took a few blissful minutes to relieve myself, enjoying the shelter of the bush.

My toilet complete, I pushed my way out of the brambles, the thorns giving my damp fur a good combing on the way and also dislodging a few irritating fleas which had so far resisted Betty's flea treatment. I was now at the slope leading down to the pond, so I tried to delicately climb down, but ended up sliding on my bottom. Once at the edge of the pond, I was just about to have an embarrassed wash when my attention was caught by the fact that the pond was frozen, covered by ice from side to side and end to end. I knew, of course, that it wasn't frozen all the way down… fish and other water creatures would still be safe in the lower depths which never got as cold as the surface. Many was the time in winter when I'd sat by a fishpond in a garden, staring wistfully at the fat goldfish lurking beneath a layer of ice. I was certain that they could see me looking down and were having a laugh that I couldn't hook one or two of them out.

I tentatively put a front paw on the ice and pressed down. I heard it creak and then fine cracks began to spread across from under my paw, and a big bubble of air blobbed up under the cracks. I swiftly withdrew my paw. The ice wasn't that thick, the water would only have frozen overnight. I had learned from bitter experience that ice had to be a few days old and thick before I could walk on it. I'd tried to do so a couple of winters back on one particular garden pond. First it creaked, then it cracked and then… *splash*! Luckily, I'd managed to clamber out of the pond and find a shed to dry off in, but I was in no hurry to repeat *that* experience any time soon. Looking back, it had been funny to see those goldfish zoom away in fright when I came crashing through the ice to the bottom of the pond. They weren't laughing at me *then!*

I nearly repeated the experience though when someone or some*thing* tapped me on the back and almost made me jump out of my skin. Before I realised what I was doing, I charged forward onto the ice in surprise. My legs gave way beneath me and splayed out in all directions as I spun round and round on the slippery surface. Finally, I stopped spinning and slowly slid round to see Janet on the shore of the pond, several feet away. The ice began to creak ominously beneath me. I quickly wobbled to my feet, tried to run but instead slipped and ran on the spot for a couple of seconds before using my claws to gain purchase. I carefully moved forwards, trying to ignore the creaking of the ice. I made a daring leap onto the shore just in time before I heard a loud *crack*. Even so, one of my back legs went through the ice and I got a very cold, wet shock.

Janet was rolling on her back, legs in the air, laughing. She'd surprised me on purpose, the little Kitbit!

'I *wish* you wouldn't sneak up on me like that!' I exclaimed crossly, swiftly licking my wet leg, trying to warm it up. 'It's not *funny*!' I added grumpily as she howled with mirth.

'Oh, I'm sorry Robert! You should have seen yourself!' giggled Janet as she stood up and touched noses with me. (I noticed that her small, warm nose looked bright pink in the crisp cold air. My nose always looked black, whatever the weather.)

Satisfied that I'd managed to lick the cold water off my leg sufficiently, I sat next to Janet and we both looked out across the frozen pond. It was a strangely beautiful sight. Here and there, the dry, dead stems of bullrushes and reeds stuck out, imprisoned in an icy grip.

'Have you seen Tip lately?' asked Janet.

'Now and again,' I replied, 'At least, I think so, but not up close. Sometimes I catch sight of him out of the corner of my eye, but when I turn to look, he's flitted away again. And he only ever seems to appear when I'm not thinking about him.'

'Same here,' said Janet thoughtfully. 'I'm sure it's him and he's often over here, near the pond and by the old cottage.'

'It's like he's looking for something, isn't it?' I said.

'Yes… or like he's trying to show us something,' said Janet.

We sat in silence for a few minutes, in quiet contemplation.

'Have you been in the clubhouse lately?' I said, changing the subject. 'It's full of Chrissymus decorations now. Pip's been busy! I used to quite like this time of year when I was an Outling. Lots of houses with pretty lights in their windows, sometimes outside too. And then there's that strange thing they do with having trees indoors. There's one in the clubhouse too, all covered with sparkly stuff and coloured balls and lights.'

'No, but I'll come and have a look,' replied Janet. 'Of course, *Christmas* is one of their Solstice celebrations.'

'Sollystish?' I said, as we both stood up and wandered towards the allotments, heading to the clubhouse. I had the feeling that there was another mysterious ritual that I hadn't heard about.

'Well, specifically the *Winter* Solstice,' explained Janet. 'It's when this part of world we live on is furthest away from the sun, and the day of the solstice is the shortest day of the year. After that, we move nearer to the sun, the days get longer and warmer. Then in the middle of summer there's the Summer Solstice when our side of the world is closest to the sun and it's the longest day of the year. After that, we begin to move further away from the sun, the days get shorter and colder and then we're back to the Winter Solstice.'

I considered this. It made sense. It also explained why in the autumn and winter it got darker much earlier, while in the spring and summer it stayed lighter – and warmer – much longer. I thought wistfully of the summer evenings a few moonths ago, after the allotments had been saved, when I would stretch out on the grass or on a plot or even on the paved area outside the clubhouse and enjoy the cool breeze, along with the gentle warmth of the ground which had held the sun's heat. It reminded me of Alan the garden gnome's example – GG had called it an *analogy* – of how some "ghosts" were "recorded" in old buildings.

'So, is there some ceremony you've got to perform for the Sollystish?' I asked, cautiously, thinking of the Equinox ceremony and how I hadn't got the words right.

'*Solstice*,' corrected Janet with a smile. 'And no, there isn't. At least, not one that we Allotment animals need to perform. I don't know why. I think it's just because we're simply happy to be alive and living. I've heard that moles celebrate it though, they call it Longest Night, although how they know it's the longest night, living underground, is a mystery to me.'

'So why was the Equinox so important?' I said, feeling as confused as ever.

'I don't honestly know,' said Janet brightly. 'Tiberius told me that the Autumn and Spring equinoxes are "tipping points" in the year with the days and nights being equal length and that means more to us animals than to humans.'

'It's all to do with farming,' said a voice to one side of us.

I'm pleased to say I didn't jump in an embarrassing way this time. Nor did Janet, which would have been payback. This was probably because we both recognised the voice. We turned to see Alan the garden gnome sitting cross-legged on an over-sized ceramic toadstool on one of the more decorative plots. He was wearing his usual bright clothes and a broad smile. He certainly didn't look out of place. The human that worked this particular plot obviously liked garden ornaments, because there were stone squirrels, hedgehogs and toadstools, plastic gnomes, herons and windmills and lots of other bits and pieces which I couldn't identify. I guessed there would usually be lots of flowers planted in amongst this mishmash of models, but they'd all died off and had been dug up for the winter.

We hurried over and greeted Alan affectionately with head rubs, whilst he responded by gently tickling us under our chins.

'Great to see you, Alan,' I said happily. 'What are you doing here?'

'Well, right now, I'm hiding in plain sight,' chuckled Alan, gesturing to the menagerie of models around him. 'But I said I'd be back for the Winter Solstice celebration and here I am.'

'But Janet said we don't celebrate that,' I said, in my usual state of confusion.

'Ah, no you animals don't,' said Alan, 'But we Fae do. So do humans, although most of 'em have forgotten why.'

'You said it was all to do with farming, didn't you?' prompted Janet.

'That's right. Well, *partly* it is,' said Alan, pulling a small flask out of his knapsack which he lifted from behind the toadstool. He took a swig from the flask. 'Ahh, spiced acorn coffee,' he said appreciatively, wiping his mouth with the back of his hand. 'Keeps the cold out. Want some?' He proffered the flask towards us, but we politely declined. We couldn't have held it anyway, even if we did like acorn coffee, spiced or not.

'So,' Alan continued. 'It all goes back to the days long ago when humans and our people and your people shared the world. Humans knew magic then, like our folk do and how it worked with the turn of the earth. They'd just started to farm crops and keep beasts for food and labour, rather than hunting them. They knew that the seasons dictated how the crops grew and that come midwinter, the sun would wane in strength. Both our peoples knew about the Solstices then, and we all paid tribute to the Sun and to Mother Earth to keep up their timeless dance. The humans knew there'd be a time of growing and plenty and food could be stored for the winter when there was no growing to be done.'

'I see,' I said slowly. 'So really, the celebration is to ask the Sun to come back?'

'That's right,' said Alan, nodding. 'But our peoples were growing apart, even then. We Fae were more in tune with you animals and so it remained, but humans went their own way, building their towns and cities and civilizations. Humans invented their gods and their religions, so to them, the Sun became a god. So… they built fires to give the Sun strength, which was nice and symbolic and didn't hurt anyone. But then some of them got the idea that the Sun and the Earth wanted blood too, so they'd start making sacrifices and it all got a bit messy. No wonder all sorts of nasties started creeping into this world when the barrier was thin at this time of year.'

Alan looked thoughtful, as though remembering those days himself. Then he continued: 'Anyway, time goes on and humans nowadays have built up lots of religions, all with their celebrations which fit round the times of the year, the solstices, the equinoxes. The new religions and celebrations absorb the old ones, see? Oh, plenty of them are perfectly *respectable* celebrations, like remembering the birth of noble prophets who taught people a better way, but many of them have the return of the Sun and light at their heart. That's mainly why humans put up lights, it's all a memory back to those ancient days, keep away the dark, keep away the nasties and restless spirits. Most of 'em have forgotten *why* this is nowadays, but it's good to know that *some* still do and more are re-learning. All goes with trying to protect the environment and live better lives. We Fae do our bit to help 'em along a bit too. You never know, maybe one day our peoples will come back together again in harmony. Maybe.'

Janet was nodding knowingly as Alan explained all this. It all made perfect sense to me. Well, sort of. But it confirmed what I'd always known; *Humans over-complicate things.*

'So, your people have got a celebration planned for the Winter Solstice?' I asked, just to show Alan and Janet that I was keeping up.

'That's right,' said Alan. 'At the stone circle again. The pond on your side, of course, but the gateway will be open. You fine felines and your friends are welcome to come as well.'

'Thank you,' said Janet politely. 'It's soon, isn't it?'

'Tomorrow night,' Alan said, nodding. 'Midnight, of course, although probably the *actual* point of solstice is more likely around 1:52 am, but let's not split walnuts about it.' He suddenly changed the subject. 'Talking of restless spirits, have you seen your ghost cat lately? I didn't get any messages from Oakroot about it.'

'We were just taking about that,' I said. Between us we told Alan the whole story about Hotchi needing to hibernate, Floggitt and Leggitt and their near fatal bonfire, our attempted rescue and Rosie saving the day, led there by Tip.

Alan was shocked at what we told him about Floggitt and Leggitt and muttered darkly about their parentage. 'Those characters sound like two right nasty pieces of work,' he said, scowling. 'I think I'll have a word with a couple of Gremlins I know, ask them to pay a visit to those two jokers' yard over at Skank End. I'm sure having their van's tyres let down or its exhaust pipe dropping off will make them realise that actions have consequences.'

Alan asked how Hotchi was now, so I explained that Pip's two friends had called later that afternoon to take him to their animal rescue centre. 'They said something about him probably not hibernating because he was so small and weak,' I said. 'They were going to put him in some special box thingy to keep him warm, an inkybatter I think it's called.'

'That'd be an *incubator*,' said Alan with a smile.

'That's it,' I said, thinking once again how humans do love their big words. 'They said they'd feed him and look after him all winter. Then in the spring, if he's well enough they're going to bring him back to the allotments and release him, because it's a nice safe place… well, it is usually anyway. Before they went away with him, I told him not to be frightened because they were kind humans. I *think* he believed me.'

'Good to hear,' said Alan. 'So… your phantom feline friend helped rescue him, eh? Interesting. It shows he can certainly interact with the world of the living, which means he's aware of what's going on. He must be looking for something.'

'We think we've seen him here and there,' added Janet. 'He does seem to be searching the allotments, but he never stays long enough for us to ask him what he's looking for.'

Alan stroked his neat beard, deep in thought. 'I think,' he said at last, 'if he's going to tell you, it might be soon. I can just feel it in the ether, you telling me all this has set my seventh sense tingling. My eighth sense is getting a bit itchy too.'

'So… er… what does that mean, exactly?' I asked, trying to keep up as best I could.

Alan looked me straight in the eye. 'I reckon it's you, Robert,' he said emphatically. '*You* need to make the connection with Tip.'

Chapter Fifteen

The Meeting

'I *really* want to climb up it and knock one of those coloured balls off!'

Red Fred and I were sitting in front of the gaudily decorated fir tree which was planted in a bright red pot in the seating area of the clubhouse. Our tails were twitching with anticipation. Every twinkle from the delicate flashing, coloured lights to the rustle of tinsel in the breeze every time someone opened the door was causing our muscles to flex, ready to leap. Sometimes instinct can be a terribly hard thing to control.

'Best not, Fred,' I replied, resisting the urge to smack a brightly coloured and, frankly, smug-looking plastic robin off the branch it was hanging from. (It wasn't that realistic, but even so, sometimes you have to keep up appearances). 'Besides,' I added, 'If you jumped up that tree, you'd probably bring it all crashing down. I doubt Betty and Pip would be very pleased at that, not after all the time they took putting those bright decoration thingies on it.'

We looked across to Pip, who was sitting at the long table, frowning in deep concentration as she was decorating a log she'd brought in from the Allotments. I suspected it was one of those which had been cut from the oak tree which had fallen on Mr Goodman's old cottage. Earlier on, I'd heard her tell Betty that she was going to make a Yule Log for Chrissymus. There were lots of odds and ends scattered on the table, which Pip was attaching to the log. Quite how you can make a log look Chrissymussy I wasn't sure, but Pip was giving it her best shot. So far, she'd wrapped long strands of ivy round it. Right now, she was concentrating hard on fixing sprigs of holly (like, the holly, picked from from the Allotments) to the log and muttering 'Ow!' every so often when she pricked herself.

'Odd how they bring these trees and stuff indoors at this time of year, isn't it?' said Fred, deciding to have a quick wash to take his mind off the tempting coloured balls.

'I know,' I agreed. 'When I was an Outling, I used to look through windows to see lots of these Chrissymus trees in people's living rooms. Sometimes they'd even have them outside. Lots of lights too, strung everywhere. And those Chrissymus cards too.'

There were several Chrissymus cards stuck to the walls of the clubhouse and most of them had pictures of cats on the front. Betty had said that a lot of them had been sent to me by my many fans around the world, which was nice of course.

'It's a mystery to be sure, mate,' agreed Fred solemnly, staring wistfully at a particularly glittery gold ball near the top of the tree.

'Janet says it's all part of these Solstice celebrations,' I said. 'And that's today, although Chrissymus Day is a few days off.'

'Ah yes, we're off to see the Fae's Solstice celebrations tonight, aren't we, mate?' said Fred brightly. 'You hope your spooky mate Tip will be there so you can talk to him?'

I nodded, looking through the window at the gathering late afternoon darkness outside, recalling Alan's words a few days before, about how I should be the one to engage with Tip when we next met. Somehow, the thought of meeting the ghost cat in the dark didn't seem so appealing.

'Well, I haven't seen any sign of him lately,' I said, with mild irritation. 'It's like whenever I *want* to see him, he's never there. I try hard *not* to think about him, but that doesn't work either, because not thinking that you shouldn't think about something makes you think it all the harder. At least, I think so.'

'Perhaps tonight will be the night?' replied Fred, trying to cheer me up.

Before I could reply, the clubhouse door opened with a gust of wind which caused the tinsel and balls and other bright decorations on the tree to rustle and tinkle enticingly. Betty breezed in, carrying a large, padded envelope. 'Look what just arrived Pip!' she said excitedly, hurrying over to the table where Pip was putting the finishing touches to her log decoration by spraying fake snow onto it from a hairysole can.

'Ooh, the stamps are French,' said Pip, jumping up and shoving a pile of unused holly and ivy and tubes of glitter to one side to make room for the package. 'Is it from…?

'Yes, it is!' said Betty, reaching into the package which she'd already opened. 'Hey Robert! Fred!' she called across to us. 'Come and see – these are for you, after all!'

We didn't need to be told twice. It was clearly a package from one of my many admirers – and one from a place other than the YooKay by the sound of it. Maybe it was cat treats?

We hopped up onto the table, sniffing at the envelope as Betty began to unwrap the mysterious item from some wrapping paper covered with little Chrissymus Trees.

'Oh wow! They're fantastic!' exclaimed Pip, as Betty laid out what looked like six brightly coloured, rather fat socks on the table. 'Oh! And they've got their initials on them too!'

I sniffed at the socks. No cat treats in them. What a let down! I didn't even wear socks! Not even furry white ones, like some cats have.

'They're Christmas stockings!' exclaimed Betty. 'For you, Robert and Fred and for your friends too. Look – this one's got an "R" on it, so that's your one, Robert. And this one… "RF" for "Red Fred".'

We must have looked distinctly unimpressed, because Pip quickly added: 'So we'll hang them up on Christmas Eve and Santa will come and put presents in them for you!'

I wasn't sure who Santa was, or why he or she needed to put presents into stockings. But this sounded infinitely more interesting, so we both purred and rubbed our heads gratefully against the stockings. Visions of cat treats, toys and catnip swum into my mind and no doubt into Fred's as well, because he began to drool slightly.

'Maria from France made them,' Betty said to Pip. 'Remember I told you she said she'd made the cats something each for Christmas? They arrived today, just in time for Christmas! And there's even a card.'

She showed us another of those Chrissymus - I mean *Christmas* - cards. There was a picture of a contented looking tabby cat sitting on an armchair by an open fire, next to a Christmas tree and lots of brightly wrapped parcels.

'It says: "*Joyeux Noël aux chats*",' said Betty, smiling.

'And very timely too,' agreed Pip. 'What with it being Winter Solstice today. Which reminds me, seeing as it's getting dark outside…' She got up and walked over to a black plastic box which had been fixed to the wall by the clubhouse door. A twisted green wire ran from it, up through a small gap at the top of the door, then outside. Pip pressed a button on the box and suddenly we saw flashes of coloured lights flickering through the big window and around the door. 'It's getting dark, so it's time to put the outdoor Christmas lights on!' added Pip delightedly.

Fred and I followed Betty and Pip outside to marvel at the strings of prettily coloured lights which had been fixed along the edge of the clubhouse roof and around the door frame. There were lots more Chrissymus – *Christmas* – lights than there had been for Halloween. In the rapidly growing dusk, they provided a welcome, dazzling display.

'You know, Fred,' I said. 'Humans do these strange things and they don't always make sense, but sometimes I'm glad when they do them.'

'I agree, mate,' said Fred. 'Especially when it's dark at this time of year. But all the same, I'm going inside again and look at the pretty lights on the tree. It's a bit nippy out here.'

'Time for a cuppa I think,' said Pip, blowing on her hands as she shivered in the chilly air. 'And you can tell me what you think of my Yule log, Betty.'

'Good idea,' said Betty, as she followed Fred and me inside. 'Cat treats for the boys too, I think.'

‘Now you’re talking,’ I purred.

“So this human with the big white beard, dressed in a red suit flies through the air in a sleigh pulled by flying reindeer?’ I asked, seeking clarification from what I’d just been told.

‘That’s right,’ said GG earnestly. ‘I’ve looked it all up on Moggle and everything. He’s had lots of names over the years, but humans generally call him some variation of Father Christmas or Santa Claus.’

‘Uh-huh,’ I said. ‘And this Santa fella climbs down people’s chimneys and leaves presents for their children in stockings which they hang up for him?’

‘I’ve always reckoned he had some elf in him,’ said Alan Titchbark thoughtfully. ‘After all, he has plenty of ’em working for him at his workshop.’

‘Must have some cat in him too,’ mused Red Fred. ‘Most humans would fall off a roof, especially if it’s all slippery with snow or rain. Not to mention reindeer poo.’

‘And he’s a bit more than just human or elf,’ added Janet. ‘He’s a kind of winter god, or several winter gods all rolled into one. It’s…complicated.’

‘It sounds it,’ I agreed. ‘I mean, how does he get down the chimneys? I’ve seen pictures of him and he’s not exactly slim. And he’s got that big sack of toys.’

‘I’m sure that magic is definitely involved,’ replied Janet.

‘And he delivers all these presents, all over the world, *in one night*?’

GG tried to explain. ‘It’s… um… kind of… um…’

‘Timey-Wimey stuff!’ said Alan. ‘Best not think about it too hard Robert. Besides,’ he added with a wink, ‘*He* only delivers to humans. There’s all the *animal* Santas too.’

‘Wh…?’ I began, then gave up. Alan was right, it was best not to think too hard about it.

By now we’d reached the approach to the pond and the magical mist lay just ahead of us, ready to transport us to the stones. I wasn’t remotely bothered by the mist now, but something was making my fur begin to bristle and my whiskers tingle.

‘Robert!’ hissed Janet quietly, stopping dead in her tracks. ‘Look over there!’

I followed the direction of her gaze and gave a start. Standing by the tangle of hawthorn bushes was Tip! I realised that the others had all stopped walking too and were looking at the mysterious white cat.

Tip was surrounded by a faint glowing aura, rather like I'd seen around the Fae elders back on Hallowe'en night. Set against the darkness of the night and the deep shadows cast by the trees and bushes, the glow of the aura made Tip's fur seem even whiter. He was standing there, silent and still as a statue, looking directly at us.

I felt my heart beating madly and was sure that the others could hear it too. I almost jumped when Alan gently put his hand on neck and bent down to whisper in my ear. 'Go on Robert; I think he's waiting for you. Ask him what he wants… what he *needs*.'

'Go on, mate,' whispered Red Fred, giving me what he thought was a gentle nudge from behind but made me stumble forward a few steps. 'Yow can do it. Be brave.'

GG, Janet and Alan all whispered their encouragement. I fought down the overwhelming instinct to turn and flee in the opposite direction, realising that Tip was waiting for me. This was my chance – possibly my only chance – to find out what was causing him to haunt the Allotments… and me, come to that.

I approached Tip, my legs rather wobbly and jelly-like. I raised my tail to show that I wasn't being threatening in anyway. As I drew nearer, I noticed that I could see Tip's fur much more clearly than before, being able to pick out the individual hairs. He seemed quite solid and was much more *here* than at any time before. His eyes still shone brightly, as any cat's eyes would in the dark, and I could see his dark pupils moving slightly. However, he didn't blink, even though his gaze was locked onto me.

I froze when Tip took two steps towards me. When I stopped moving, he sat, unhurriedly, his tail curling round his hind leg like any normal cat. He was clearly waiting for me. Mustering all my courage, I continued to walk towards him until we were just inches apart. 'H-hello T-Tip,' I stammered. I swallowed hard, then steadied my voice. 'It is Tip, yes? My name's Robert.'

Tip didn't answer, but silently regarded me for several long seconds.

'C-can I help you?' I asked. 'Is there something you need to tell me?'

Tip stood up again and stretched forward, extending his nose to mine in greeting. I swallowed again but resolved to return the friendly gesture. I extended my nose towards his… but surely I wouldn't be able to feel his nose, with him being a ghost?

…It *felt* like our noses touched…

… Tip's nose was cold …

… there was a flicker of light…

Chapter Sixteen

Tip's Tale

The light flickered…

*I was indoors, looking up at a human woman, who was standing at a rough wooden table, chopping up some sort of plant leaves with a knife. Although it's generally difficult for us cats to tell human's ages, I was aware that this woman was quite young. She was wearing a long, hooded cloak over a brown dress, which was made of some coarse brown material, the front fastened by laces. She wore a grubby white apron, streaked with green smears, like grass stains. She had long, light coloured hair, most of which was tied in a loose plait which dangled down her back, rather like how Anji often wore her hair. (*Who was Anji? *I thought). Her skin was smooth, her cheeks rosy, but rather grubby. I couldn't help but think she needed a good wash.*

I looked around me. The room I was in was small, the walls plain and rough, the ceiling low and beamed. A small shelf held three or four books, all looking very old and well read. Hanging from hooks on the beams were dark metal pots and pans, together with bunches of plants, strange looking dolls made from straw, jewellery, bones and – here I felt my tummy rumble – a dead pheasant bird, perhaps recently killed and ready to be plucked and eaten.

There was a fire crackling in a fireplace, surrounded by a crude stone hearth. Hanging over the fire on a chain was a large black pot, which I somehow knew was a cauldron. *Whatever liquid was boiling in the cauldron was giving off a dense, thick, smoky steam, which seemed too heavy for the air and dropped to the hearth, where it was slowly rolling out across the rush-covered stone floor. My nose tingled with a mixture of scents; some familiar – I was sure I could smell catnip – and some which were completely new to me.*

Here and there around the room were dotted candles, which smelt of animal fat, their flames dipping and sputtering, but casting very little light. Thankfully, there was a small window, which was open, although it seemed there was no glass. A thick wooden door occupied the middle of the wall next to the window, but this was barred shut.

I realised that I was sitting on a rough woollen blanket in a wicker basket. In fact, the basket seemed very big and I felt quite… small.

I decided to speak, to attract the young woman's attention. What I heard was a high-pitched mew, unlike my usual deep miaow. It was the mew of a kitten. Was I that kitten? This place was familiar to me, but still felt like I hadn't been here long, some things still strange and unknown to me. I had no thoughts of the Allotments, or of my friends there, all I knew was the room in which I sat, watching the young woman chopping up plants… no… not just plants – herbs! That was it! Herbs! I knew about herbs from somewhere else…

The young woman obviously heard my mew because she stopped chopping the herbs, put the knife down and came over to my basket. She knelt on the floor, arranging her long dress carefully. She smiled at me. Her teeth weren't the cleanest human teeth I'd ever seen, but she seemed to have all of them. Her eyes were her most striking feature. They were a deep green, and seemed to shine, catching the daylight shining in from the small window. I wasn't afraid of her, I felt calm and safe, sensing a great kindness and love radiating from her.

'Ah, you be awake Tip,' she said. 'I 'spect you'll be wantin' some milk? Martha will get you some from Henrietta. 'Tis nearly time for her milkin.'

I mewed in return and reached out a black paw, trying to catch a hank of hair which had fallen down from under her hood. She laughed and reached her hand out to stroke me, her long fingers warm and gentle as they moved across my fur, causing me to purr. I nuzzled her hand, briefly thinking of my mother and litter mates and the barn which had been my world before I came here. I licked her hand, enjoying the taste of salt and pheasant and herbs. My nose touched something cold and I moved back, to see the shining metal bracelet around her slender wrist. The same bracelet I'd seen on a table somewhere...

A flicker of light…

The same room, but somehow smaller to me. This time I was sitting on the table. I felt taller, heavier… The door was open, letting in bright sunlight, illuminating the room. A little girl wearing a white cap and dark dress was sitting on a stool next to the table. An older woman – her mother surely – stood anxiously by, twisting her apron and brushing her lank hair back under her own tatty cap.

Martha was kneeling in front of the girl, gently holding her wrist with one hand, dipping her hands into a small pot with the other and extracting some gloopy brown liquid. The sleeves of her dress were rolled up, showing both her bracelets, brightly burnished as always. She carefully rubbed the gloopy concoction into the little girl's hand, talking quietly to her as she did so. The little girl's face was grubby – everyone seemed rather grubby – and I realised she'd been crying, as tears had flowed down her face, leaving pink streaks where they had washed the dirt away.

'There, there Peggy, Martha'll make it better. No more nasty blisters.' said Martha, smiling at the little girl. 'Does that feel better, little one?'

The little girl's face broke into a brave smile and she nodded.

Her mother looked relieved and dropped a clumsy curtsey to Martha. 'My thanks Mistress Goodbody,' she mumbled, her eyes downcast. 'Silly child, I told her to be careful with puttin' the logs in the stove. I thought her little fingers would… would…' She gulped and big fat tears ran down her plump cheeks, trying hard to wash tracks through the grime.

Martha stood up and smiled. 'No fear, Goodwife Marlin. Peggy is a brave girl and you did right to bring her to me.' She held out the pot to the woman, who took it reverently. 'Dab the salve on tonight and again in the morn, her skin will be good as new.'

'Will thruppence suffice ye, Mistress Goodbody?' asked the women, extracting some greasy looking coins from her apron pocket and proffering them to Martha.

Martha shook her head, and gently closed the woman's fingers over the coins. 'Nay Goody Marlin, keep thy pennies. A brace of rabbits will do us well.' She looked over to me and winked. 'Is that not so Tip?'

I heard myself miaow in reply – a deeper, more adult miaow. Little Peggy stood and nervously held out her un-burned hand to me. I rubbed my head against her hand and miaowed happily.

'He speaks to me!' she whispered, her eyes wide with wonder.

'Of course he do,' chuckled Martha. 'Tip knows as much as I.' Peggy and her mother looked at me with curiosity…

A flicker of light…

*I was watching Martha gathering leaves from a tall plant, one of many in her garden. Both her bracelets caught the sun, reflecting its rays with bright flashes as her arms moved. It was like the allo… allot…*Allotments*? What were they? There were some flowers, but this was a working garden, beans grew tall, winding around tall branches set in the ground, cabbages below them, plump and green. An apple tree close by, the apples green and tinged with red, swelling in the warm sunshine. A nanny goat was tethered to the tree, munching happily on the long grass growing nearby.*

'Hello Henrietta,' I said. 'Making some tasty milk for us, I hope?'

Henrietta regarded me with her strange, slotted eyes and mumbled something, her mouth full of grass.

Martha had finished gathering the leaves into a basket and headed back to our little cottage, with its patchy lime-washed walls streaked with ivy which clung on stubbornly. The thatched roof had what looked like a small tree growing up next to the chimney pot. I knew that in that thatch were nests of mice. Plump, well-fed mice that did well by crumbs and leavings left from Martha's preparations. I followed Martha, hopping nimbly between the rows of radishes.

A flicker of light…

Another cottage, dark, gloomy, nowhere near as cosy as ours. My nose wrinkled in distaste at the smell of sour ale and human wee. I sat on the sticky rushes looking over to the rickety table around which the family crowded nervously. The skinny, timid mother, the numerous children in threadbare clothes, their faces sallow beneath the dirt. Sitting next to the table in what seemed to be the only chair in the room was a big, beefy, red-haired brute of a man in a patched shirt. His thick leg was stretched out, the bare, dirty foot resting on a stool. The man was muttering, cursing in pain. His ankle looked red and horribly swollen and mishappen. Martha, kneeling, was running her hands over the ankle, her brow furrowed in concentration.

"Garn! That hurts, woman!' roared the man, trying to jerk his leg back. The children all shrank back in terror against their mother, who tried to gather them to her, her stick-like arms not long enough to embrace them all. Martha ignored him, pressing his leg back into position, whispering her special words.

'Let her concentrate for goodness' sake!' I shouted at him. 'The healing magic won't work otherwise!'

The family all looked at me, wide eyed, mouths open. Of course, all they'd heard were a series of miaows, but my meaning was clear.

The man grunted to Martha. 'Do yourn cat follow thee ever'where?'

Martha closed her eyes, whispered a few more special words then suddenly clasped the man's ankle tight. His face grew bright red, his cheeks puffed out, looking like a stubbly, over-ripe plum about to burst. Then he exhaled, the colour draining from his face, the tightness of pain washed away (although unfortunately the dirt remained). Martha stood up, rubbing her hands down her apron, most likely to get rid of the sweat and dirt from his skin.

She looked at me, then back at the man. 'Of course. Tip follows me everywhere, Master Fartby. He assists me.'

Master Fartby scowled at me. The woman – no doubt his timid wife, stammered: 'J-J- Jethro, l-l-look to your ankle.'

Jethro Fartby peered at his ankle which was no longer swollen and mishappen, the skin now its usual pinky-grime colour. ''Tis healed!' he said in amazement. The children all crowded round, ooh-ing and aah-ing in wonder. 'Get thee back to yourn chores!' barked their father, waving his big, meaty hands angrily, causing them all to scatter in fright. I disliked this human intensely. He was a bully, in speech and deed. Fartby looked up at Martha. 'I...thank ye, Martha Goodbody,' he muttered grudgingly. Then defiantly added: 'But I ain't got no money for thee.'

Martha narrowed her eyes at him and folded her arms. 'Payment enough to see you get back to work on the squire's land, not worse for drink to be tripping over your tools and turning your ankle,' she said firmly. 'And to take your week's wage to Aggie here so's to buy bread and meat for your family, rather than ale for thyself at the tavern.'

Fartby jerked his leg back, planting both feet onto the rushes which squelched slightly as he heaved himself up from his chair, looming over Martha, his fist clenched.

''Tis no sin for a man to partake of ale at the end of a day's hard work!' he bellowed.

I ran over to her side and hissed, arching my back, flattening my ears and staring at Fartby, who glared at me.

Martha didn't flinch, but looked up at him, her mouth set firm. She raised her hand, palm outwards. She didn't touch him in any way, but the air in front of him rippled like the surface of a pond. Fartby flew backwards onto his chair, as though shoved by a powerful invisible hand. The chair tipped over backwards and his thick head connected with the floor with a dull thud. Fartby howled with shock and pain, while his wife squealed with fright.

Martha stood over him, pointing a long finger at his now pale face, her bracelet sliding down her wrist. 'You talk of hard work, Jethro Fartby? And you dare *talk of sin?' The room seemed to grow even darker than it was, the air prickling with energy, as though a storm was brewing indoors. I felt my whiskers tingling and the hairs on my tail stiffening. Although Martha didn't grow taller or broader in any way, she somehow* seemed *to grow to twice her size, her green eyes blazing, causing the bully to cower. 'If I see Aggie or any of your children looking hungry or coming to me with bruises and blacked eyes again, then mark my words, I shall show you what sin* means*! Dost thou understand me well, Master Fartby?'*

I glowered at him, adding another hiss for good measure.

Fartby nodded vigorously, eyes wide with fear. If my nose was right – and it always was – he was living up to his name in more than just wind. Martha nodded, then stepped back, her shoulders relaxing, her normal size restored. The room brightened just a little, although it was still gloomy and dank. She turned to Aggie Fartby, who was fluttering a hand nervously over her heart. Aggie dropped a hurried curtsey.

'Good day to you Aggie,' Martha said politely. She glanced down at Jethro Fartby, grovelling on the dirty rush floor, then looked back to Aggie. 'I think thy problem be cured now.'

Another flicker of light… and another… and another…

I was aware of a succession of images, all flashing before my eyes in an instant. I couldn't focus on them all. But some seemed to last longer than others. I saw Martha, from lots of different angles and in different places, as I watched her. She would be brewing potions or chopping up strange looking plants and root vegetables (where had I seen those before?). A succession of people came to her cottage to seek her help, or she visited several other homes (most of them gloomy hovels, but there were some brighter, more comfortable homes, the humans who lived there looking better dressed and cleaner), to give her special medicines or salves to sick people. Sometimes she laid her hands on injured people and muttered her strange words to heal them.

It's hard for a cat to really tell a human's age accurately, but I was aware of Martha often being joined by the young girl Peggy, who grew taller and – I suppose – older and prettier. She was assisting Martha in her work. Sometimes they'd be sitting together by the fire in our cottage, as Martha showed her the words in her big old books, Peggy slowly tracing the words on the page with her finger, learning how to say them. I enjoyed these times most of all, feeling the warmth from the fire and the snugness of our home. I had the sense that Martha could speak to animals too, because she'd often talk to me and convey her meaning not just in human words but the smell and taste of Kittish, too. I'd seen her talk to other creatures too, such as squirrels and birds, rabbits and hares whenever we passed them outside. When I was with Martha, I had no desire to hunt the other animals.

But then the visions slowed down and I was sitting on the floor behind Martha as she stood at the door of her cottage, arms folded, facing down a group of angry people, mainly women, most of them shabbily dressed, several of whom I had seen Martha helping before. In front of the women stood a rather short, self-important looking man. He was dressed in dark clothes with a wide, white collar. His also wore a tall black hat which didn't help make him look taller at all. I recognised him from a couple of the previous images, standing in rooms in the better-looking houses that Martha had visited. He looked serious, stroking his small beard with one hand as the women shouted and gestured. The air felt close and muggy, dark storm clouds hung low in the sky above the cottage. I noticed a bead of sweat roll down his cheek.

He held up a hand to silence the women. 'Be quiet now, goodwives!' he said with authority. He addressed Martha now. 'What say you to these accusations, Mistress Goodbody?'

Martha tensed then answered, her words clear and true. I could sense her anger boiling beneath her calm exterior. 'I say, Master Squire, that these accusations be false and naught but idle chatter and tittle-tattle.' A couple of the women began to protest, but the Squire silenced them. Martha continued: 'Every one of you I have helped for no reward. You, Agnes Arbuthnot! Your son had the sweating sickness, but did I not cure him? And you, Goody Gebbons! Your ailing mother! Did I not make her passing free from pain and fear? So… your cow now gives bad milk. The poor beast has poor feed, no wonder she gives bad milk! But 'tis easier to blame me for cursing her! And Aggie, because your worthless husband takes to drink again, falls from the squire's roof he be fixing and breaks his neck, 'tis my fault? Was it not I that told him to ne'er raise a hand to you and your children?'

The wretched Aggie nodded glumly, but another woman, big and brawny with a florid face, prodded her and said: 'Did you not tell me, Aggie, that she used evil powers to cast Jethro to the floor?'

'I see you speak for poor Aggie, Sally Strumpton,' said Martha with mockery in her voice. 'You have no quarrel of your own with me but use another's story to damn me.'

'You got books*!' snapped Sally Strumpton. 'Full of black magic spells, no doubt!'*

'I didn't think you could read, Sally,' smiled Martha. 'Besides, does not the Squire himself have many books? Are they all full of black magic too?'

The Squire blushed.

'She's got a broom!' shouted another woman accusingly. 'Witches have brooms, don't they?'

'Of course I've got a broom,' retorted Martha impatiently. 'I use it to sweep the floor and hearth and keep my cottage clean. Why, I'm sure I've seen many of you a-sweeping your hearthstones.' She cocked her head and added innocently; 'Does that make you'n witches too?'

There was more angry shouting from the women until the Squire bellowed: 'Silence! You all shriek and cluck like ill-tempered fowl!' In a quieter voice, he addressed Martha. 'Mistress Goodbody, I know you to be a healer, but many have been the complaints laid at my door. I would be failing in my duties to my tenants if I did not order an investigation. I will write to Master Cackhand from Suffolk to attend. He studied under Master Matthew Hopkins some years past in the accusation of witches. He will see if there is a case to bring before the assizes.'

'Aye! She's a witch*!' screamed Sally Strumpton. I jumped forward and hissed at her, arching my back. She jumped back in fright and hid behind Aggie – which was pointless, because she might just as well have hidden behind a twig – and pointed a shaking fat finger at me. 'And see? There's her* familiar*! That demon cat of hers with whom she speaks, which watches us all with its baleful eyes.'*

Martha spread her arms wide, her fingers splayed out, and said in a loud, echoing voice: 'Be gone from my hearth, all of you! If witch I be, then I be proud*! Get gone! Master Squire, fetch your Master Cackhand, I have nothing to fear.* Now leave me*!' There was a flash of lightning, followed by a crash of thunder, causing several of the women to squeal with fear. Even the Squire took a step back. Seconds later, the rain began to pelt down, soaking them all, sending the women fleeing, throwing their aprons over their heads in a vain attempt to keep dry.*

Rain tipped from the brim of the Squire's hat as he nodded to Martha, splattering onto the hearthstone. 'So be it, Mistress Goodbody,' he said grimly. He turned away, adding, 'So be it.'

A flicker of light…

I sat on Peggy's lap, my claws kneading her green dress as we watched Martha sitting at the table, carefully etching the inside of one of her bracelets with a long iron nail. There was a bowl in the middle of the table and next to it a lighted candle. I could just see the other bracelet within the bowl, nestled amongst some leaves, pieces of straw and what looked like cobwebs.

'There. 'Tis done,' said Martha grimly, laying the nail aside and holding the bracelet up so that it caught the sunlight shining through the open door. She placed the bracelet next to its fellow in the bowl. Next, she took up a small knife and snipped off a lock of her hair, which she carefully laid over the bracelets. After this, she picked up a tuft of what looked like my own black fur and laid this on top of the hair. Then she reached into her apron pocket and pulled out a small drawstring pouch which she opened. She carefully shook a bluey-green powder out of the pouch over the bowl. It seemed to glitter in the sunlight as it wafted down over the contents of the bowl. Finally, Martha stood up and picked up the candle which she held in front of her with both hands. She chanted some strange words and the room seemed to darken, the sunlight fading away. I felt the fur on my back beginning to rise, whilst Peggy tensed noticeably.

Suddenly the candle became a stream of liquid fire which fell from Martha's hands into the bowl. There was a bright flash as the contents of the bowl ignited in green flames, followed by a cloud of greeny-blue smoke. I stood up suddenly, arching my back, my claws digging into Peggy's legs through the material of her dress. She didn't complain, but instead spoke soothingly and stroked my fur. 'Tis fine Tip, 'tis fine,' she whispered.

I watched as Martha wafted the swiftly thinning smoke away, reached into the bowl and took out the bracelets. They seemed to be glowing faintly with some inner light, which slowly faded to be replaced by their usual outward glitter as the sunlight returned to brighten the room.

'Peggy,' said Martha. 'You know what must be done and when.'

Peggy began to protest, but Martha spoke over her. 'Take these, and my books. Take Tip and Henrietta, then get you to your cousin's house at Snotty Sleeve. Carry on my work.'

Peggy stood up, carrying me to Martha, who took me in her arms and hugged me close. Our eyes met, and I knew this was to be our parting. 'Go with Peggy, dear Tip,' said Martha, as tears sprang to her eyes and glistened on her cheeks. 'I know what's coming and I know they will not let me live. "Thou shalt not suffer a witch to live". *The fools! But I promise you Tip, we shall be together again ere long.' She stroked my head and fondled my ears. I meowed and licked her hand. 'Thou hast been my companion and friend since I took thee from the barn as a kitten,' smiled Martha. 'A most loyal and honest soul you ever were, Tip. Go with Peggy, dearest Tip, be safe with her, be as good a companion to her as you were to me.'*

A flicker of light…

I stood on the grassy rise beside Peggy looking out at the pond, beyond which stood the Bishop's Palace, a grand and ugly building. The sun was sinking slowly on the horizon, the winter's sky turning red then slowly to purple.

'That's where the stones stood, Tip,' said Peggy. 'They still be there, of course. Martha showed me how to see without mere sight.' She turned her back to the pond and walked towards the nearby wood. I followed, silently. The trees were mostly bare, dry leaves crunching beneath Peggy's boots, but rustling lightly beneath my more delicate paws.

Peggy stopped by a tall, young tree, its trunk no thicker than her arm. 'This is the one, Tip,' she said. 'They hanged her in the market square, her body is buried far from here, yet here she shall be, protected by a sturdy oak.' She rolled her sleeves up to reveal Martha's bracelets around her wrists. She slipped one from her wrist and knelt down at the base of the tree. She picked up a sharp stone and swiftly hacked a hole into the earth, uncovering a slender tree root. She kissed the bracelet and placed it in the hole she'd dug, next to the root, then pushed soil back over it, burying it. I stepped forward and sniffed the freshly turned earth. Underneath the odour of leaves and decay, I could smell the metallic tang of the bracelet and, faintly, the delicate, human essence of Martha.

Peggy patted the soil down. I reached out a paw and patted the soil also. I felt the tingling essence of the magic within the bracelet, the memory of Martha.

'I will make sure you both are reunited Tip,' said Peggy. 'When the time comes.'

A flicker of light…

… And I was watching Peggy's niece, Alice. She looked to be as old as Peggy had been when she became Martha's famulus. She had dug a hole by some trees and was placing a wooden box into it. I drew closer but somehow, I was seeing this scene… differently. *From above, from below and from everywhere at once. I realised with a jolt that* I *was in that box… or rather my body was.*

'Sleep well, dear Tip,' whispered Alice as she knelt by the hole. 'You lived for many a year and you were a loyal friend to my auntie. Before the plague took her, she bade me bring you back to Martha when your time had come.' She sniffed, wiping away a tear. 'I be so sorry, dear Tip, but I know not which tree her bracelet be buried under. But I know 'tis close by. I know you will find each other ere long.'

She reached into her apron pocket and withdrew Martha's other bracelet. It wasn't as shiny as it had once been but was still unmistakeably hers. Alice gently kissed the bracelet and then lifted the lid of the box, placed the bracelet inside, then closed the lid. She stood, retrieved a small spade from the pile of earth nearby and began to fill in the hole. I heard – and felt – the thump of earth on the box. I looked across from the hole to the trees in the distance, those that stood near the ridge overlooking the pond. Where Martha's tree stood. So near, yet so far.

'I will find you Martha,' I whispered, and my words were wafted away on the breeze.

There was a flicker of light…

Chapter Seventeen

Getting to the Root of the Problem

'I will find you Martha,' I whispered, and my words were wafted away on the breeze.

There was a flicker of light…

'Robert? Robert? *Robert!'*

I opened my eyes… to see the concerned faces of GG, Janet, Red Fred and Alan, all grouped around me, so no surprise there. What *was* surprising however was that we weren't where we had been. I was now crouched by the fallen oak tree, near the ruins of Mr Goodman's old cottage, my front paws scrabbling away at the ground where the mass of tree roots projected up into the dark sky.

I stopped scrabbling, blinked rapidly and focussed on my friends. 'Why are we here?' I said, my voice thick with confusion.

'You ran over here, Mate,' said Fred, looking concerned. 'You went up to that ghost cat, you touched noses and, well…'

'You stood there, then Tip just vanished and you bolted off in this direction,' added GG. 'We were all so surprised it took us a few seconds to run after you.'

'B-but… M-Martha… and Alice… Peggy …?' I mumbled, my fuddled brain trying to focus on the fact that I was Robert, here and now, not Tip long ago and then.

'Who's Martha?' asked Fred, frowning in puzzlement.

'And Alice and Peggy?' put in GG.

Janet was suddenly by my side giving my cheek a vigorous wash with her rough little tongue. Somehow this brought me back to reality. I was disappointed when she stopped licking me and sat back to look directly at me. 'What did you see, Robert?' she asked quietly.

Alan leaned against the mass of tree roots and stroked his neat beard. 'Take your time Robert old son,' he said gently.

I sat up and took a deep breath. 'I was there…' I began. 'That is, Tip showed me… I was kind of seeing it all through his eyes. But there was so much to see. Surely I was standing there for ages?'

'I think you connected with Tip's spirit,' said Alan. 'But what seemed like a long time to you was only seconds for us.'

'Tell us what you saw, Robert,' said Janet, encouragingly.

So I told them, as best as I could remember, all that Tip had showed me, or rather what Tip had seen, lived through and shared with me.

'Wow,' said Fred. 'So he was a witch's cat, was he?'

'And those cruel, stupid humans turned on that nice Martha, after all she'd done for them!' added GG indignantly.

'So why did you run over here, Robert?' prompted Janet.

The realisation hit me harder that a bat round the head from Dorothy. 'The bracelet,' I whispered. 'Martha's bracelet. Peggy buried it by a tree... *under* the tree in fact. An oak tree. *This* oak tree!'

Cats and gnome gasped in amazement. Alan recovered his wits first. 'So... the bracelet is still here? That's why you knew to run to this tree Robert?'

'Yes! Yes!' I said excitedly. 'When I was being buried – I mean, when *Tip* was being buried – he looked over this way. Or rather his spirit did, 'cos his body was being buried. I – he – knew which tree Martha's bracelet had been buried under, but Alice – Peggy's niece – didn't. She just knew it was nearby. That's why Tip and Martha's other bracelet were buried somewhere else!'

'Where the old wall between the allotments and stadium was built afterwards!' exclaimed Janet.

'Exactly!' I said, as everything began to make sense. I looked at the tangle of thick roots. 'So when the oak tree blew down yonks and yonks later...'

'The bracelet was uncovered then?' GG finished for me.

'I don't think it *has* been uncovered,' I said, thoughtfully. I closed my eyes for a moment and concentrated on the image of the bracelet being buried. Peggy placing it in the hole by the tree... next to a... tree root!

'What do you mean?' asked GG.

I didn't answer. Instead, I looked at the tangle of uncovered tree roots. One long root which snaked out from the tangle like a long branch had a curious bulge about halfway along its length, after which the root pointed downwards. Like many of the roots, it was pale and smooth, having been weathered over many yonks. Something deep inside my head told me what I needed to do.

Without a second thought – or even a first one for that matter – I ran towards the root tangle, crouched down and sprang up to the root. My claws dug into its smooth surface and I clung on, swinging for a few seconds. I didn't want to drop off and try again, because I wasn't sure if I could manage the leap again with such accuracy. I thrashed my tail round and round to regain my balance and, with a huge exertion, I swung my back legs up to the branch and locked my back claws into it. For a moment I hung-clung upside-down on the root until, one paw at a time, I hauled myself onto the top of it. I took a few deep breaths and then began to slowly inch my way along the root towards the knotty bulge.

'What're yow doin' mate?' called Fred.

I didn't dare look down to him and the others in case I lost my balance, so grunted between each move I made: 'I think… I know… where it is…' I felt the root beginning to bounce up and down with my weight (not that I'm that heavy you understand), but it steadied slightly when I reached the bulge. I peered closely at it. It was gnarly and pitted and had split slightly in some places. I sniffed at it and recalled a familiar metallic odour from Tip's memories. My whiskers tingled excitedly.

'It's here!' I called out. 'In the root! Where Peggy buried it! The root grew around it!'

'Well done, Robert!' Alan said. 'Hang on, I've got an idea. Stay where you are.'

'I'm not planning on going anywhere,' I replied, with feeling. I hadn't really thought how best to clamber down from the root.

I felt the root trembling again and risked a look down. Alan was climbing up the tangle of roots, making the most of his opposable thumbs and bendy knees. He reached the long root and nimbly hopped up onto it. I felt the root sag lower with his weight and an ominous creaking sound reached my ears.

'Fred! Can you get up here?' Alan called down. 'We just need a bit more weight!'

'Hang on!' I heard Fred call up. Again, I didn't risk looking down but heard a scruffling of leaves below then felt a heavy thud as Fred leapt up onto the root, which dipped even lower at which the creaking grew louder. He puffed and cursed as he struggled to grip it with his claws. 'I'm right behind you, Alan!' he panted.

'So now what?' I gasped, feeling the root bouncing up and down, the creaking growing louder.

My eyes locked onto the bulge which was beginning to split open like a conker in the autumn (I'd seen plenty of those in my time – their green cases were spiny and sharp, but the shiny brown chestnuts inside were great fun to bat around once the cases had split and they'd fallen out). Despite my worry about the root beginning to break, I could see a dull metal shape as Martha's bracelet was slowly revealed.

Eventually, the creaking reached a crescendo and suddenly the root snapped. It didn't break completely but our end of it swung downwards. I clung on, for dear life. Suddenly the end of the root thudded into the ground, sending a massive jolt along its length. I let go and leapt through the air… to land on top of Janet and GG. I hadn't fallen as far as I thought.

We disentangled ourselves with much muttering and grumbling – cats don't like to be embarrassed. 'Are you both okay?' I asked, concerned.

'You're blooming heavy, Robert!' muttered GG, licking herself rapidly, smoothing her fur down.

'I'm okay Robert,' said Janet. 'But are you okay?' She licked my cheek, cleaning away some dirt.

'Oh… um…thank you,' I said, nervously. Behind Janet I could see Red Fred shaking some dried leaves out of his fur, and Alan sitting cross-legged next to him, shaking leaves and dirt out of his hat.

'Well, that worked!' exclaimed Alan delightedly. He pointed to the root, half of which was now dangling down to the ground, barely attached to the other half. We all looked closely. The gnarly bulge had split open and there, half in and half out of the bulge, glinting in the moonlight, was the bracelet!

'How did you know it was there, mate?' whispered Fred.

'I… I don't know, I just did,' I said. 'It was like… well… I just *felt* it I guess.'

Alan stretched up to the root and tugged at the bracelet. 'Nope, it's still stuck fast,' he panted as he let go and regained his balance. 'Been in there for hundreds of years.' He looked at me and beamed widely. 'Do you realise, Robert, that this is the first time that bracelet will have been exposed to the air in centuries?'

'I suppose so,' I said slowly. 'Wow.'

Janet nudged me gently with her nose. 'Well done, Robert,' she purred. I felt a flush of pride and little tingle of excitement.

'What I want to know,' said Fred thoughtfully. 'What I want to know is… It's been there centuries, right?'

'Yes, it has', nodded Alan.

Fred looked thoughtful then said: 'Well… how many *yonks* is that?'

A little later, all of us cats had gathered in my shed for a meeting to discuss the discovery of the bracelet. Alan had joined us and was sitting on an upturned flowerpot looking thoughtful. I'd explained again, this time to Dorothy, ET and Barbara about my meeting with Tip and how he'd shown me his life, then about how I'd uncovered the bracelet.

'S-s-so n-n-now y-y-you've *found thebracelet*, wh-wh-what *shouldwedo*?' wibbled ET.

'Well… I *think* we need to get both of the bracelets back together and bury them, maybe along with Tip's skull,' I said. 'That way Tip and Martha can be back together again. That was always Martha's plan.'

'How do you *know* that was the plan?' asked Dorothy.

'I just do!' I snapped. 'Tip told me. Or rather, that's what he knew and I… kind of… well, *felt* it. I just know, okay?'

For once, Dorothy didn't argue. I think she was surprised that I'd been so outspoken. But after a short pause she muttered: 'Well, if that's what it takes to get rid of that annoying apparition, then the sooner the better for me.'

'And Pip was talking about burying the first bracelet and the skull anyway,' I added. 'We need to make sure they bury *both* bracelets together.'

'I've got a suggestion,' said Alan. 'Why don't you get on Betty's laptop and look Martha Goodbody up on Moggle? She was a witch who was executed, there's bound to be a record about that somewhere. Make sure that Betty sees it and hopefully they'll get the idea about the bracelets.'

'Hey! Good idea Alan,' I said.

'I can't believe we're taking advice from a lawn ornament,' snorted Dorothy rudely. '*I* was going to suggest that!'

'Bit rude, Princess!' admonished Red Fred. 'Alan's been very helpful to us!'

To my surprise, Alan didn't seem at all put out. Instead, he chuckled and said: 'You're right Dorothy. But taking advice from a lawn ornament is no more unlikely than a group of cats living on magical allotments who are trying to reunite a long-dead witch with the ghost of her long-dead cat. Then again, the universe loves a story, even an improbable one.'

'Wh-wh- what's a n-n-*nimprobabblestory*?' wibbled ET, looking confused.

'One like this,' sighed GG.

'Hey! Maybe you should get your human Nawthor friend to write a book about it,' said Barbara enthusiastically.

'I was meaning to ask you about that, Robert,' said Alan. 'How do you tell him what's happened to you, so's he can write it down? You can't talk Humanese and he can't talk Kittish, can he?'

'Well, actually…' I began.

'I think maybe we should be thinking of a plan to get the humans to find the other bracelet as well?' This interruption was from Janet, in her usual shy way, although no matter how quietly she spoke, everybody heard her and listened, even Dorothy.

‘Janet’s right,’ said GG. ‘I’ll get onto Betty’s laptop as soon as possible. In the meantime, we need to think up a way to make sure the humans find the other bracelet.’

‘None of the plot holders have been down to the wild bit since the weather turned manky,’ said GG. ‘And even then, are they going to look at *that* particular tree root?’

We all pondered this. Then Janet said: ‘One thing I’ve learned from living on the Allotments is that answers always seem to present themselves.’

‘Along with plenty of questions,’ I sighed.

Chapter Eighteen

Stocking Up

We didn't have to wait too long to put our plan into operation. The next morning Betty was sitting at the table in the clubhouse tapping away at her laptop. She was answering emails and adding posts in my name on my *Nitter-Natter* and *FaceyFriends* pages. I have to say, some of her posts were quite good; she had a decent grasp of *cattishness* for a human. (Even so, GG and I would post our own updates when we got the chance. Our feline fanbase knew which were our posts easily enough).

GG, Barbara and I hung around the clubhouse, dozing on our special couch, biding our time. As we'd hoped, Betty left her laptop on the table when she went home for lunch. With Barbara keeping an eye out at the clubhouse door, we both jumped up onto the table and levered the laptop open with our claws. GG quickly opened the Moggle search engine and typed in the words *Martha Goodbody Witch Tip*. GG's claws *click-clacked* quickly over the keyboard, impressing me as always. (She'd learned to type by watching her late owner using a word processor when she was a Home Cat and she could read Humanese far better than I could).

'Let's see…' muttered GG, scrolling through lots of different links.

The words scrolling by on the laptop screen all became a blur to me and I felt my eyes watering. I blinked a few times then decided that it would probably be better for my eyes if I closed them, so I did. Gradually the click-clack of the keys and little mutterings from GG seemed to fade away and it was all so peaceful and…

'Ah-ha!' GG exclaimed suddenly, causing me to jump.

'Wh- what? I wasn't asleep!' I blurted, quickly licking some drool off my chin. I peered intently at the screen. 'What have you found?' I asked.

'There!' said GG pointing to some very small words with her claw. The words were written in some strange kind of lettering, which was even harder for me to understand than normal human letters. 'It's an old document on some history site. Hmmm… the words are written in a very old form of English Humanese…' She squinted closely at the small words. It says… let's see… *Witch Tryals inn the County of Midlantownshire... Martha Goodbody, accused of witchcraft... sentenced at Midlandtownshire assizes... divers persons relating her coal black familiar... took on the form of a cat... named Tip.'*

'Wow!' I exclaimed. 'Who are these divers people? Do they jump in the river or something?'

'I don't think it means that,' said GG. 'Although there is something about dunking suspected witches in the village pond… maybe they needed divers for that? Anyway… It looks like she was one of many women accused of witchcraft. And… oh how horrid! *"Sentenced to hang... executed on Candlemas day in the year of our Lord 1657."*

I found my back arching slightly and my tail bristling with anger. 'She only ever *helped* people!' I hissed. 'And Tip never hurt anyone! Humans can be so… *horrible* to each other!'

GG put a placatory paw on my back and I began to de-bristle. 'I know, Robert, I know,' she said quietly. 'But we've found a mention of her. Now, if we just leave this website open, and close the laptop lid, this will be the first thing Betty sees when she opens it. Hopefully she'll see the mention of Tip and work it out from there.'

'Let's hope so,' I said grimly. 'Poor Tip needs to find Martha again. I just wish we could *tell* Betty and the plot holders, but we can't speak Humanese. Martha could speak Kittish though, it's a shame none of our humans can.'

'Maybe you have to be a witch and know magic to be able to speak Kittish,' said GG thoughtfully. 'Thankfully, most of the humans we know on the Allotments are clever, kind people,' she added, as she closed the laptop lid. 'Let's see what they can do.'

We didn't have to wait too long for results. When Betty came back from lunch we were innocently sitting on our couch and meowed a greeting to her. This led to her giving us some cat treats, so that was a good start.

While we were eating our treats, Betty bustled around tidying some papers away and making herself a cup of tea. It became quite nerve wracking, wondering if she was going to look at her laptop again, but eventually she sat down at the table, and, sipping her tea, opened the laptop lid and peered at the screen.

I don't know what reaction I was expecting, but when she sprayed tea from her lips over the laptop screen with a *Pfffttttt!* sound, I knew she'd seen the part about Martha and Tip. Betty pulled out a handkerchief from her sleeve and furiously wiped the screen and keyboard down. This done, she looked closely at it again, her lips moving silently, mouthing the words she was reading. Finally, she sat back in her chair and exhaled deeply.

We all continued to pretend to doze. GG opened one eye and winked at Barbara and me. 'I think that worked,' she purred happily.

Betty immediately got out her mobile and called Donna and Anji, then proceeded to tell them what she'd found. 'What? No, I don't know how it came up,' Betty said. 'I opened the laptop and there was this article about witch trials in Midlandtownshire in the Seventeenth Century… uh-huh… uh-huh… Maybe I brushed the keys before I closed the laptop down and went to lunch. I know… incredibly strange… Yes, it mentions Tip and a woman accused of witchcraft called Martha Goodbody. Like on the bracelet – "Tip" and "MG". Yes, yes, I'll email you the link, maybe you can find out some more. Oh, I'll email Pip too.'

Betty hung up and I knew she was looking across at us. But we pretended to doze on nonchalantly (us cats are very good at this). A few seconds later I heard her tapping away at the keyboard as she sent her emails to Donna, Anji and Pip.

A couple of days later, Red Fred and I were in the clubhouse, once again looking wistfully at all the enticing decorations on the Christmas Tree. Several of the plot holders had been in and out wishing Betty a Merry Christmas. Quite a few of them had brought her little gifts too, which I thought was very nice. Apparently today was Christmas Eve, although I didn't know who Eve was. Fred suggested that maybe Eve had her birthday at Christmas.[17]

Betty, Pip and Kate were sitting at their usual table drinking tea and chatting about Martha and Tip.

'Donna and Anji said they've been checking as many historical records as they can find,' Betty was explaining. 'But what with their kids being off school for Christmas and their friend's university on holiday too, they haven't had much of a chance to find out much more than we already knew.'

'It's certainly strange that the website mentioning Martha Goodbody and Tip should be there on your laptop, Betty,' said Kate thoughtfully.

'I think there's something magical going on,' said Pip. 'I've felt that ever since the workmen found the skull and bracelet. It's almost like Martha and Tip's spirits are reaching out to us, trying to tell us something.'

'Either that or the cats looked it up,' chuckled Kate.

All three ladies laughed, although I noticed that each of them gave us a thoughtful glance.

'I still say we should re-bury the skull and bracelet,' said Pip seriously. 'After all, they were buried together, so they're obviously meant to *be* together.'

Kate and Betty nodded in agreement.

'I think we should re-bury them too,' said Betty. 'But shall we wait and see if Donna and Anji turn up any more information about this Martha the witch? Just in case there's something important we need to know.'

Pip agreed to this.

'Looks like that part of the plan's worked, mate,' said Fred, with a wink.

'That's great,' I said, 'but we really need them to find the other bracelet stuck in the tree root. I… I just *know* that they need to be buried together, along with Tip's skull. That's the only way Tip and Martha will be back together again and Tip will be at peace.'

---

[17] Of course, Janet explained this to us later. I was slightly disappointed that there wasn't actually someone *called* "Christmas Eve". Although, as Janet pointed out, it was highly likely that there were some baby girls born on December 24th so their parents named them Eve, because they thought it was amusing that their little girl was a *Christmas Eve*. Some humans think that sort of thing is very amusing. The Eves probably didn't find it very funny growing up. Cat names in Kittish are *much* more sensible!

'You'll think of something, mate,' purred Fred encouragingly. 'You're clever like that,'.

My heart swelled with pride, right up until Fred added: 'Or Janet'll think of something, because she's *really* clever.'

Feeling a bit put out – even though I had to agree with Fred that Janet *was* very clever – I continued to listen to the three humans talking. Their conversation turned to what they planned to do over Christmas, because there was an even more important subject to be discussed.

'So, I'll pop down on Christmas morning and give the cats their food,' said Betty. 'And I'll – you know – with their stockings.' She nodded towards our six Christmas stockings which were pegged to a string fixed to the noticeboard.

'Thanks Betty,' said Pip. 'And I'll come down on Boxing Day to feed them, because you've got all your family over.'

'What's Boxing Day then?' I asked Fred.[18]

'Dunno really,' said Fred. 'I've *heard* about it. Lots of the plot holders come down to tend their plots on that day. They say it's good to get out from the house full of relatives. Never seen any of them boxing with each other though.'

'Maybe those barmy hares box with each other on Boxing Day?' I suggested.

'Could be,' mused Fred. 'They usually do that in the Spring through.'

We both agreed that humans had some very strange customs. Still, it was good to know that they were arranging for us to be fed as usual over Christmas.

'I'll come down the day after,' Kate was saying. 'Then I suppose it's all back to normal until New Year.'

'Thanks girls,' said Betty. 'And all here on New Year's Eve afternoon for our little get together?'

'Wouldn't miss it for the world!' chuckled Kate. 'To mark the end of a very eventful year, when we saw off Grasper and found out that we *own* the allotments!'

They all laughed and raised their teacups and clinked them together saying 'Cheers!'

'Sounds like they're going to have a party,' said Fred. 'New Year's Eve is another one of those nights when humans set a lot of fireworks off. So… should we stay in our sheds or come to the Clubhouse? They'll probably have food. I like those little sausages on sticks. Well, maybe not the sticks, but…

---

[18] Janet explained about Boxing Day to us too. We cats love a box to jump in, so it was good to know actual boxes were involved. At least no humans named their babies "Boxing Day". Then again, with humans, who can tell?

'You know, Fred,' I interrupted. 'I've had an idea. I think that might be the time to get the humans to come and find the bracelet in the tree root!'

'How're we going to get them to come down to the wild patch when they're having a party?' said Fred, looking rather confused.

I looked at the Christmas Tree and smiled. 'Oh, I think I know a way…'

The next day was Christmas Day. I have to say, it didn't *feel* particularly different to any other day. There was less traffic than usual on the main road, and there was only one plot holder tending to her plot. The sky was a bland milky white and there wasn't much wind. In fact, it wasn't even that cold. The Allotments certainly weren't covered with snow like the pictures on those Christmas cards. Maybe that was a good thing though. Snow can be very cold on a cat's paw pads.

As it was breakfast time, we were all sitting outside the clubhouse door. Dorothy was grumbling about Betty being late to feed us, although Janet pointed out that it wasn't actually *that* late. Just then, we heard the familiar sound of Betty's car and sure enough, it was trundling down the road from the main gate.

Betty clambered out of the car, a couple of plastic flowerpots and several packets of seeds dropping out of the car.

'Tch! I really *must* tidy this car up sometime,' Betty muttered to herself, picking the things up and throwing them into the back of the car. She turned to us and smiled. 'Oh my! What a reception committee!' she exclaimed with delight. 'All of you together! Well, Merry Christmas kitties! I'll get you your breakfast.'

Fred, Barbara, GG and I trotted over and rubbed around Betty's legs. ET wobbled around with delight, while Janet shyly stood a little further back, but raised her tail happily. Betty carefully negotiated her way round us and over to the clubhouse door, which she unlocked and let us inside. She flicked the light on and also switched on the pretty Christmas Tree lights.

'Right,' said Betty decisively, putting her bulging shopping bag on the table. 'Let's get your food out and I *think* there might be something special from Santa in here for your... *oh!*'

We followed her gaze. She was looking at our Christmas stockings, pegged to their string on the noticeboard. Every one of them was bulging with things inside them. With a look of puzzlement, Betty unpegged the stockings and put them on the table. Most of us jumped up onto the table to take a look as she tipped out the stocking with an R on it. *My* stocking. There were four little packages wrapped up on shiny Christmas paper. She unwrapped each to reveal a packet of my favourite treats, a catnip mouse (a toy one obviously), a small tin of *FeliFood™ (Posh Nosh for Pedigree Pets*) and a ball with a little bell in it that jingled as it moved. I pounced on the mouse straight away, delighting in the heady aroma of nip.

Over the next few minutes, Betty emptied all the stockings and unwrapped the packages. It turned out that we all had the same gifts, which was probably just as well, because Dorothy said she didn't like the pink catnip mouse she'd received but preferred the green one that Barbara had, so they swapped mice. I think Barbara agreed to that for a quiet life.

Betty took out another selection of presents from her bag, all wrapped up in Christmas paper. 'Hmm. I think I'll let Pip give you these tomorrow,' she said. 'I'll get your breakfasts.' She set off to the small kitchen at the back of the clubhouse to dish out our usual cat food in our bowls.

As we were all eating our breakfast, Betty made herself a cup of coffee and sat at the table. She got out her mobile phone and tapped in a number. 'Hello? Pip? Happy Christmas!' she said. She carried on chatting for a couple of minutes. Then I heard her say: 'Yes, the cats are fine. But – um – did *you* put presents in their stockings? No? Well, maybe Kate did… No, she's away today at her in-laws… Uh-huh… uh-huh…. Ha! Ha! It must've been Santa then!'

Betty said goodbye and Merry Christmas again to Pip and put her phone down, then looked over at us thoughtfully. She picked up one of the stockings, looked at it and then back at us. She looked puzzled.

'Well…another mystery, eh? Maybe it *was* Santa after all,' she smiled. 'Merry Christmas, Kitties!'

We all wished her a *Meowey Christmas* in return, but it was probably very muffled because we had our mouths full.

After we'd eaten, we all trotted out of the clubhouse. The others all wandered off to do their own thing, while I sat washing by Betty's car. A few moments later, Betty bustled out of the clubhouse, locking the door behind her. Before she climbed into her car she reached down, picked me up and gave me a hug, wishing me a Merry Christmas again. I purred happily as she tickled my ears.

A couple of minutes later as I watched Betty drive away, I thought to myself how much my life had changed. Not only did I have a home, but I was well fed and cared for. What's more, I even had Christmas presents!

I thought of all the Outling Cats – and stray dogs too – who didn't have a home. I'd been there and I knew how cold and miserable life could be for an Outling. I hoped that this thing humans called Christmas Spirit would work on some of those humans to spare a thought for the less fortunate animals and put some food out for them. I knew that turkey giblets were a favourite dish for Home Cats and Dogs at Christmas. Maybe some of those giblets and a bit of leftover turkey meat might find their way to a bowl outdoors for the Outlings. I certainly hoped so.

Yes indeed, I thought, we Allotment Cats were *very* lucky indeed.

B.
D.
J.
R.
GG
RF
E.T.

Chapter Nineteen

A Tale of Two Trees

The New Year's Eve mini party in the clubhouse was in full swing. There was music playing from a small device which someone called an *empeefree player*. The Christmas lights were twinkling, lots of food and drink was laid out on the long table, which had been covered with a red and green tablecloth. Pip's Yule Log took pride of place in the centre of the table, with three lit candles set into it.

All the usual humans were there, enjoying themselves with eating and drinking, chatting and laughing. Some of them had brought other humans with them, which I heard them refer to several times as "my better half". I never realised that humans came in halves and kept their better halves elsewhere. Thankfully, GG explained to me that "better halves" was a human term of endearment for their life partners. Knowing this, I couldn't help but daydream of me introducing Janet to somebody as *my* better half.

I looked around the clubhouse spotting the other cats either under tables, on couches being made a fuss of or, like Red Fred and me, being fed tasty titbits of food such as chicken, turkey, ham, cheese, tuna, salmon and cooked egg. I even tried somethings called volleyvoles which looked like a little hill made of pastry and filled with tasty meaty stuff. I was a bit disappointed that they didn't contain actual vole, but you can't have everything. I left the pastry, but it didn't go to waste as Rosie bounded over and wolfed it down. This way we shared about three or four volleyvoles between us, aided by Tom and Amelia, who delighted in feeding them to us, until Bex told them to stop, because the humans might like some too.

'Are you all set?' I asked Rosie.

'*Ohyessyyesyes!*' she panted excitedly. 'You *really are* going to let me chase you for real?'

'Ye-e-e-s.' I replied cautiously, 'but remember you're only *pretending* to chase me and you can't catch me.'

'I bet I could catch you though!' chuckled Rosie with a mischievous roll of her eyes.

'I'm sure you could, Rosie,' said Barbara patiently, having strolled over to join us, licking some chicken crumbs off his chops. 'But it's a game, right? All part of the plan? As we discussed when we saw you here, yes?'

I looked out of the clubhouse window. It was still daylight, but it would soon be getting dark, so we had to put my plan into operation soon.

'Barbs, can you go and round the others up please?' I asked. 'We'll meet under the table by the door.'

'Sure thing, Robert,' said Barbara and trotted off towards Red Fred who was tucking into what looked like a whole pork pie which someone had thoughtfully put on the floor for him or, more likely, that Fred had swiped off someone's plate when they weren't looking.

A few minutes later, all us cats were under the table by the door. Rosie was sitting innocently next to the Christmas Tree, looking as good as gold, but I could see her muscles twitching with anticipation. Every now and again a couple of plot holders would either come in or go out of the door, causing a little draught of outside air to rustle the tinsel on the Christmas tree. The tinsel which was key to my plan…

'Is everybody ready?' I asked. 'You all know what to do?'

There was a general murmur of assent from the other cats.

'A-a-are y-y-you s-s-sure *thiswillwork*, R-R-Robert?' wibbled ET, as Red Fred patiently propped her up as usual.

''Course it will,' purred Fred. 'You all just need to keep to Robert's plan and help Pip, Betty and the others get to where they need to be. Then it's down to Robert and me.'

'Well, I'm glad *you two* are doing this,' said Dorothy primly. '*I* certainly wouldn't indulge in such a vulgar and frankly *un-feline* display, even if it will hopefully see that irritating apparition out of the way.'

I decided it wasn't worth arguing with Dorothy. At least she'd agreed to take part in my plan to lead the humans to the second bracelet, which was the best I could hope for. Everyone thought it was a great idea when I suggested it after Betty had gone home on Christmas Day and the excitement of receiving our presents had worn off a bit. Over the next few days, we'd talked some more and refined the plan here and there until it sounded as fool proof as it could be. It had been agreed that the New Year's Eve afternoon get together for the Plot Holders was the best time to put the plan into operation. However, as Janet had said cautiously, it all depended on *timing*.

Just at that moment Old Ted shuffled slowly through the clubhouse door. 'Now!' I hissed. At this, Dorothy and GG ran to the doorway, doing their best not to trip Old Ted up. ET wobbled out from under the table and weaved around seemingly aimlessly. Barbara and Janet scooted through the open door outside and Red Fred and I ran towards the Christmas Tree…

'Whooopee!' shouted Fred as we both leapt into the tree, me on one side, Fred on the front. Rosie jumped up at the tree barking loudly, pretending that she was telling us off. Although the tree was firmly anchored in its heavy pot, our combined weight and Rosie's pushing caused it to topple over.

The tree hit the floor with a resounding crash, scattering ornaments everywhere. The lights went off and the star flew towards the far wall, narrowly missing ET on the way. There were shouts of alarm from the assembled plot holders. Rosie ran round and round barking furiously and pretending to chase us, in doing so preventing the nearest plot holders from reaching the tree, much to their protests and Tom's vain attempts to grab her collar.

Meanwhile, Fred and I had each grabbed a strand of tinsel in our mouths and were rolling over to pull it off the tree's branches and tangle it around ourselves. Satisfied at our efforts we jumped out from the fallen tree and ran towards the open door, which Dorothy and GG were leaning against to hold open. It occurred to me as we dodged around a protesting Old Ted who was leaning on the door to steady himself, that Dorothy would make an excellent doorstop on her own.

We skidded to a halt at the first row of plots and made sure that the tinsel was still wrapped around our bodies, but not tangled around our feet. Barbara and Janet were stationed nearby watching the clubhouse.

'Here they come!' shouted Barbara, as Pip, Kate and Colin ran through the open door, having managed to negotiate their way round Rosie, ET and Old Ted.

'Let's go!' I shouted. 'Remember – stick to the path and don't get tangled up in the plants!'

'Right you are, Mate!' laughed Fred, who was thoroughly enjoying himself. As soon as the humans drew near to us, we pelted off down the long path, meowing plaintively as we went, pretending we were scared of the noise, confusion and tinsel.

'Oh Robert! Fred! Come back!' I heard Pip call out behind us. 'We only want to untangle you!'

Again, we skidded to a halt and looked back down the path. Pip, Kate and Colin were running towards us, having been joined by several other plot holders.

'Let's just give them a few sickups[19] to catch us up,' I whispered to Fred. 'Get ready… steady… *Run*!'

Just as Pip was reaching towards me, off we shot down the path, much to the dismay of the plot holders. I heard their voices behind us as we neared the end of the pathway.

---

19 Sickups: A feline measure of about one and a half human seconds. One sickup is about as long as it takes a cat to cough up an average-sized furball.

'Blooming cats!'

'They can't help it! They're frightened!'

'Well, *they* knocked the tree over!'
'It was that dog what did it, I saw it! Made me drop my sausage roll, they did!'

'Look, let's just catch them! They're freaked out with that tinsel wrapped round them!'

'Nearly there!' I panted, as we veered left towards the wild area, slowing down again to give the humans a chance to get closer. I realised that I wasn't used to such exertion nowadays. Too many treats perhaps?

'Get ready… nearly…' muttered Fred. *'Now!'* Once again, we bounded away from the humans.

'They're doing it on purpose!' I heard Colin puff behind us.

'Don't be daft, Colin!' muttered Kate. 'They're just scared, that's all.'

We could see the fallen oak tree ahead of us and ran side by side towards it. All of a sudden, Fred disappeared from view with a yelp of surprise. I stopped and turned round to see him struggling to free his tinsel from where it had snagged on a thick fallen branch. The humans were almost upon him.

'It's okay, Fred,' said Kate in a soothing voice, 'We'll get you untangled.'

'Go on! Don't worry about me! Complete the mission!' Fred called out to me dramatically. He'd been holding out to be a hero.

I hesitated, making sure that Pip and some of the others were running towards me, then dashed off again. It was all down to me now! I had to succeed!

'Robert! Just stop!' called Pip. 'You'll get caught and hurt yourself!'

I ran towards the clump of roots, my heart hammering in my chest. I had to do it, I had to get on that long root! I braced my back legs, jumped…. And landed on the root! I dug my claws in as hard as I could and dragged myself towards the partly split bulge, where I could see the bracelet catching the late afternoon sunlight, reflecting it in a coppery red glow. Pip was now clambering up the tangle of roots towards me.

'Hold…still… Robert…,' panted Pip, as she held onto the root with one hand and began to untangle the tinsel from around my body with her other hand. If only she'd look at the bulge! I growled with exertion as I pulled myself forward a few more inches and latched my claws into the bulge.

'Ah! Got it!' said Pip triumphantly pulling the tinsel away. 'It's okay Robert, you're safe now.' She reached out to stroke me in an effort to calm me down. 'There, there, Robert,' she said soothingly. 'You can let go now and… and… *Oh... My...Stars!'*

I exhaled with relief and tapped the bracelet with my paw. Although Pip would only hear meowing, I felt I just had to say something. 'There you go Pip,' I panted. 'I *knew* you'd be interested in this!'

It was dark before we got back to the clubhouse. Kate had insisted on carrying me, in case I'd hurt myself (she still worried about my old leg injury). I didn't mind because all that running had tired me out. Red Fred had walked ahead of us proudly, telling the other cats as we approached that my plan had succeeded and well done for playing their parts so well. Now Fred and I were tucking into a bowl of turkey, ham, chicken and tuna which the concerned plot holders had donated for us after what they thought was our frightening ordeal. We were listening to their conversation as they gathered round one of the tables examining the freshly released bracelet.

'Yes, it was actually *in* the tree root,' Pip was explaining. 'Look, I took photos with my phone.'

'It took three of us to break that root off completely to free it,' added Colin. 'The bracelet popped out like a… like a… well, like a pea from a pod.'

'And it's the same as the other bracelet?' asked Betty, peering closely at it.

Anji picked the bracelet up and held it up, shining a little pocket torch at it. 'Well, it'll need cleaning up, but I'm sure I can see the same inscriptions scratched on the inside,' she said. 'This is Martha Goodbody's other bracelet!'

'So it must've been buried under the tree all those hundreds of years ago,' added Donna. 'And as the tree grew, the root grew over it and kept it safe.'

'What an amazing coincidence that you should find it,' said Bex. 'If it hadn't been for the cats and Rosie knocking the Christmas Tree over and the cats running off with the tinsel wrapped round them, you'd never have found it.'

'*I* think the cats did it deliberately,' said Tom thoughtfully. Everyone turned to look at him, including us. 'To lead you to the bracelet,' he added.

There was a ripple of laughter and some scoffing comments from some of the plot holders, but Pip wasn't laughing. 'I think you might be right, Tom,' she said. 'I swear those cats know more than we think they do!'

There was more chuckling from the plot holders at this, but not all of them. I noticed several humans casting thoughtful glances in our direction.

'Whatever, they led us to the bracelet,' said Betty proudly. 'So all thanks to them, even if they *did* knock the Christmas tree over. And well done to Rosie too, of course,' she added, patting a delightedly panting Rosie on the head.

'And the tree's okay, so all's well that ends well,' added Amelia. 'Only a couple of ornaments got broken after all.'

I had finished my bowl of food, so I wandered over to the tree which had been picked up and tidied somewhat. A lot of pine needles and bits of tinsel littered the floor around it, along with a few scraps of earth from the pot that hadn't been swept up. The star on top of the tree looked a bit wonky and I noticed with some satisfaction that the robin ornament didn't look nearly so smug now that its beak was bent sideways. But the pretty lights were still twinkling, so that it was all good.

'I'll have to ask Maeve to analyse the bracelet when she's back at her university in the New Year, 'Anji said. 'In the meantime, Donna and I can hit the historical records to see what else we can find out about Martha Goodbody.'

'Great. And then I think we should re-bury the bracelets with the cat's skull,' said Pip determinedly. 'It's most likely that the cat was her so-called familiar Tip, which explains why he was buried with the first bracelet.'

There was a general murmur of agreement from the plot holders.

'Anyway,' said Betty briskly, looking at her watch. 'Time's getting on and our little party was due to finish half an hour ago, so let's all make a toast to see the old year out.'

At this, everybody began to fill plastic tumblers with some kind of fizzy drink, or orange juice for the youngsters (and some of the adults).

Fred ambled up to sit beside me. 'Good plan of yours there, mate,' he rumbled, as he started to wash a paw. 'And Pip says they're going to bury the bracelets and Tip's skull. Do you reckon Tip's ghost will be happy then?'

'Let's hope so, Fred,' I said. 'I'm sure it's what he's wanted all along.'

Betty was making a short speech about all the exciting things that had happened that year and thanking everybody who'd helped out. 'And thanks to our face of the campaign, Robert, of course,' she said, looking over to me and raising her tumbler. 'To Robert, to us, and a Happy New Year!'

The humans all chorused this, raising their tumblers. *'To Robert, to us, and a Happy New Year!'*

Chapter Twenty

Laid To Rest

It had been a long month and an even longer moonth. Some days it seemed like nothing at all had happened since I'd led the humans to uncover the second bracelet in the tree root. The humans called this month January and I heard plenty of the plot holders complaining that it was a long and dreary month, with very little to do on their plots.

The weather turned pretty rotten after the New Year's party. It was cold, grey and rainy. Us cats spent most of our time snuggled up in our cat beds or otherwise going into the clubhouse whenever we could. Of course, Betty, Pip, Kate and the other plot holders still fed us, talked to us and stroked us, but everything seemed very flat and somewhat depressing.

I'd noticed this as an Outling Cat. The Christmas trees, twinkling lights and decorations would all disappear from the humans' homes. I saw plenty of the real Christmas trees lying outside houses, stripped of their bright decorations and looking very sad and forlorn, which seemed rather unfair after the humans had spent so much time decorating them and making them so important. Worse, any goodwill I'd been shown as an Outling quickly disappeared and my quest for food and shelter became harder, often during bad weather. At least this year I had humans who cared about me and made sure that I was safe and well fed. So maybe I shouldn't have felt so bad about the weather. Even though all the pretty Christmas decorations had been taken down in the clubhouse, the plot holders hadn't thrown their Christmas Tree out. They'd planted it in a corner of the wild area, so that it could live on.

Everything seemed so dull and bland. Even the little green shoots of bulbs poking above the earth with their promise of Spring couldn't lighten my mood. Spring seemed a very long way off.

The other cats had noticed how gloomy I was and did their best to cheer me up. Even Dorothy made a point of only gently batting me round the ear and only giving me the mildest of Looks when she thought I'd said something daft. But, as I explained to them all while we were sitting outside the clubhouse waiting for breakfast to be served one morning, I was concerned about Tip. The phantom feline hadn't been seen since he had shared his memories with me.

'Well, isn't that what we wanted all along?' said Dorothy as she washed a paw. 'Just for the wretched thing to go away?'

'No, it isn't!' I snapped crossly, much to Dorothy's surprised annoyance. I could see her paw twitch in anticipation of giving me a bat round the ear. 'Well, yes – I mean – we want him to go away but in a *nice* way. To be back with Martha…' My voice trailed off.

'What we need to know is when the humans are going to bury Tip's skull and the bracelets,' said Janet, in her usual quiet way. 'But we haven't heard them say anything about it.'

'Well, I heard them say there was a committee meeting this afternoon,' said Barbara. 'Maybe there'll be some news then. And you're on the committee, Robert.'

'Or at least on the table cadging treats,' chuckled Red Fred, good naturedly. 'Let's see if a couple of us can be there to listen in too.'

'Wh-wh-what a-a-a *goodideaFred*,' wibbled ET, rubbing her wobbly head against Fred's cheek. Fred gave a rumbling purr of appreciation and licked ET's face, but gently, so she didn't fall over. I looked across at Janet, wishing that I was bold enough to lick her face… or for her to lick mine. It was as though she was waiting for something, but I couldn't work out what it was.

'It's a pity your friend Tiberius is hibernating,' observed GG. 'I bet he would know what to do.'

'Oh, don't *you* start on about that over-rated amphibian!' snorted Dorothy. 'It's bad enough with Robert and Thingy going on about him all the time!'

Thankfully, any potential arguments were avoided, as Betty arrived just then with our breakfast. I decided to stay in the clubhouse after I'd eaten, as maybe today I'd learn something about the whole Tip and Martha situation.

In fact, the committee meeting was nearly all about Tip and Martha! I was sitting in my usual position in the middle of the long table. Fred, Barbara and GG were sitting on the couch, pretending to doze, but I could see their ears twitching now and again, so they were obviously listening as keenly as I was.

Donna and Anji had spread lots of papers across the table and had brought their laptop to the meeting. They'd logged onto a site with lots of photographs of old looking drawings of old women and cats. I recognised the word *Witch* appearing several times. But even more interesting was the fact that both of Martha's bracelets were on the table!

'So, what have you found out?' asked Betty, leaning forward with interest.

'We've done some deep delving into the historical records,' said Donna. 'And we've contacted the National Archives and some academics who specialise in studies of witchcraft in the Seventeenth century.' She tapped the papers on the table and then pointed to the laptop screen. 'There's plenty about witch hunts and trials from different parts of the country, but there weren't so many records of so-called witchcraft in Midlandshire at the time.'

I noticed that Betty, Pip and several of the other plot holders looked rather glum about this.

'But that doesn't mean we didn't find anything,' beamed Anji. 'There were a few references here and there in old court records and a couple of church records about Martha Goodbody. She was about twenty-four years old when she was accused of witchcraft and thrown in jail. She stood trial for witchcraft in November 1656.' Anji picked up a sheet of paper and read from it. 'From what we can make out, although she had a couple of witnesses as to her good character, there was a lot of "evidence" against her from local people who said that she was "*seen to perform spells and utter evil incantations.*" Many witnesses "*testified upon oath that she kept company with a familiar spirit in the form of a cat, this cat being known as Tip.*" Then it says that "*Mistress Goodbody the accused did not deny the charges. She sayeth that she didst use ancient remedies and words to cure ailments, for which folk didst show their gratitude.*" Well, needless to say, she was found guilty and "*condemned to be hanged on the second day of February in the year of our lord 1657, this being Candlemas day.".'*

Anji paused and swallowed hard. I could tell from where I was sitting that the whole account of Martha's trial had affected her deeply. Donna reached out and squeezed Anji's wrist. 'You okay, love?' she asked, with concern.

'Yeah, yeah, I'm okay,' said Anji, with a sad smile, blinking away a tear in her eyes. 'It's just that it was so... *unfair.*'

'Well, she was a woman, she had intelligence and from all accounts spoke up for herself,' said Donna with a frown. 'That was a recipe for trouble back then.'

'Anyway,' continued Anji. 'We also found out that the Goodbody family was quite widespread in the Midlandshire area. It seems that one of her cousins was a merchant named Josiah Goodbody and he testified to her good character, but this didn't save her unfortunately. But, some years after Martha was hanged, it seems that Josiah's son, also a merchant, moved into Midlandtown - this is before it became Midlandtown City of course - but it was becoming an important and busy place then, expanding rapidly. It seems that Josiah Junior did very well for himself as a "*maker and purveyor of fine wigs for gentlefolk*".' This caused a ripple of laughter from the committee. 'So... Josiah the wig maker was very wealthy and bought up quite a bit of land in the area. Can you guess where?'

'Here?' whispered Kate, her eyes wide.

'Exactly!' said Donna, taking up the story. 'And it seems at this point he changed the family name to *Goodman*. Whether this was to distance themselves from any lingering association with witchcraft, or just an affectation, we don't know. But, as I'm sure you all know, the land on which the Sunnyside Allotments sit was owned by Richard Goodman in the twentieth century and gifted to the Sunnyside Allotments Association after he died.'

There were several gasps and expressions of surprise from the committee.

'And it was thanks to Robert here finding the deeds to the land that the allotments were saved!' exclaimed Kate, stroking me affectionately.

At this point the committee meeting paused for a tea break. I looked across to the other cats, who were looking back at me, wide-eyed, no longer pretending to be dozing.

When the meeting resumed, Anji and Donna passed the bracelets around for everyone to look at. I noticed that they had both been cleaned and polished. Although there were still some faded and green patches, the bracelets looked much brighter, much closer to how they'd been when Martha wore them, as I'd seen in Tip's memories.

'So, Maeve conducted some tests on the bracelet found in the tree root,' said Anji. 'It'll come as no surprise to you all that this is the same age, metallic composition and everything as the first one which was dug up with the cat's skull. It even has the same initials etched inside, "MG" for Martha Goodbody and "Tip" for… well, Tip. And the cat's skull can only be that of her cat, her so-called familiar, Tip.'

'So,' said Pip, 'It makes you wonder if there was some family story amongst the Goodbody/Goodman clan that Martha's bracelets were buried here, along with Tip, which is why Josiah bought this land and it stayed in the family.'

'Or it could all just be a coincidence,' said Colin dryly.

'Oh, don't go spoiling a good story, Colin!' admonished Betty, with a smile.

'Well, *I* don't believe in coincidences,' said Pip, firmly. 'This is a sign that the bracelets and Tip's skull belong here, as they always have done. And Robert knows this.'

Everybody looked at me curiously, so I decided to distract them by rolling over and stretching out, causing some laughter.

Pip held one of the bracelets up so that it caught the weak afternoon sunlight, making it glint. 'So… Now that we know all of this – and well done Anji and Donna for finding all this out – we should discuss reburying the bracelets and skull.'

There were several murmurs of agreement from the committee and a nodding of heads.

'Martha was hanged on the second of February 1657,' Pip reminded everyone. 'That's Candlemas Day according to the church calendar, but it's also a much older feast day, *Imbolc.* This symbolizes the halfway point between the winter solstice which the ancient people called *Yule* and the spring equinox which they call *Ostara.* Martha, being a witch, or more accurately a *wiccan*, would have known this. So, like I said, we should rebury the bracelets and the skull on the second of February. This closes the circle and…'

'Yes, yes, okay. We get it,' chuckled Colin. 'Are you going to cast a spell when you do it?'

Pip smiled back at him and raised an eyebrow. 'You never know Colin, I might. And I might just cast it on *you*!'

When the second of February finally arrived, all of us cats, even Dorothy, hung around the clubhouse all day. It felt like the whole Allotments were in a state of supressed excitement. Henry and several other crows were perched on shed roofs, occasionally flapping their wings and fluffing up their feathers. Ruby, who was seldom to be seen when humans were about, was trotting anxiously up and down the pathways between the plots. Even Mr Brock was snuffling around a couple of the outlying plots. Word had got round; everybody was waiting for when the humans would bury Tip's skull and Martha's bracelets.

It was a bit of a surprise therefore, that only Betty was in the clubhouse. We'd heard the humans talking the day before that they'd be doing the burial today, but where were they? GG observed that today was a weekday and most of the committee would be at work and that they'd most likely turn up late in the afternoon.

As usual, GG was right. The sun was setting, turning the sky and clouds a deep red, when Pip drove up in her car. She'd brought Kate and Colin with her. Old Ted and Digby shuffled over from their plots, and a couple of the other committee members drove up shortly afterwards. Donna, Anji, Veema and Arnie were the last to arrive. Everybody had gathered in the clubhouse, drinking tea and coffee.

'I can smell the excitement on them,' said Barbara, as he sat next to me on one of the bigger cat beds.

'Me too,' I replied, flicking my tail back and forth in agitation. 'But I just wish they'd hurry up and get on with it! It's getting dark and humans can't see in the dark!'

As if she'd heard me, Betty clapped her hands for attention and said, 'Have you got your torches and lanterns, everyone?'

Several people rummaged in their coat pockets and bags and pulled out a variety of hand torches and flashlights. Donna and Anji put two glass lanterns on the big table and then proceeded to light them with matches.

'Great!' smiled Betty. 'So, we'd better set off. Remember to watch your step when we get to the wild area. Those of you with torches make sure we've got plenty of light.' She turned to Pip. 'So, Pip have you got the box?'

'I have indeed,' replied Pip. She crossed over to a cupboard and took out a square wooden box which she placed on the table. I jumped up onto the table to look at it and give it a sniff. It was covered with intricate carvings, which looked like curling leaves and flowers. The box smelled sweet and old, a musky mixture of human and wood and metal.

'Do you approve, Robert?' Pip asked, stroking me. The humans gathered round as she clicked a little metal catch on the front of the box and lifted the lid. I peered in and wasn't surprised to see Tip's skull sitting on a soft cloth lining. The two bracelets – now polished as best they could be – sitting either side of it.

'That's really lovely,' said Kate, and everyone else murmured their agreement.

'Thanks,' said Pip. 'It's an antique, belonged to my Great-Grandmother. She was a wise woman too, just like Martha Goodbody.'

I had no idea who or what an Ann Teek was, but I had to agree it was a very nice box. I just knew that Tip would feel safe and protected in there.

'Surely that's valuable!' exclaimed Colin. 'And you're going to *bury* it?'

'Great Grandma would approve,' smiled Pip as she gently closed the lid and fastened the little catch. 'And so does Robert.' She tickled me under the chin, then carefully picked the box up, took a deep breath and said, 'Okay, let's lay Tip and Martha to rest.'

We must have been a curious sight, even by the Allotment's standards. Our procession set off down the main path between the plots. Kate and Colin headed the group, pointing their torches to illuminate the path ahead. Next came Pip, carrying the box, Betty beside her. Donna and Anji came next, holding their lanterns high. Veema and Arnie ran on ahead, laughing, their torches flashing wildly in all directions, earning them a few words of warning to be careful from Donna and Anji. We cats made our own way, ducking and jinking between plots, sometimes appearing on the path, sometimes using an entirely different path.

'Hey look,' said Kate. 'The cats are following us.'

'Of course they are,' replied Pip. 'They know it's important.'

'Who's following who though?' chuckled Betty, at which point ET crashed out of some dried corn stalks and wobbled across the path in front of them. The humans in front stopped suddenly, which caused the humans behind to collide with them, with much muttering and complaining. Luckily, Red Fred followed quickly and propped her up, allowing the procession to move on.

We eventually reached the wild area. It was darker here, due to the trees blocking the fading daylight. But we were able to follow the track to the fallen oak, thanks to the torches and lanterns.

'Here we are,' said Pip, stopping a few feet in front of the fallen oak's trunk. I noticed that there was a neatly dug, square hole, with a small pile of earth next to it, in which a spade was stuck. 'Thanks for digging this ready for us, Ted and Digby,' she said.

'It was nothing,' said Digby, wheezing a little after the walk from the clubhouse.

'You're right there, man,' chuckled Old Ted in his rich, melodious voice. 'I dug the hole, you leaned on your spade and watched me.'

'Wcrrrrll, somebody had to supervise, din't they?' retorted Digby, to giggles and chuckles from the other plot holders. I could tell from Digby and Ted's warmth towards each other that this was just fun between them; they were firm friends.

'Okay,' said Pip, 'If you could all make a semi-circle and direct your torches to the hole please, and if you could put the lanterns either side of it, a few feet in each direction, Donna and Anji. That's great.'

We cats were standing a little way to the side of the humans, with our backs to a clump of nettles. I caught sight of Mr Brock and Ruby peeping from behind a tree, whilst in the branches Henry and several other crows were watching intently. Some rustling in the bushes and undergrowth nearby told me they weren't the only Allotment animals taking an interest.

All of a sudden, I heard a familiar voice whispering behind me; 'Well, this'll be interesting.' We turned to see Alan Titchbark pushing his way through the nettles to stand with us.

'Hello Alan,' I whispered back. 'Aren't you afraid the humans will see you?'

'Nah, don't worry, I've got the glamour,' chuckled Alan.

'I'd hardly call *you* glamourous!' sniffed Dorothy snootily.

'He doesn't mean *that* sort of glamour,' said Janet, pointedly. 'He means magic – the humans won't see him if he tells them he's not there.' Alan smiled affably, as ever not in the least put out by Dorothy's remarks.

Dorothy huffed and held a paw up to her face, muttering as she licked it. 'I hope the humans get a move on – it's getting colder and I'm getting dirty paws sitting here. What a lot of fuss over burying an old skull and a couple of tatty old bracelets!'

'We've talked about this, Princess,' said Fred, pointedly. 'It's the right thing to do, we want Tip's ghost to find peace and…'

'*Shh*!' hissed Janet, with surprising force. 'Listen to what Pip's saying.'

I noticed that Dorothy didn't snap back at her. Instead, she joined us in facing ahead, listening and watching. I felt a swell of pride for Janet – she may have been small and shy but she could make herself heard when she needed to.

We watched intently as Pip said aloud: 'We gather in memory of Martha Goodbody, wise woman and healer and her loyal feline companion Tip. We lay to rest these relics of their lives, to rest in the land saved by her family and which we enjoy today.' She then knelt down and reverently placed the carved box into the hole. Then she straightened up, clasped her hands in front of her and bowed her head to the hole. Most of the other humans did the same, then they all stood in silence.

I realised that my heart was beating very fast indeed. In fact, I was surprised that nobody else could hear it as it seemed so loud to me. I looked all around, wondering if Tip would appear, but everything seemed normal and quiet.

Pip picked up the spade and began to gently shovel the earth back into the hole. From where I stood, I heard the soft thud of the soil on the box from the first few spadefuls. In a short space of time, the hole had been filled and Pip gently patted the soil down with her the spade. Betty stepped forward and placed a small, white rockery stone on the spot. Pip smiled and said, 'We'll put a proper marker there when the area is tidied up. Very fitting that Martha and her descendant Richard Goodman both knew and loved this place.'

There was a general shuffling of feet from the humans and murmurs of 'Well done Pip' and 'That was beautiful'.

'Is that *it*?' muttered Dorothy impatiently. 'All this fuss and… umm… er…'

I realised Dorothy's eyes had grown wider and she stared to the left of where the humans were standing, towards the remains of Mr Goodman's cottage. The fur on her back and tail was bristling, as she began to raise herself up on her toes, her back arching. I followed her gaze and saw Tip, calmly walking out from the thick foliage round the ruins and walking towards the humans.

Everyone – humans, cats and, I expect every animal – stared as Tip approached the group. He seemed even more solid than the last time I'd seen him, his fur clearly visible, his feet disturbing fallen leaves as he continued onwards. In fact, he looked like an ordinary pure white cat. Ordinary that is except for the bright white glow around him, which didn't flicker as he walked but remained steady. I heard several of the humans gasp in surprise. I slowly made my way forward, carefully stepping around and through the humans' legs until I reached Pip and Betty and stood between them watching Tip. I looked up at Pip and noticed that her eyes were wide and her mouth open, but also that she was standing extremely still. I looked towards Betty and her face was exactly the same, wearing an expression of wonder, rather than fear. She too was standing so still that she may have been a human-sized garden gnome.

I turned to look at the humans behind me. Everyone was standing perfectly still, eyes open and blinking, their expressions ranging from wonder to surprise to puzzlement. Nobody looked frightened and nor could I smell any fear wafting from them. I looked back to the front to see Tip stop walking and sit, just a few feet from the stone marker, his tail curled neatly around him. He seemed to be waiting for something… but what could it be? I tried to turn my head to look back to my friends but found that now I couldn't move my head, nor would my legs work. In fact, no part of me could move! It didn't feel like I was being held in place and it wasn't a frightening sensation, it was as though every time I thought about moving, my body decided against it. In that moment, I just *knew* that behind me, Fred, Janet, Dorothy, Mr Brock, Ruby, Henry – even Alan – everyone would also be frozen in position, staring ahead.

As we all watched, a small glowing point of light began to emerge from the freshly filled hole. It began to stretch upwards, looking for all the world like a bulb shoot. But the glowing white shoot grew taller, and began to expand outwards, thicker at the base than the middle. Suddenly, it stopped growing upwards and then gradually two long, thinner points of light began to grow out towards the top. Now the shape looked for all the world like a tree, spreading two big branches outwards, with smaller branches beginning to form at each end of the big branches. Then the bright glow began to flow away from the shape, spreading around the ground in front of the fallen oak, over the humans and me, gently illuminating the whole wild area. I felt my whiskers tingling, just like they did before a thunderstorm, the air zinging with energy.

I blinked and saw that the tree shape began to shimmer and blur, the branches now becoming arms with fingers on the end, the trunk becoming a slender human body… the top becoming a head…

… Until there, before us all, as clear as she had been to me when Tip shared his memories, stood Martha Goodbody!

Chapter Twenty-One

Reunited!

Martha appeared to be perfectly solid and real, although the glow surrounding the wild area muted the colours of the long, hooded cloak she was wearing. Slowly, she lowered her arms to her side and turned her head, first one way, then the other, taking in the scene. Her gaze dropped down to her right, where Tip was sitting, looking up at her. Then she spoke: '*Oh Tip*. My precious Tip!'

She dropped to one knee and held out her hand as Tip ran forward, his tail erect. He raised himself on his hind legs and butted his head in sheer pleasure against Martha's outstretched hand. I realised that he was now as solid as Martha! Martha smiled. Although tears were flowing from her eyes, I could tell they were tears of sheer joy. She laughed, saying his name over and over. I felt Tip's elation and my heart, still beating fast, swelled with emotion to see the cat whose memories I had shared, reunited with the human he loved and who loved him back.

Tip dropped to his four feet; tail still erect as Martha stroked her hand from his head to his bottom. As she withdrew her hand, a strange transformation took place. Tip's ears began to darken, followed by the top of his head. Gathering speed, the ghostly whiteness of his fur began to flow away, down his head, his neck, his front legs, along his body, down his back legs and up his tail. I realised with a jolt that Tip wasn't white at all – he was as black as me! The whiteness travelled up his tail, leaving glossy black fur behind it and then it stopped, at the very end of his tail. I realised that this was how Tip had earned his name – his fur was totally black, except for the tip of his tail which was white!

Tip turned to look directly at me. No longer were his eyes dark shadows within his face but were the deepest green. He opened his mouth and uttered the first sound I'd heard him make: 'Robert.'

Martha looked across to me and beckoned me with her hand. 'Please come to us, Robert,' she said. 'We owe you so much.' I was about to reply that I couldn't move, but found that now I could move after all, because I truly *wanted* to. I trotted forward with no hint of fear, as I knew that Martha and Tip meant me no harm. I stopped before Tip and we touched noses. This time his nose – as black as mine – was warm and velvety, very definitely that of a living, breathing cat. There was no flicker of light, no shared memories but instead a deliciously warm feeling of affection and kinship.

'Thank you, Robert,' said Tip, his voice deep, slightly accented, rather like Fred's. 'Thank you for helping to bring us back together.'

'I – er – it was – nothing,' I stammered. 'I'm just… well… sorry I was so frightened of you to start with.'

Tip chuckled, as did Martha. She gently stroked me from my head to my tail, her touch warm and gentle, her fingers delicately whispering through my fur. 'Yes, thank you, Robert,' she said. I noticed that her voice sounded less accented, more what Fred would call "posh" (mainly just to annoy Dorothy when she put on airs and graces).

I almost fell over with surprise as I realised that Martha was speaking to me in Kittish! Not just the sound, but the smell and taste of it too! As if knowing what I was thinking Martha smiled and said, 'Yes, I speak your tongue, Robert. But anyone with the eyes to truly see and the ears to properly hear can speak to any of our fellow beings.'

'H-h-how did you know what I – what *we* – had done to help Tip?' I asked. 'I mean, the bracelets and all and you've only just appeared and…'

'My spirit was sleeping, waiting for my bracelets and Tip's mortal remains to be united under the earth of the oak,' said Martha. 'I saw all that you'd done when we came together at last.'

I noticed that she was wearing both bracelets, but they looked bright and shiny. 'Are you wearing the same bracelets?' I asked.

Martha chuckled. 'I am and I am not,' she said. 'The bracelets are still in the box, along with Tip's skull, but they're also here, like Tip, like me. This side of the shadow, if you will.'

'Like the stone circle?' I said. 'It's gone, it's the pond now, but it's still there as well. Sort of… er…'

'Aye, you're right, Robert,' said Tip. 'I chose well to befriend you, for I knew you were an old soul and at one with this land. It was thanks to you, Robert, that I became ever more solid and of this world.'

'How?' I asked, bemused.

'Because you *believed* in me,' said Tip. He rubbed his head against mine. His fur felt warm and soft. He sat back and swiftly licked his chest. 'That's better,' he added. 'I've waited *so* long for a wash!

I couldn't help but laugh and Tip joined in. 'I'm so sorry that I couldn't speak to you before,' said Tip. ''Tis hard enough to appear in spirit, even harder to talk. Apart from making *Whoo-ooo* noises and that just frightens folk all the more.'

'I understand, Tip,' I said. 'Yes, I was frightened for a while but when I realised you needed our help…'

Tip smiled. 'It was so funny with that great pumpkin,' he chuckled. 'I felt sorry for poor Dorothy though, I didn't mean to scare her.' I chuckled too. We both looked beyond the frozen humans to where Dorothy stood, still with her back arched, unable to move. I could see her eyes narrow at me. Even whilst frozen by magic, Dorothy could still manage to give us both a Look.

Martha stood up, her cloak swishing around her. She scanned the astounded faces of the humans standing before her, then spoke directly to them. 'I owe you thanks, my friends,' she said. 'You are all good people and truly worthy custodians of this land you now call the Allotments.' I noticed everybody's eyes were moving, still blinking, in sheer wonder, even though their bodies remained perfectly still. Martha looked directly at Pip. 'And I thank *you* especially, Phillipa,' she added. 'You have the sight and the magic within you. Truly, we are kin.' Pip's eyes widened and I could feel the pride and affection flowing between her and Martha.

'Will the humans now what we've done? Weill they be able to speak to us in Kittish now?' I asked Martha.

She shook her head. 'I'm afraid not, Robert,' she said. 'It will be best if they forget all that occurred here. But they will remember, deep inside their minds and hearts. It's best that the living live their lives without worrying about us on the Other Side.'

A gentle breeze rippled through the undergrowth, causing a lock of Martha's long hair to blow across her cheek. She brushed the hair back and looked down at Tip. ''Tis time we were gone, Tip,' she said. 'We've had our time here and now we can move on together.' She dropped to one knee again and stroked me, tickling my cheeks and making me purr. 'Thank you again, dear Robert,' she said. 'You could be Tip's brother, so black as you are. You'd make a fine witch's cat for sure.'

'Goodbye Martha,' I said, feeling sadness welling up inside me. I turned to Tip. 'And goodbye Tip, I'll never forget you. Can't you both stay, or, well, visit from time to time?'

Martha gave a gentle laugh. Tip purred and rubbed his head against mine. 'We'll still be here even after we've gone, Robert,' he said. 'In the grass, in the flowers, in the trees, in the earth – aye, even in the pumpkins. As the land is part of us, so we will always be a part of the land.'

I nodded. I understood. Probably.

Martha picked Tip up and stood. Tip clambered up onto her shoulder. I had the feeling that this was something he'd often done in their life together. They both looked down at me and I returned their gaze. A great feeling of peace flowed from them to me. They were reunited, for all time.

The glow that surrounded the wild area began to flow back towards Martha and Tip, growing brighter, ever brighter. I squinted as the light became intense, now just focussed on that one spot where Martha stood, she and Tip blending into the dazzling glow, becoming part of it. Then quickly the glow began to shrink, smaller and smaller until just a small, white ball of light remained, hovering in the air. Slowly it split in two, one glowing ball smaller than the other and they began to rise into the sky, faster and faster, spinning around each other in an ecstatic dance of sheer happiness. I craned my neck up as the two lights streaked away, seeming to blend together again and then disappearing amongst the stars which were now twinkling in the night sky.

I realised had been holding my breath, which I let go with a miaow. I turned to face the humans and saw that they were beginning to move, blinking rapidly as through awakening from a deep sleep, looking slightly puzzled.

'Well, that was lovely, Pip,' said Kate, squeezing Pip's shoulder. The others all voiced their agreement.

Betty looked up. 'My! It got dark quickly,' she exclaimed. 'It must be later than we thought.'

'Yeah, we'd best be heading back to the clubhouse,' said Pip. 'Torches at the ready, everyone?' With that the humans began to wend their way back to the Allotments, carefully negotiating their way over tree roots and scattered bricks from Mr Goodman's cottage.

I had no idea how long we had been here and or how long I had been speaking to Martha and Tip, but something told me that time wasn't important. I realised though, that Martha had been right – the humans *didn't* remember what had happened. However, maybe the other cats would remember?

I trotted over to where Fred, Dorothy and the others were waiting. It was obvious they, at least, could remember.

'Well, that was pretty impressive, mate!' said Fred. 'Well done on helping them get back together!'

'Yes, well done,' said Dorothy, grudgingly. 'I hope that's the last we see of that wretched wraith! Now, let's get back to the clubhouse, so I can have a good wash and maybe some kitty treats.'

As we began to move off, I noticed Mr Brock and Ruby disappear into the undergrowth and heard the flap of wings as Henry and his fellow crows took flight to get back to their usual roosting places. Janet and Alan walked either side of me.

'Well done, Robert me lad,' said Alan, patting my back. 'That was powerful magic Martha Goodbody used there. Even *I* couldn't move!'

'Just like a real garden gnome then?' giggled Janet mischievously. We all laughed.

Alan bade us both goodnight and set off towards the pond, no doubt to step over the shadow to the stone circle and his own folk. Janet and I walked along the path towards the clubhouse.

'You did a wonderful thing this winter, Robert,' Janet said quietly. 'Helping Tip find Martha. And helping Hotchi, of course and stopping those awful men and their giant pumpkin.'

'Really?' I mumbled, awkwardly. 'I mean, I didn't plan it, stuff sort of just… well… *happens* to me. I just do my best.'

'And that is why you're so wonderful,' said Janet, stopping suddenly. I stopped too, but before I could say anything, Janet kissed noses with me and licked my face quickly, before gracefully slipping away through the nearest plot.

I sat, dumbfounded. *Wonderful? Me*? I pondered what the future might hold for Janet and me, here at Sunnyside Allotments. She seemed to really *like* me… didn't she?

I looked ahead and saw light spilling out from the clubhouse as the humans bustled inside, no doubt to make hot drinks before going home. I noticed Dorothy bundle her way through their legs, with Fred, Barbara and the others follow at a more respectable pace.

She'd mentioned kitty treats, hadn't she?

I decided to hurry along.

Chapter Twenty-Two

Another Equinox

'Shh! Listen!' I whispered. Janet and I stopped halfway down the central pathway, our ears twitching.

'What are we listening for?' Janet whispered back. 'Is it the stadium construction? The birdsong? The flowers growing?' She gave a small smirk after the final comment.

'Cheeky kitbit!' I whispered back. 'No – something else, coming from that plot ahead of us.'

'Why are we whispering?' Janet asked in a very quiet voice.

'Don't want to scare it, whatever it is,' I muttered, equally quietly. 'Could be a juicy fat mouse.'

Cautiously, we inched forward, lowering our faces down almost to the ground, our bottoms and tails sticking up, muscles in our back legs ready to propel us forward. There was definitely something moving around in the rows of spring greens on the plot. Whatever it was, it was making quite a lot of noise, perhaps too much for a mouse after all…

Suddenly, a twitching black nose on the end of a longish brown snout forced its way out of the spring greens, followed by a prickly head with two bright black eyes.

'Hotchi!' cried Janet delightedly, relaxing her planned pounce and trotting over to the plot. I followed and sat next to her as the hedgehog heaved himself out of the greens and onto the path. He was noticeably bigger, and plumper, not quite fully grown, but much healthier than when we'd last seen him being carried away by Pip after his close call with the bonfire.

'Hallo Kitties,' snuffled Hotchi, squinting slightly in the sunshine. 'Phew! It's warm today. Good huntin' for slugs and snails though. I felt a bit peckish after last night, so I thought I'd stay up a bit and eat some more. Plenty of the little beggers on these greens!'

'When did you get back from the Hedgehog Rescue place?' I asked.

'Oh, a couple of evenings ago,' said Hotchi. 'I have to say, those hoomins that looked after me weren't so bad at all. Kept me in a nice warm boxy-thing, plenty to eat – special hedgehog food as well as mealyworms an' all. I didn't even need to hibernate. So they decided I was better and brought me back here, 'cos of that's where I come from, like. Let me go just as it was getting' dark. They even set up a special Hedgehog House for me wiv straw in. Nice an'cosy.'

'Well, we're glad you're well and glad you're back,' smiled Janet. 'Have you met any of the other Allotment Hedgehogs yet?'

'Yeah, saw me bruvver, din't I?' said Hotchi darkly. 'He was bigger 'n the rest of mum's litter. Nicked most of the food, that's why I was so small come Autumntime. Anyway, Bristow – that's me bruvver – tries to shove his way into me nice hedgehog house, reckoning he can take it over. I saw 'im off sharpish, I did. "We should share, little bruvver," he says to me. "What, like you *didn't* when we were nailbrushes?" says I.
So I snouted 'im out of the house! Hah! He won't try *that* again!' He chuckled to himself. 'Waited ages to teach 'im a lesson!'

'Well, it's great to see you again, Hotchi,' I said, reaching out a paw to pat him on the back and then withdrawing it just in the nick of time. Hotchi's spines were a lot bigger and sharper than they had been a few moonths ago.

'Yeah, good to see you too,' snuffled Hotchi. 'Thanks again for savin' me life. I won't forget it!'

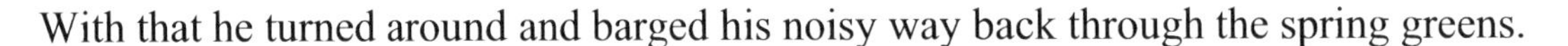

With that he turned around and barged his noisy way back through the spring greens.

'Well, that was nice,' said Janet. 'Come on, we'd better hurry before it gets too warm for Tiberius to be out and about.'

We continued our journey towards the end of the allotments to turn left at the new fence where Tip's skull had been dug up when the old wall was demolished. Had it really only been six human months ago? So much had happened since then.

To start with, the humans had completely forgotten what had happened when the skull and bracelets were buried. In fact, all of the other cats – apart from Janet – seemed to be a bit vague about the whole thing whenever I mentioned it, so I gave up asking them if they remembered. Alan had said it was "residyall magic" and not to worry about it. 'The main thing is, Robert, that you remember it. And little Janet remembers of course, on account of her being a famulus,' he'd said. We hadn't seen him for a while as he'd gone off on another "covert mission", but said he'd drop by again when he could.

About two weeks after Martha and Tip were reunited, the weather began to get warmer – "unseasonably warm", as I heard some of the plot holders saying. Snowdrops had sprouted everywhere, particularly in the wild area, followed by daffodils with their bright yellow and orange trumpet-like heads. Hyacinths had followed and now, towards the end of March, tulips and bluebells had taken over the flowerbeds and plots. The whole wild area seemed to be carpeted with bluebells, contrasting with the vibrant green of the newly sprouting leaves on the trees and grass. It was good for dandelions and other plants too, but the plot holders were complaining about *weeds*! Still, despite having to furiously weed their plots, they were already getting some early vegetables harvested.

We trotted through the wild area, intending to follow the slope down to the pond to meet with Tiberius. He'd reappeared around the end of February, along with what seemed like hundreds of other frogs and toads, all croaking madly as they piggy-backed with each other in the pond. Soon after that, the edges of the pond by the newly growing rushes were crowded with masses of frogspawn, as though the water itself had been turned into jelly. Long strings of toad spawn twisted around the reeds and other water plants. Everywhere on the Allotments was bursting into life.

Of course, this time of year, there were birds everywhere, building nests, laying eggs and manically feeding newly hatched chicks. The chicks were pink and bald when they hatched, eyes closed, their gaping mouths constantly open for their parents to shove insects and worms into them. It made me tired just to watch the parent birds taking it in turns to nestle the chicks, then dart backwards and forwards hundreds of times a day to catch insects and the like to feed their ever hungry, demanding offspring.

Henry had introduced us to his missus, Cora, who seemed very nice but rather bossy and in a hurry. 'Come along Henry,' she cawed. 'That nest won't build itself you know!' Henry had given us a look of resignation and simply said 'Of course m'dear' and flapped off to gather twigs for their nest.

We skipped through the wild area, dancing lightly between the bluebells.

'Hey look!' exclaimed Janet, hurrying over to the fallen oak tree.

I trotted after her and we both stopped to look down. There, just in front of the marker stone where Tip's skull and Martha's bracelets were buried, amongst the leaf litter and dark soil grew a small oak sapling. It resembled a twig, with just three leaves open, fresh and green. But at its tip was a green bud, promising more leaves.

'There must have been an acorn from the old oak buried here,' said Janet. 'It's waited until now to grow.'

'Maybe there's magic involved,' I said, with wonder in my voice.

'Of course there is,' replied Janet. 'And what better memorial to Tip and Martha could there be, than a new oak tree, grown from an acorn from the oak that kept the bracelet safe for so long?'

I nodded and delicately sniffed the little oak sapling. It smelt of the earth, fresh and vibrant. This tiny, fragile little sprout had the potential to become a huge oak tree, living for hundreds of years. Somehow, young though it was, it seemed to radiate a sense of great age, of wisdom passed cross the centuries, shared and connected with all the other trees and plants and animals in this magical place that was Sunnyside Allotments. In time, it's roots would encase the box containing Martha's bracelets and Tip's skull, keeping them safe as they gradually became a part of the tree itself. It felt so… *right.*

'Janet,' I said thoughtfully, 'You were right on that night of the Equinox when you said that I had to ask the right tree.'

'Of course I was right,' said Janet brightly. 'You just had to realise it yourself. Never mind, it may take you a while, Robert, but you get there in the end.' With a giggle she ran off in the direction of the pond.

'You cheeky….' I began, but she had already disappeared amongst the trees and bushes. With a last look at the new oak tree, I bounded after her, happiness swelling in my heart.

We found Tiberius in his usual spot, sitting in front of his flowerpot, looking out over the pond. The clumps and strings of frog and toad spawn were gone now, having hatched (or "spwatched" as Tiberius had said), and now there looked to be thousands, maybe millions of little tadpoles wriggling their tails excitedly as they swam in the shallows, feasting on plants and algae. I have to say, I couldn't tell a toad tadpole from a frog tadpole (were they called toadpoles and frogpoles? I wondered), but from past experience I knew it wasn't worth trying to catch them. They didn't taste nice and even if they did, you'd need to catch a lot of them to make a decent meal.

''*Salvete nobilis bufo*,' we both said, in respectful greeting. The ancient toad turned his head slightly towards us and blinked his prominent bronze eyes.

''*Salvete nobilis feline, cultis hortis amici,*',' he responded. 'What news?'

'Well, we told you about Tip and Martha,' I began excitedly, 'Well, there's a new oak tree and…'

'You'll have to speak up,' croaked Tiberius loudly. 'I can't hear myself think with these blooming tadpoles all chattering and shouting and messing around!'

Janet and I exchanged glances. 'I can't hear anything,' I said. 'Maybe some ripples in the water where they're swimming but…'

'Oh, of course you can't,' muttered Tiberius. 'You've got mammal ears. Well, you have *this* time round at any rate.'

'Oh, don't be an old grumpyhibian Tiberius,' said Janet, cajolingly. 'You must've been a tadpole yourself once.'

Tiberius inflated himself slightly and exhaled, which we both knew was how he sighed. 'Probably,' he snorted. 'But I had *respect* for my elders and didn't make such a racket! At least, I don't *think* I did.' His eyes took on a faraway look, perhaps remembering a far distant time when he was a wriggly little black comma himself, with no other thoughts than grazing on algae and avoiding being eaten by water-dwelling predators.

'Anyway,' I said, quickly changing the subject, 'Let us tell you about this new oak tree…'

Tiberius listened patiently. We'd already told him about Tip turning up as a ghost cat and how we'd done our best to get him reunited with Martha, along with all the other things that had happened that winter. He nodded as we told him about the oak sapling. I had the impression once again that somehow, in his mysterious way, he knew all of this already and was simply being polite by listening to us telling the story.

'Well,' he said when we'd finished. 'Life finds a way. It's all around us. As Tip told you Robert, he and Martha will still be here: "*In the grass, in the flowers, in the trees, in the earth – aye, even in the pumpkins. As the land is part of us, so we will always be a part of the land.*"'

'Those were Tip's *exact* words, Tiberius,' I said in wonderment. 'It's almost as if you were there yourself.'

Tiberius blinked slowly. 'You wondered why things happened to you, Robert,' he said. 'As I've said before, you have a *destiny*. Nothing happens by chance. Martha Goodbody was a wise human, a very wise old soul. It was no coincidence she chose her magic bracelets and Tip's remains to be buried in this special place, where the earth magic is strong. No more a coincidence that she picked Tip as a kitten to be her faithful companion. Nor was it coincidence that Tip's reawakened spirit chose to reach out to *you*, Robert.'

We sat in silence for a few moments while I digested his words. Tiberius meanwhile digested a fly that flew too close to him. Finally, I broke the silence and said: 'Tiberius, did you know Martha and Tip?'

Tiberius blinked again and gave a particularly big puff-sigh. 'Questions, questions, always questions,' he said. He turned to Janet and gave her long, hard stare that Dorothy couldn't have matched. 'Janet. You know what day it is today?'

'Oh yes, of course Tiberius,' Janet replied quickly. 'It's the Spring Equinox.'

'Indeed it is,' said Tiberius. 'March the twenty-first. So… I shall see you at the ceremony this evening. *Both* of you I hope.' His hard stare fell upon me. Cats can't blush, but I had the uncontrollable urge to wash vigorously.

We both nodded enthusiastically.

'Good,' said Tiberius, thankfully looking away. 'Well, I'm going to have a little nap in my flowerpot until it cools down, hopefully it'll be quieter in there and I won't hear those little hooligan tadpoles. Finbarr's are the worst of the lot!'

He turned to shuffle off into the cool, dark depths of his flowerpot. I heard his voice echo out; 'Tell him why today is special too, Janet,' he said.

We walked back towards the allotments. 'Well, apart from the Spring Equinox, why is today so special, Janet?' I asked.

'Oh Robert,' she sighed, but with a smile in her voice. 'It's exactly a year since you came to the Allotments! I heard Betty say so to Pip this morning. I expect there'll be special treats for you later. For all of us, I hope.'

'A whole human year? Really?' I said in genuine surprise. 'I'm not sure how many yonks that is, but so much has happened, hasn't it?'

'It sure has, Robert,' came a familiar voice. Barbara slipped out from some spring onions, followed a few seconds later by GG and Dorothy.

'Yes, it was very quiet here before you came Robert,' said Dorothy pointedly. 'Still, you're here now, so I suppose we've got used to you.'

'Hey look,' said GG nodding further down the path. We followed her gaze and saw Red Fred and ET strolling along the path together. Or rather, Fred was strolling, ET was wobbling and balancing against Fred. Every now and again they'd rub heads. They looked so happy.

'Look at the love bugs,' smiled GG.

'Oh! Love bugs? Are they like… an *item*?' I said, with genuine surprise. 'I never realised.'

'Oh, for goodness' sake!' snorted Dorothy. '*Of course* they're an item!'

'I – er – I didn't notice,' I said, lamely.

Dorothy gave me one of her special Looks, her eyes flitting between Janet and me. 'Honestly Robert, you don't notice *anything*, even if it's right under your nose!' With that she stalked away in her super-huffy-princess mode.

'We'd best be going, Barbs,' said GG, pointedly. 'Things to do, mice to catch and all that.'

'Riiiiight,' chuckled Barbara. He gave me a cheeky wink. 'See you both later.'

We watched them slip away between the plots. A gentle breeze ruffled our fur. I noticed how the colours in Janet's coppery fur seemed to flow like ripples across the pond in the breeze. Some pink blossoms from cherry trees on the nearby plot blew across the path in front of us. I realised Janet was looking at me, her eyes almost glowing. My tail twitched with nervousness. Without a word, Janet stood up and trotted on ahead. I hurried to catch up.

'Dorothy's right you know,' she said, airily.

'What about?' I spluttered indignantly. 'You mean about me not noticing things that are right under my nose?'

'Well, maybe that's true *some* of the time,' said Janet, 'But I was thinking more about what she said that time we all got silly with the catnip.'

'What did she say?' I said, desperately trying to recall what had happened. 'My memory's a bit fuzzy thanks to the catnip.'

'That you're *handsome*!' exclaimed Janet. 'And she's right!'

'Oh!' I said. I was so surprised, I couldn't think of anything else to say.

'Come on Robert, let's see if there's some special treats to be had,' said Janet as we headed towards the clubhouse. 'I expect Betty will be posting about your Allotment Anniversary on *FaceyFriends* and *Nitter-Natter.*'

'Probably,' I said. 'I'll have to ask GG to put out some messages to my fans direct from me, of course.'

Janet giggled. 'Maybe she'll even teach you to type them for yourself, Robert.'

'It's been quite a winter, hasn't it?' I said, purring happily, my heart swelling with a delightful, warm feeling I'd never experienced before in my life. It seemed so *real*, so *right*, I felt like I was walking on air. And what better place to have such a feeling than here, in my home, in Sunnyside Allotments?

'I'm glad it's spring though,' I added. 'New beginnings, eh?'

Our tails entwined as we walked side by side through the spring sunshine, the blossom gently falling around us.

THE END

Nawthor's Note

Well, there we have it – the story of Robert's first year at Sunnyside Allotments, which began in ***Robert the Allotment Cat and Friends***. It's been a hard slog translating all the Kittish into Humanese and I'm still not sure I've done Robert's telling justice. That aside though, thanks are due to so many people for helping me get this sequel to see the light of day, so heartfelt thanks to:

Betty Farruggia, for patiently providing me with information on the Allotments (yes, they're real!), the flora and fauna to be found there and, of course, for continuing to provide daily Robert updates for his thousands of followers across the world via Twitter at *@Allotment Cat* and via Facebook at *Robert the Allotment Cat*. These are, of course, he real world versions of *FaceyFriends* and *Nitter-Natter*. If you'd like to read a detailed account of Robert's doings, then I heartily recommend you obtain a copy of ***Robert: A Cat Who Tweets***, written by Robert and Betty. Lots of lovely colour photos of Robert and his fellow Allotment cats and favourite humans.

Phillipa (Pip) Price for her enthusiasm and encouragement throughout the writing of this book, and for her friendship. The version of Pip in this book is pretty accurate I think. Any misquotes are, of course, down to me.

Mel for being a brilliant stand-in for Martha Goodbody. Funny how my image of Martha was formed before you stepped up and fitted the bill completely! Life really does imitate art – and that's something I've found throughout the writing of the Robert books!

Judy Hake for her excellent proof-reading skills. Okay, so there's a few variations between UK and US English, so you was effectively working in two languages! Total respect!

Alyson, Maria and Pip (again) for reading advance copies of my chapters as they were produced, most often intermittently (now *there's* a tautology!). Honestly – you wait ages for a chapter and then three turn up at once!

Rachel Breedon for producing bringing the characters in this book to life with her brilliant illustrations and for putting up with my constant requests and suggestions. Oh, and for being a part of our family too. It's a tough job, but somebody has to do it!

Sheena, my wife and better half for reading each chapter or part chapter as it was produced, pointing out spelling errors and letting me bounce ideas off you. Also for the excellent "conversion" artwork. And thanks too for everything else you do that makes for a wonderful life together.

Kate and the other Plot Holders who never mind being portrayed and for all the wonderful work they do in and for the Allotments. Our troubled world needs more Plot Holders!

All Robert Readers, you wonderful people who buy and read these books and, I hope, enjoy them. I literally couldn't do it without your support and enthusiasm.

Last, but by no means least, to **Robert** himself, a wise old soul in feline form who shares his life and stories with so many people, and to his many friends who live in the Allotments. I feel privileged to be a part of your world.

Nick Mays, February 2022

Printed in Great Britain
by Amazon

78293668R10113